C. A. Merriman was born in London and educated at Kent University, and has now lived in Wales for thirty years. The author has previously published four novels, one winning the Ruth Hadden Memorial Award, and three collections of short prose. These works have been widely acclaimed, garnering awards from the Arts Council of Wales and the Rhys Davies Short Story Competition. C. A. Merriman's milestone motorbikes have been the AJS 500, the Suzuki SP 370, the Kawasaki GPZ 900R, and the Kawasaki KLR 600.

## ALSO BY C. A. MERRIMAN

*Leaving the Light On*
*Fatal Observations*
*Silly Mothers*
*Of Sons and Stars*
*State of Desire*
*Broken Glass*
*Getting a Life*

# Brotherhood

## C. A. Merriman

PARTHIAN

Parthian
The Old Surgery
Napier Street
Cardigan
SA43 1ED
www.parthianbooks.co.uk

The author wishes to acknowledge the award of a bursary from the
Arts Council of Wales for the purposes of completing this book.

ISBN 1-902638-33-6
Typeset in Sabon by JT

Printed and bound by Dinefwr Press, Llandybie .

With support from the Parthian Collective

Parthian is an independent publisher that works with the support
of the Arts Council of Wales and the Welsh Books Council

Edited by Isla Telford

A cataloguing record for this book is available from the British
Library

Cover design: Jo Mazelis
Photography: Scott Clark

# BROTHERHOOD

# 1

Biker funerals are shit. Don't let the romantics kid you otherwise. You see photos sometimes in the magazines, AWOL or BSH, showing processions of bikes, black leathers, black helmets, grumbling along at walking speed behind the cortège, and it looks kind of impressive. A heavy, armoured convoy look. Excites the macho sentimentals. Wow, you think, maybe I should die too, give them the excuse.

No you don't.

In reality it's shit. Especially in the drizzle. Especially when you're grumbling so slow your clutch paw aches. Especially if you know this isn't the real thing, just a bunch of mates on bikes, following the cars. And especially if you suspect, from the looks you got from those cars before you set off, that you're not a hundred per cent welcome.

At the crematorium, mind, no one blinks an eyelid. The mourners got their attention locked elsewhere and the staff must be used to all sorts. Inside the building the decor reminds me of the registry office in town, which I visited only a couple of weeks ago, witnessing the union of my deathwish sister to her scabby shit of a husband. Same orangey wood, garden shed colour, same dinky flower displays. Same piped music, except a tad more downbeat. Could have done with something even more funereal for the wedding. Swear the chairs are the same too. Ceremonial issue, maybe, seats too small for the average bum, backs too vertical for the average spine, so no risk of anyone falling asleep. Here there's segregation operating. Family far side of the aisle, interestingly most the same shape, variations on skeletal crow, especially pronounced today since most are in black, friends our side, bikers mostly in black but otherwise all shapes, sizes, colours. One exception. Dale's managed to place himself opposite. A blondie among the crows. Just wandered down the aisle at his usual dreamy amble and slotted himself into a space. And half the boys this side are now daggering him with their eyes, because the chairs left and right of him have been immediately occupied by the best looking women in the room. How does he do it? At a fucking funeral. The woman the far side has to be one of the family, because she's tall, thin and dark, but she makes a pretty crow, no hat, eyes outlined like an oriental and chin-length hair shiny as a pool ball. The woman this side is ten years older, mid-thirties, I'd guess, still dark, but rounder than family. Tartier look to her, too – showing a lot of tit for half eleven in the morning. She's the one I'd go for, given the choice.

Bethan is nudging me. She whispers, "Why the hell is Jonno here?" and nods forward to where the man is standing, exuding bristles from the back of his pig-bum neck, just across the aisle from the grieving parents. Poor sods, they look grey and shrivelled, like the juices've been sucked out of them. Mentally I reply, "In my opinion he's trying to show the rest of us that whatever his differences with Stu, we're all brothers under the leathers," but I know it won't come out right. Keep it short, that's what I've learnt. So I just murmur, "Guilt."

I decide to disengage my brain altogether then, until the coffin's gone. Gives me the creeps, imagining Stu inside that box. I'm not fond of small spaces – goes back to freaking out as a kid, stuck in a roof bunk of a pitch black campervan. Also my eyes water easily and if I blubbed here, when no one else is blubbing, it would seem kind of fraudulent. Plus I'd look a prat. So I concentrate on Bethan's hand, holding the wordsheet to some hymn about knights winning their spurs that we're about to sing. Very neat hands, Bethan has, like the rest of her. Thumb nail short and clean, two solid silver snake rings, plain and classy, round the base of index and middle. Bethan has natural class, and thinking this makes my insides ache. Sense of loss must be catching. One day, I know, she's going to wake up in the morning and look at me lying next to her, and suddenly realise that she's wasted a year of her very precious life on a loser, who's never going to be anything but a loser (unless the world changes radically, very quickly) when she could have any winner she wanted. She'll get up, shaking her neat pretty head in astonishment, pack her things, wake me to say goodbye – got good manners, too – and be off. I'll definitely blub then.

Well, Bethan's hand don't seem to be doing the trick. I'm more misty-eyed than ever. I need to switch off altogether, but it's frustrating the way brains can't think nothing. There are lots of occasions when nothing would be useful, but the cells keep wriggling and worming, taking you places whether you want to go or not. Like the mind's not really you, but something that's been implanted in your head to control you. Or confuse you.

At last; we're standing up to sing. That's the only way to turn the brain weevils off: occupy them with something else. The hymn's got an OK tune but I keep my voice low because I doubt I'm hitting the right notes. Bethan seems to know the song, though; she's not half a beat behind the music like most of the others.

I'm having doubts about us coming here. None of us knows the family well. No one's known Stu more than six months. I bet the family see us as a manifestation of his downward spiral. His wife dumps him, he loses three jobs in quick succession, gives up working, buys himself a monster bike and starts hanging out with us. We definitely weren't to blame for any of that, but we're probably a reminder they could do without.

When the singing's over we sit down and Dire Straits *Brothers in Arms* comes over the speakers. Kind of corny. Kind of affecting. The coffin's sliding away backwards. I suddenly need to get out of here. Bethan's read my mind; her hand finds mine between the chairs and gives it a tight, soon-be-over squeeze. Being a nurse, I suppose she's used to death and grieving relatives, and people who aren't really grieving, and just want the hell out. And then the music changes and the audience stirs. People start to rise and Bethan releases me. Over. Thank shit for that.

Out in the foyer there's a general milling about. The family are going on somewhere we're not invited to, but that's fine by us. We've done what Stu would have wanted and I've stopped panicking; 'course we had to come. Bethan elbows me and says I should say something to Stu's parents. "What?" I hiss. "Just that you're sorry," she hisses back. "You don't have to give a speech." I realise then that that's what everyone else is doing: offering condolences to the parents. The milling around is really a loose queue. I wait my turn, feeling jumpy and practising my words, and when I'm finally face to face with Stu's Dad mumble, "Really sorry, Mr Jones." Stu's Dad extends his arm and shakes my hand. I don't think he heard what I said, but he looks quietly dignified and majorly cut up. He says, "Glad you could come, Jay. Glad you could come," and makes me feel a heartless shit. It's not till a minute later, on my way to the double doors, that I realise he used my name. I'm so bad at names I always assume others are too. I've met him, what, half a dozen times, and always just to nod to, usually outside his gaff when I've been calling in on Stu. But he remembers my name. I'm more than touched.

After the heaviness of inside the fresh air hits us like liberation. Even the drizzle has stopped. The family are sorting out cars for their journey but there's nothing to keep us. Time to be off. Twelve swift miles up the hills to Brynmawr, where we're planning our own wake in the Crucible. We start the bikes up but keep the revs low in the car park, out of respect. Six bikes for seven of us. We wind out of the grounds on to the main road, sorting ourselves into our usual order. Andy and Jonno first, Andy because he's got the bike most likely to shed essentials, and Jonno because he's got no documents. In fact he's banned, right now, and not for the first time. Always having to change his bike and respray his helmet. Then there's Sparky and Damien on their little Yams, and finally

Dale and myself, with Bethan pillion behind me. Got to have big bikes sheepdogging at the rear – means no one gets left behind, and because Dale and I look after our machines and pay our taxes, if a cop fancies a chase we can drop back and give them a couple of bodies to check out and lecture, while the others tail it for home.

Bethan and I end up right at the back. Following Dale's a treat. He's got Guzzi Le Mans. You either like Italian or you don't. Dale does, and even cruising like this he rides like a pro. Outside work, riding's where all his energy and judgement go. Perfect road position, perfect crouch, perfect anticipation. He's the fastest rider here, given his head, but still the only one of us, besides myself, that Bethan will go two up with.

Today we're all riding slow and sober though, because of where we've just come from. Death is a calming influence. But the irony is that Stu didn't kill himself on his bike. He should have done, because he was a crap, crazy rider, and he didn't respect himself or the machine. But he didn't. He died because he wanted to raise hell – and owning a bike was part of that – or, failing hell's ascension, he was going down to meet it. It's a sad story. Three weeks ago he shredded his hand punching the glass out of a door in the Talywain, after rough words with Jonno, and while he was off the road, bandaged up and tamping, he took to the whisky big time. Then last week, in the middle of the night, for a reason that only another piss artist would understand, he decided to explore his parents' cellar, one hand strapped, the other carrying the whisky bottle. They found him at the bottom of the stone steps. He'd have survived, if he hadn't hung on to the whisky. A shard of glass caught him just south of the breast bone, and because he was too out of it to yell for help, he bled to death. Only twenty seven, and the stupid sod bled to death.

At the roundabout outside Brynmawr I peel off for home. The others live in town so they can leave their bikes in the Crucible car park and collect them later, but I'm tucking my Z1000 safe in its shed and getting Bethan to drop me off on her way to work. It's a steep climb up to the open mountain, and the most scenic part of the journey. Wide empty road, only hazard the occasional sheep, and a brown-green moorland horizon that looms nearer and nearer until suddenly deciding to show you how insignificant you are by dropping to the far edges of the world. The Beacons to Herefordshire. Four fucking counties.

As usual my Mam's guard-chickens have collected by the small-holding gate to see off visitors. As usual they're affronted that despite their squawking threats we insist on coming in. Screams and flappings and general fowl hysteria. Opening the gate Bethan has to be very firm with the cockerel, because he's got spurs like stilettos and he'll give you a vicious stab in the calf if you turn your back on him. After she's kicked him out the way she jumps on quick again and we leave them bickering with each other. Major postmortem on why the defence failed. Nasty, stupid creatures.

We bump carefully down the track, approaching the house I expect to live in all my life. Well, for at least as long as my Mam stays alive, and since she's only fifty five I hope that'll be quite a while. Maybe not as long as it could be though, because she's been diabetic since she was twenty, which is a heavier illness than most people imagine, and due to cock-ups along the way she's already got problems with her eyes. In ten years she'll be blind and I'll be thirty eight and we can be a couple of hopeless cases together. Ever since Mam's eyes started to go my little sister has lived in terror of being trapped at home with her, which is maybe why she's settled for the scabby shit husband, but I can think of worse fates than living on a seven-acre hillside small-holding with a funny, tough-minded Mam to look after, and all this space to make use of, so I'm not complaining. And at present, and for as long as she wants to, Bethan lives here too, and if she was still around in ten years I'd count it paradise.

I stop in the yard to let Bethan off. The main part of the bungalow was built just after the war and consists mostly of roof. Mam says that Dad's family, who built it, did it sneakily without telling anyone, and decided long and low was the answer, so it was hardly visible from the road and any casual off-road eyes would think it was a sheep shelter. This may just be a good story. Since then bits have been added as they've been needed, using materials to hand, so there's a workshop barn built with stone from the collapsed ex-railway viaduct down the road, a breeze-block outside toilet (because the one inside is too far from the back door, and Mam got fed up with Dad pissing in the yard) and several lean-tos in rustic corrugated iron. The overall result is a mess, but a warm, dry, functional mess.

I wheel the bike into one of the lean-tos and lock the doors, and we go inside for Bethan to change into her uniform and get the car keys. Mam's in the kitchen playing with the litter of puppies Floss the Doberman produced six weeks ago, and pretending to book-keep – her part-time job – on the table. Not a job you'd naturally associate with failing eyes, but she's OK close up. Uses a very black pen. There are six pups living in the kitchen at the moment, a most unhygienic state of affairs, though at least they're in the shed at night. Since they're jointly worth more than two thousand pounds, enough to keep Mam's car on the road for another year and pay this year's council tax, we're putting up with it. They should all be gone in a month, anyway, assuming Mam can bring herself to part with them.

"Buried him, then?" she says, as we come in. Her new glasses shock me slightly, as I expect they will for a while, till I'm used to them.

"Cremated," I say. "Yup." I pick up one of the pups and rub it against my cheek. Oh, those squirming muscles. Those silky jowls. Yeah, every house should have one.

Mam says, "Stupid boy," her mouth tight. I light up a ciggie and inhale deep. Ah, been waiting a while for that.

Bethan flaps at us, making for the doorway, "Excuse me," she says. "I got to change."

*Excuse me.* That's the sort of thing Bethan says. Ingrained with

7

manners. She says it when she gets pissed too, just before she throws up. I remember about the fifth or sixth time she came here, when she knew her way around, and she said to Mam in the kitchen, "Can I have a glass of water, please?" and Mam said, "D'you think I'm made of money?" sounding quite tetchy, and they both started laughing. First joke they shared that wasn't through me. Soon afterwards Mam was warning Bethan not to expect me to sign over all my worldly wealth to her because what with my writing problems I might have difficulty listing my possessions, and Bethan laughed over that, too. Make a bit of a team, these days. Or gang. Wonder sometimes who Bethan moved in with.

I stay chatting to Mam for five minutes while Bethan gets changed, and do chores I'll be too wasted to do later, like filling the Rayburn and taking the rubbish out to the wheely bin. I tell Mam not to cook for us this evening – I'll be full of beer, and Bethan'll eat at the hospital – and she says fat chance anyway, because she's going out with Randolph. Randolph is our closest neighbour, half a mile nearer town, and also Mam's best friend. They share interests in dog breeding and fence maintenance and occasional nookie. Randolph has a million grown-up children scattered over the hillside who had serious anxieties about their inheritance when Mam first got pally with him, but now it's obvious that marriage isn't on the cards they see her as an asset, keeping him single and solvent. As well as his sheep he owns a coal merchant business in town and it's his book-keeping she helps out with. Tonight she and Randolph are going to a commoners meeting at seven, and then on to the pub.

Bethan reappears in her hospital uniform. She wears her brown hair twisted into a roll at the back of her head and looks so clean and useful that if Mam weren't here I'd go for a quickie on the kitchen table, right now, pups or no pups. Nothing like messing up a nurse, or being messed up by one. But I got a wake to go to, and she has work.

We drive into town in Mam's Subaru estate. Mam isn't allowed to drive, because she can't tell a bollard from a policeman at fifty yards, but she's had a car all her life and hasn't got her head round her limitations yet so we call it her car, which it is, legally, only mostly it's Bethan who uses it. In the winter I do as well, because winter's my working season and we're above the snow line here and the bike and my body are too precious to risk on snow and ice.

Bethan turfs me out at the War Memorial town square and it's just seconds round the corner to the Crucible. It's so gloomy in the bar it could be evening, and probably will be by the time we emerge. Jonno's playing pool with a local kid on his lunch break and is stripped off to a singlet, displaying about a yard of disgusting bum-blubber every time he leans across the table to take a shot. His clothes – jacket, sweatshirt, face scarf, gauntlets – are scattered everywhere. There's just too much of Jonno. Like a huge, bad-tempered, half-trained animal, always in your face. Dale is leant against the bar, watching him with narrow eyes.

"Right, then, Dale," I say.

"Aye, OK,"

"Where the others?"

He jerks a thumb into the darker recesses of the bar. Sparky and Damien are talking to a lad called Trevor, who used to be a serious pill-head till he got his act together courtesy of one of Her Majesty's institutions, and now he's an outreach worker for a drugs project. I see another boy is blowing smoke into his face from a large cigarette, just asking to be outreached. Comes in for a lot of stick, Trevor does, poacher turned gamekeeper, but it's mostly good-humoured.

Jonno starts roaring because the lad he was playing has beaten him and doesn't have time for a return game. The kid's half his weight and looks nervous until Dale snaps, "Pack it in, Jonno," which brings Jonno stomping over to us for a refill. The lad gives us a quick nod and escapes. Dale looks much more concentrated, much less dreamy than usual.

"What were you doing down the crematorium, Jonno?" he

asks. "And what you doing here, pissing around?"

Most people are cautious about lecturing Jonno. Not Dale. It's not brave, because you know he hasn't geared himself up to say it. He's just thought it, and said it. Jonno's chest swells with indignation.

"Should show a bit of respect," Dale says.

Not sure what Jonno's done to deserve this. Sounds like Dale has suddenly had enough, for some reason. Because a mate's dead, maybe.

"Weren't my fault," Jonno says. "Didn't push him down the cellar."

"Didn't say you did, thicko," says Dale.

"So?" Jonno looks mystified. Dale rolls his eyes and puts his glass to one side.

"Not sure I'm up for a piss."

"Ah, hey," complains Jonno. "You gotta stay. That's what we're here for. You got to get ratted."

"Shit," sighs Dale. "The man's dead."

"Yeah." Jonno nods in urgent agreement. "Fucking dead."

Dale sighs again. Unbridgeable gulf between these two. Dale may be quiet and a dreamer but he's bright – builds race engines for a living, and earns good money for it – and he possesses a full deck of emotions. Right now he seems to be feeling sad, and that's making him irritable. Jonno is as dull as dung, and has only two main states of being: conscious and unconscious. Everything else is whim. Even when he's angry it's like he's playing, just letting rip for the hell of it. Maybe that's why he and Stu couldn't get along; there's room for one scatter-gun in a group, but not two.

Damien and Sparky wander up, and then Andy too. Andy's been trying to stem a haemorrhage of oil from his bike out in the car park and seems to have been doing it mostly with his beard. Grubbiest person I know. Dale relents and agrees to stay, and buys everyone another round. A couple of ales later tongues begin to loosen and mellow, and we start to do what we came here for: to reminisce about Stu.

"Generous, he was," Sparky says. "And always flush."

"Yeah," says Damien. "Couldn't fault him on that."

"It were his share of the house," says Andy. "What his wife gave him. Shouldn't really have been spending it. Still...."

"Had a nice dog," says Jonno, who maybe is scratching around for compliments.

"Cracker," I say. It's the name of the dog. I hadn't meant to speak, but I opened my mouth on the thought, and it just popped out.

"For fuck's sake." Dale snorts into his beer.

"Were a nice dog," protests Jonno.

"Yeah yeah."

"What d'you think it's like," says Damien, "bleeding to death?"

There's silence for a moment as we all contemplate bleeding to death.

"Was probably unconscious," says Sparky at last. "Didn't he hit his head?"

"Think you go cold," I say. "Cold and sleepy."

"Don't sound too bad." Sparky's cheered.

"Sounds shit," says Dale. "You don't get much shitter than dead." We all agree on this.

"You think we should have a run?" suggests Sparky. "Sort of commemoration? Where'd he like to go?"

Everyone perks up. "Hay Bluff?" Andy suggests.

"Na," says Damien. "Roads too slow. Too many sheep."

"And too near," says Dale. "Be there in half an hour."

"He liked the sea," I say. Don't know where I remember this from, but I'm sure it's true.

"Port Eynon," says Damien. "Got a camp site there. And a pub."

"How 'bout Cricieth?" says Dale. "Stay over. Do it proper."

"Where's Cricieth?" asks Andy.

"North. Long way north. Good three hour run. Four, if you

come."

"Oi!" says Andy. "How 'bout Weston?"

"Naa," says Damian. "Fucking motorways all the way…."

Could go on for hours. Favourite topic of conversation, where we go for runs. There's always pros and cons. Lucky Bethan isn't here, so we don't have to listen to her teeth grinding. We're still talking about it – just dismissed Three Cliffs, because someone says the camp site won't take bikers – when I have to go for a piss. The gents are off the front entrance and on my return I'm blocked by a woman's back. She's not moving, just hanging about the entrance.

"Scuse me," I say. She's staring into the interior. She turns round.

"You," she says, as if she's been waiting for me.

"Yeah?" I do a double take. "Hi." The pretty crow who was standing next to Dale at the crematorium. She's amazingly tall. I'm looking straight into her face. Maybe a black swan, not a crow.

I give her a smile but she don't smile back.

"I was looking for you," she says.

"Oh aye?" I assume she means you plural, not me in particular.

"I'm Stu's sister." She says it with aggression, and as if she expects me to quail. Not sure why.

I move my head up and down. "Stu was a good man."

"No he wasn't," she says contemptuously. "He was a nutter."

"Well – "

"So why didn't you look out for him?" Said so furious I feel slapped round the face.

"Er…."

She turns back violently to view the bar. "Who's the one who had a fight with him?"

I shake my head quickly. "Nobody. You got it wrong."

"His hand was bandaged. It happened in a fight. Mum told me."

"He punched a window. Did it himself. No one hit him."

"You say."

"It were his hand," I point out. "Whatever, he was doing the hitting."

She stares at me as if she'd like to argue with this but can't. Then says, "What's your name?"

"Jay."

"And...." She nods towards the others. I'm embarrassed that they're laughing, and willing them to look more sedate." Theirs?"

I hesitate.

"Come on. Christ. You thick or something?"

"No." She's just lost her brother. Think calm.

She gets out a pen and paper. "Write them down. Surnames too." She's so keen I have to push her hands away. "You do it."

She looks me hard in the eye, and I see something click in her mind.

"OK." A little smile to herself. Twigged she's talking to a dullard. She waggles the pencil. "You tell me."

I could just walk away. Say *fuck you*, and walk away. But I don't. Her brother's dead. I mutter, "Why d'you want them?"

"None of your business."

"Sounds like it is."

She sighs. "Last time I saw Stu he was fine. OK, he's a nutter. But not mental. Not..." She screws up her face, tailing away. "Something happened to him."

"Before us," I say. "Honest. When d'you last see him?"

Her eyes slide away and her lips tighten. "A while." She don't want to discuss this. She waggles the pencil again. "Those names."

"I'll introduce you." See if she's got the nerve face to face.

She has. She folds up the piece of paper and I take her over to Dale. Everyone stares at her as we cross the floor, because strangers don't come in the Crucible except by mistake, and lone women never, but she keeps her shoulders back and her stride firm.

Dale says, "Hiya," when I introduce him, and then I realise I don't know the woman's name. Stu's sister, I say.

"Eileen," she says.

The only other Eileen I know is over eighty. Eileen, Eileen, I say to myself, to fix it in my brain.

Dale doesn't say, "Stu was a good man," or any crud like that. He stands more upright and with a crooked friendly smile says, "You want a drink, Eileen?"

As she considers this her eyes rest on him, and the fire leaves her. She came in here tamping, but suddenly she's letting go. She nods at him, and moves her throat, as if she's swallowing the last of the bile, and almost smiles back.

Dale has this trick. It don't work with men. When blokes first meet him we think *no competition* and disregard him. All that floppy blond hair, shiny like a girl's, smooth dreamy face, shit, makes him look soft. But then you see him with women. Bethan says noticing him is nothing for women to congratulate themselves on. Same self-serving antennae at work. In her opinion, it's because he looks (looks, note) so innocent. Not a quality that rates with men, but it does, apparently, with women. The bad ones want to corrupt him, the good ones want to mother him. Simple as that. Dale, of course, being Dale, says yes to all of them. But no woman lasts longer than a month, because he's still saying yes to the next one.

This woman Eileen can keep her cool. She's introduced to Damien and hardly flinches when he grins at her. Two front teeth missing and the rest so green with algae he should be called Popeye. Makes his breath noxious – it's a wonder he don't pass out in his crash helmet. The kid's OK, though. Only twenty one and had a hard life – his Mam's an alky and it was his stepfather who punched out the teeth – and no one could blame him if he was a rager and took it out on the world. But instead he's a willing little runt and getting his life sorted. Driving security vans for a living now.

Sparky insists on shaking her hand. Sparky is into manners, but not like Bethan is. Bethan is well-mannered because she was brought up strict. Sent to her room if she didn't say please and thank you. Sparky's well-mannered because that's how he holds the sky up. He dresses neat too. About ten years ago, when he was nineteen, the sky fell in on him so hard he couldn't get out of bed and he had to go to hospital to have his brain electrocuted. Five times they did it. Sounds cruel, but it's kept the sky up there ever since. His Mam only worries now when he starts wearing a tie or mentioning God. Whisks him off for the tablets and they pull him back. He was in the year above me at school and his family are famous for their brains. His Mam was county chess champion for years and has to be the cleverest dinner lady in Wales. Dunno which joker christened the boy Sparky – not us, for sure – but it's stuck, and he don't seem to mind. Most people assume he's an electrician, anyway.

"Where's your Mam and Dad, then?" Dale asks.

Eileen takes a quick gulp of the gin and orange he's bought her. "Some club down Pontypool. Just tanking up the relatives. Seen enough of them over the last few days. They're so...." Her mouth twists, like it's in pain.

Jonno suddenly appears from the gloom at the back of the room and barges through to the bar.

"Andy says Cricieth sounds the best." He ignores Eileen and slams his empty glass down on the counter. "Just give him a chance to change his carbs, he says. Oi! Stella in that. Whose shout?"

"This is Eileen," Dale says. "Stu's sister."

"Oh aye." Jonno isn't attending. Eileen gives him a moment and then slits her eyes in a way that would make my flesh shrivel. But Jonno's flesh is as block-solid as his brain and looks just as full of itself as usual. Her eyes switch to me and I can read *is that him?* in their darkness. I don't intend to send an answer back but the set of her mouth tells me she's guessed. Well, Jonno's a big boy. He can look after himself.

"I'm his twin, actually." Her voice so silky now it's like a razor through soap. She stares at Jonno, who's still failed to notice her, and then says, "Is this man retarded?"

Dale laughs. I do too. Jonno sticks his chin out. "Eh? What?"

"The lady wants to know if you're retarded." Dale lifts his pint. His eyes glint over the glass.

"What lady?" says Jonno.

"This one," says Eileen.

"Thought you said you were Stu's sister?" Jonno sounds genuinely confused.

Dale gets the giggles. Even Eileen suppresses a grim smile.

"What I want," Eileen says, "is to ask about Stu. Anything you know." Her eyes flicker over us. Me, Damien, Sparky. Even Andy, who's hovering behind Sparky, pulling greasy tangles out of his beard. "It was someone's fault," she says. "Not saying yours, but someone's. I've got to know. I should've come over before –" She suddenly chokes up. Her chin quivers and her lashes moisten.

Feet shuffle. Eyes find interesting blobs in the beer, or on the ceiling. Here we are, at a wake, and we're embarrassed by grief. Female grief, anyway. Got to say something.

"We're planning a run," I say, and hear how pathetic it sounds. "A bike run. For Stu."

She looks at me and her gaze slowly softens. Takes pity on me. "That's nice," she murmurs. "Really nice."

She clears her throat, smiles quickly, and the moment's over. Eyes refocus. The girl's got a grip again, so we have too. Dale takes over. He spots an empty table at the back of the room, and lifts his arm to guide Eileen to it.

"You ask what you like, girl," he says. "We'll see you right."

He takes her over. Sparky follows. But the rest of us don't. It's too early to get anchored at a table and there's nothing we could say that Dale or Sparky couldn't improve on. They'll sort her out. If she really wants a word we're not going anywhere.

It's releasing, Eileen going off. The pool table's empty now. We have a whip round and get a pile of coins on the baize before the wasters who've been in bed all morning drift in. Andy and me first, Damien and Jonno next. Jonno'll beat Damien, so the winner of our game'll play Jonno. Now, there's an incentive.

Half an hour later the place has filled up. We're well stuck into the games and the ale. I assume Eileen's still here, because I see glimpses of Dale over by the bar and he never comes over. Poor cow, I think, when I remember her. Glad she's not bending my ear, mind. And then the ale takes over. Think I forget about her, tell the truth.

# 2

In our house – unless there's work to go to – no one gets up early. Bugger the chicks, Mam says, does 'em good to have a sense of home. Stops them laying in the barn, too, or goring the postman. No one gets up when they wake. What's the fun of lazing in bed if you're not conscious and appreciating it? Mam sorts her medication out early and then likes a full hour before she hauls herself into the kitchen. I get up when I hear someone else has. It takes someone else to get me going. There's long periods of quiet, before that. Sometimes I imagine the three of us lying awake in the house, occasionally sparking thoughts into the air. Just occupying the place.

It's best when there's nothing on your mind. When your thoughts aren't tramrailed and can drift free. I'm a good drifter. At the moment I'm staring at a postcard Bethan has stuck in the mirror by the side of the window. Not sent to me, just bought because she thought it was funny. I suppose it is funny. Well, anyway, I'm glad she finds it funny. It's one of those Winnie the Pooh postcards and it shows the bear at his friend the owl's front door. There's a notice beside the door which says, 'PLEZ CNOKE IF AN RNSR IS NOT REQID'. The bear don't know it's spelled wrong, and nor do the owl. Maybe the postcard's more reassuring than funny. It means that, to Bethan, the fact that my writing's like the notice isn't a big deal. It's just something she knows about me, and can make little jokes about.

I'm less touchy about it these days. Or I try to be. It's like I tell people: the reason I can't spell isn't because I'm dull, it's because I have a special brain. Two brains, actually, that's how I see it, one inside the other. The inner one's fine – pretty OK, it seems to me. The outer brain's the problem. It lets the world in, but muddles everything going out. Like a one-way scrambler. I can do all the input: reading, seeing, hearing, understanding. Yeah, I can read fine, soak the squiggles up. Writing's another matter. I can't order the components, that's the trouble. In fact, can't order full stop. I can reach about H in the alphabet, just on momentum. Months of the year, in order: it's a struggle. Multiplication tables: forget it. Six times six is thirty six; but I know this only because I've just worked it out. Seen six blocks of six, and added them in my head. Sequencing problems, that's what they call it. They started calling it that when I was in Mrs Owen's class, just after I'd tried to explain that I couldn't learn poems like we were meant to over the weekend because the words got stuck in my head and couldn't get out again. Not sure she understood what I was saying because I didn't speak very clear in those days, and I kept being told to start again, at the beginning this time, and take it slow, but anyway they thought they'd better have me tested because I was obviously weird. Eight, I was. You should have seen those results. Not that I did, till a long time after. Abstract reasoning – stratospheric. Well, OK, 'far above average'. Ditto vocabulary, once they'd translated the mumbles. (Dad was a word freak. Knew the word 'precocious' before I was five.) Reading – average. Nothing special, but all right. But spelling, hand-writing, hardly out of the mud. So when I went to the comp they wrote dyslexic on my forehead – rather them than me – and sent me to special classes. Let me off foreign languages and chemistry. Told the other kids to stop calling me stupid, which of course they took instant note of.

My teacher took me to a talk once for dyslexic kids, where the woman speaker said there was no cure, and we should all organise our lives around what we could do, and not bother to struggle with what we couldn't. We should identify our talents, and work on those. I have talents. These are: I can find my way out of anywhere.

Mr Homing Pigeon, that's me. No one can get me lost – I may not be able to sequence, but there's nothing wrong with my eyes or my memory, and it's like I've got my own radar. I can fit objects together, because I can see the connections between things, and the overall picture, even if I'm shit at explaining either to anyone else. I can control machinery, as long as I'm in control. Like motorbikes. I can appreciate beauty. I can't draw, but I can see the pretty pictures things make and I can see them everywhere, micro, macro: the whorls on my thumb to the moon like a turtle egg, popping up out of Skirrid Fawr. I can sleep anywhere. Us dyslexics need a lot of sleep. Because we can't order we don't pattern, and each day's a new exciting experience. Things don't become routine, which can be good, if what you're doing's fun, or shit, if it's not. Whichever, we get tired quickly. New, new, new, it's zapping into us all the time.

But there's no even half-decent jobs that don't require output. There were no apprenticeships around when I left school, and even trade courses at college, like welding, you got to do some writing. Applications, for a start. I mean I can weld anyway, enough to get by, but employers want certificates. There's no job that matches my talents. I could be a silent appreciator of beauty somewhere unexplored or mazelike, but I've never seen an ad for this. So I do like the lady said. I don't struggle. I organise my life around what I can do, and what I want to do. I work half the year in one of the factories round here. Wiring amplifiers, or punching out plastic, or deep-freezing chicken legs. Factories off every roundabout; plenty of chance to ring the changes. But half a year's long enough to spend killing yourself on shiftwork and going blind with boredom. Some can do it, some can't. October to March, with as much overtime and weekend work as I can screw out of them, then a few days cheek to whichever bastard deserves it most, so I'm handed my cards, and I'm off. You can stand it for six months if you're working towards something: a whole spring and summer of freedom. Mam gets my dole for board, and I got enough saved on top to keep a big legal bike on the road. My life's determined by the peculiarities of my brain, and part of me thinks it's dealt me the crappest hand ever, and the rest says bollocks, don't snivel, Jay, there's plenty others worse off.

Beside me Bethan is still asleep, and now she's purring. It's probably a sinus problem but it sounds cute. She does it when she's about to surface, and in a minute she'll stretch her body as long as she can make it, chin tipped to the ceiling, make a squeaking noise, and then she'll be awake. See, I can sequence Bethan. Nine months it's been now, since she moved in. Sometimes feels like forever, sometimes only yesterday. We met just over a year ago. On a night, in fact, like it's going to be tonight, judging by the blue outside. A hot May night, when I was with the boys at the Chainbridge, everyone outside so we could admire the stars and take pops at May bugs which were zooming around our heads like motorised acorns. Inside there was a hen party going on, as raucous as they get. The women were waiting for the stripper to turn up and getting excited about it, which made pushing inside to get beers intimidating or gratifying, depending on the resilience of your balls. Most of us had been groped or pinched and Dale had already been told he was the popular choice for stand-in if the real guy didn't turn up. Jonno, on the other hand, had bulldozed his way through the crowd several times and hadn't even had his bum fondled, and he was sour about this and harbouring retaliatory thoughts. So he gets Sparky and Damien to stop popping at the May bugs and start collecting them instead in one of the crash helmets. When he's got a dozen or so he wades into the throng inside and shakes them out. Just one May bug can be impressive in an enclosed space – fast as a bat, with no sonar to stop crashes – and a dozen in furious hurtling mood creates havoc. In seconds half the hen party's outside, and the other half has fallen over furniture, or banged themselves senseless into walls, or are just rooted to the spot, screeching and flapping their hands over their hair. We think it's quite funny but the women don't, and neither does the landlord.

We're made to troop inside and clear the bugs out and pick up broken glass while several furious braver women, which includes Bethan, stand at the doorway and shout at us. Dale picks up the broken glass wearing a frown, as close to anxious as he ever looks, because the stripper still hasn't turned up. Thirty women panting for male flesh and in payback mood are a scary sight. But just as the women are crowding back in again, all snide and mouthy, the real performer turns up. Bet he'd never been kissed by welcoming blokes before. Don't know what the act is like because we're banished outside, but they're power-freaks, these guys, can twist a crowd with their little fingers, never mind their dicks, and it's only seconds before the roof's lifting with appreciation.

And after that night, like always happens when axes are out, we keep bumping into Bethan and her mates. Luckily, though, our offensiveness dims over time. After a while they stop scowling at us and start laughing instead. Remember the May bugs night, they cackle. We become quite pally. At least two of the women get Dale's togs off privately, and I take a real liking to Bethan, though I keep this to myself at first. But I hang around close enough to discover she's a sensible, law-abiding girl, even if she does throw the ale down, and I can't stop trying to impress her that I'm an OK citizen too. Like I swear off fighting, for instance, and then realise I haven't bruised a knuckle for years. Not since meeting Dale. Interesting, that. Start to think I might even deserve a girl like Bethan. Then she finds out about my writing problem, and while I'm holding my breath she chats on about how she's got a cousin who's dyslexic and he can't even read, but he's really clever, and wicked fun. Suddenly I'm bathing in green light, and from then on I'm at her beck. She goes anywhere, I do too. She wants anything, I sort it. Leave her in no doubt I'm smitten, and she don't brush me off. I start giving her lifts home – she's in one of the hospital flats in those days – and it's only a fortnight before she invites me to stay over. I'm sober – been drinking pop till I'm pissing bubbles so she'll ride with me – and she's wine-tipsy that night, which results in brilliant sex, and in the morning we do it again, slower and both sober, and it's even better. While she's lying there with me all over her, she suddenly twitches and groans and says she'd like to die now, please, if it's all right with me. I've never had a woman say that to me before, and after we've finished each other off I become a bit moist-eyed with affection. She gets very tender and whispers that I hide my light under a haystack, and she's so glad she bothered to lift the hay. It's kind of stayed lifted too, while we've been together, and even Mam's noticed I'm a more radiant person than I used to be.

I can hear the pups chirruping out in the shed. It's too late for the postman, so it must be someone else. Not expecting any visitors till midday-ish, when some of the boys are coming round to ride in the field on the trail bikes we keep up here. It could be burglars, but Floss is back in the house now the pups are weaned and she isn't barking, which suggests someone she knows has spoken to her. "Floss, it's me," you say, as you stand in the yard, and it's uncanny how many voices she can recognise. Could even tell mine the time I tried it after a balloon gulp of helium.

I hear the front door bang. Sod it. That means it's my sister Carly, the only person who doesn't live here who has a key. What's she doing here? Should be at work. In my opinion it's a cheek for her to waltz in and out of here without knocking, like it's her own gaff, when she and scabby shit husband've got their own place and we wouldn't do the same to them, but Mam says this attitude is mean-minded and typical brother.

I leave enough time for Carly to put the kettle on and rouse Mam, and then heave myself up. Just because I won't relax now, knowing she's out there, whinging and dumping her troubles. As I'm pulling on my boots Bethan makes her squeak and says, "Wha..?" and I say, "Just Carly," and she groans and pulls the duvet up over her head. Bethan and Carly don't really hit it off. Carly can't see Bethan's angelic qualities – even called her a gold digger once, what a joke – and Bethan can see Carly's demonic ones only too clearly, so they're never likely to be bosom mates.

In the kitchen Carly's grizzling on already, with her big bum on the table. Actually it's not so big these days, she's lost stones since her teens, but old insults die hard. Leather jeans, she's wearing today. It's usually them or crotch-length skirts. Blonde flecks in her tufty brown hair like it's got a deficiency disease. As she swings round to me I see she's got a black eye. Explains the day off work. No prizes for guessing who gave her that.

"Look what Russell's done to her," Mam says, though she don't sound devastated.

"More fool you," I say, referring to the fact that she knew what the bloke was like, and still went ahead and got hitched to him. And I bet she started it. I'm not generally in favour of hitting women, but as Carly's brother I've come in for abuse from her myself, and she swung a heavier punch a few years ago than she does now. You have to be very saintly, or a masochist, just to stand there and take it. Russell is neither, just a scabby shit wanker.

"What's he say?" Carly whines at Mam. "He's mumbling."

I do not mumble. Bethan can understand me. Mam can understand me. That woman Eileen understood me last night. I left my mumbling behind years ago but Carly won't have it. She knows how to wind me up. Of all the ones who've called me stupid, she's the worst.

"Shut up, Pigface," I say.

"Mam!" Carly wails.

"Now now." Mam fills three mugs with tea. "You go let the chicks out, Jay. Leave the pups a while. Take this with you and have a mooch, there's a good lad."

"Mam," I moan. I sound just like Carly, that's what she does to me. But I know what'll happen. She'll bend Mam's ear long enough to make it wilt and then she'll bounce out, bright as a daisy, having offloaded all the shit on to someone who'll worry about it for days, but can't do a thing about it. Makes me mad.

"Jay…." Mam's using her weary, do-this-for-me voice.

I grab the mug of tea and slam out the back door. Stride across the yard. Letting out the chicks I wait until the cockerel's strutting down the ramp, just swelling himself up to do his first liberated doodle-do, and then give him a swift kick up the backside so he loses face in front of his stupid wives. Blame Carly, I tell him.

I stay vicious checking the nest boxes – two broodies asking to have their necks wrung – and then stand up straight, and tell myself to get a grip. Imagine Bethan watching me. Embarrassing.

I take my mind off by wandering over to the field fence to baa at the sheep. Sheep aren't that bright. Unduly influenced by colour, in my view. We once had a white car, an old Passat estate; major mistake. Had to drive at the speed of light through the nursery field or else we picked up a bleating trail of lambs who'd decided, in their very limited wisdom, that that big white hard grumbling thing on the track was a much more promising mam than the smaller woolly baaing thing they'd only recently been born from. Caused mass desperation among the ewes, and several of the lambs burnt their noses trying to get milk out of the exhaust.

This year all the sheep are Randolph's, and he's responsible for checking them out and replacing their licks. Mam just maintains the fences and pockets the rent. Keeps her in needles and spectacles and not a lot else. In a couple of weeks they'll be out on the mountain top, making the most of the scrub till the bracken takes over.

I toy with the idea of a quick game of Grandma's Footsteps with the ewes. Always cheers me up. They've been fed over the winter, so they associate humans with food. You stroll through the field, not looking behind you, just listening to the crescendo of baas as they fall into a flock behind you, and then when the noise becomes very close and loud you stop and turn round. Instant silence. Not a foot moves. Not an eye meets yours. Tum te tum, they go, weren't following you, honest. You start to chuckle, turn away, and resume walking. Rustle rustle behind you. A tentative bleat, then another, and another, till the whole flock's baaing again. Wait till it's deafening, then swing round again. Sheep freeze. Point at one of them, twitching a foot – hey, caught you that time, girlie, you're out. They look so, um, sheepish. Can do it for hours, if your stomach muscles are up for it.

I'm just thinking, yeah, why not be a lunatic on your own land, when chicken squawks tell me someone's up at the gate. Bugger me, them fowls are keen. And oh shit, it's a blue Escort. Just when I was lightening up. But trouble never comes in ones, here's scabby shit husband Russell.

I stroll round the front to meet him, debating my welcome. I could haul him out of his car and hammer him to a pulp on the concrete, or I could shake him by the hand and congratulate him on his restraint in not pulping Carly. It's a tough one.

He's seen me and I have to say he don't look scared. His greasy little face even flashes me a quick smile.

"She here?" He bounces out of the car, eyes darting. Only a small guy, same height but a lot slighter than Carly. He's been picking his pimples again. He's got no more pimples, I daresay, than the average twenty year old, but he feasts on them till they make you want to throw up.

"In the kitchen with Mam," I say. "You given her a shiner, you gobshit."

"Fucking hell, Jay, had to stop her. Look at my arms." He pushes up the sleeves of his sweatshirt to show me a lattice of scarlet nail tracks from bony elbow to skinny wrist. "An' here," he says, turning his face.

"Shit." What I thought were pimples are little wounds.

"Fucking ciggie," he says, "when I was asleep. The woman's mental."

"You married her." But, fuck me, I'm shocked. What kind of woman sticks a lighted fag into her husband's sleeping face? A mental woman, he's right. Thing is, we're all so used to Carly that her rages are just part of her. She's not mental as in can't cope. She's got a job, a steady one, down the benefit office. She dresses sharp, pays good money to have her hair messed up. She's not fat any more. Big, but not fat. No one calls her Pigface now except me. Trouble is, Russell don't know what he's taken on. Carly's twenty-six and has a problem. Big problem. And he's a useless kid.

"You come to take her back?" Shit, I hope he has. Be the shortest marriage on record, else. And they deserve each other. Russell's still doing community service for nicking cash out of jackets and handbags down the pensioners club. Who nicks from people on sticks? Someone with the maturity and judgement to marry Carly, that's who.

Luckily he has come round to make up. I follow him back to the kitchen and watch him being more of a gent than I expect, not showing Mam his arms or telling her about his face, but nodding contritely when Mam tells him he and Carly are too big to be fighting. Mam's sight is so poor she can't see the wounds on his face. But Carly's softened now and says not to blame him, 'cos it weren't really his fault. She's done her dumping and the rage has lifted. She's actually holding his hand by the end. Mam hasn't eaten yet, which she should have done by now given her condition, and she looks exhausted.

After they've gone Mam stuffs herself with cereal and I wonder whether to tell her about Carly burning Russell. I know it'd only upset her more, but I can't get it out of my head. There were at least three burns. So she must have held him down. Must have really meant it. Creepy. If I was Russell I'd become an insomniac.

I decide to tell Bethan instead. She's a nurse; might even have something sensible to say about it. I burst into the bedroom and start saying it.

"Stop!" Bethan's still lying in bed and puts a hand over her eyes as if I'm hurting her. "Slow down. Who burnt who?"

"Uh. Carly. Russell. While he was asleep." I touch the side of my face, showing her where. "Three times."

Bethan groans, without lifting the hand. "Maybe he'd done something really shitty before he went to bed."

"Even so."

"Yeah." She sighs. "Expect they were pissed. Had a bloke in casualty once, his mate had bitten his ear off. Best mates, they were, too. She gone now?"

"Yup. And Russell."

"Great." She swings her legs out of bed. "It's not your problem, Jay."

"Well...." Not sure I agree. But I can tell she don't want it being *her* problem. Well, can't blame her. Expect she gets enough at work. I leave her to get dressed and go and have a crap. Maybe Carly was pissed, I think. Maybe being pissed excuses it. Maybe.

Lunch time Andy, Sparky and Damien arrive to play with the trail bikes. Dale's at work down in Cwmbran and Jonno wasn't invited. He's probably working anyway; he's part of a team of heavies shift-guarding an empty factory for a new owner. Four fifty an hour, he gets. Doesn't have to do anything except play with the rottweilers, but it's still a criminal rate. Even the places I work pay at least six, and that's without shift allowances or bonuses. Jonno hasn't much choice though, the benefit office stopped his money again. Andy's finished work for the day, being a postman, and he's come with his wife Maureen, who's as clean and plump as he is grubby and skinny, and she's brought a picnic so she can sit on a rug and chomp while we play in the field. Maureen and Andy have been married twelve years, since they were both twenty-two, and have two school-age kiddies who've miraculously survived being brought up in the deathtrap they call home. Last time I visited their place there was no electricity upstairs – Andy was putting in a new circuit and had run out of cable – and too much electricity everywhere else, because he'd jammed a nail in the fuse box to stop the power cutting out every time they used the washing machine. Don't touch *anything*, I told Bethan, on the way there.

Sparky's here because he don't work, being on invalidity, and I'm not sure how Damien's got the time off. Maybe security van drivers work shift hours, or maybe Andy just said, "Let's go to Jay's tomorrow," and Damien said, "Yeah, let's." Easily led, Damien is. He's got very pally with Andy and Maureen since he moved in with them a month ago. Just a temporary arrangement, while he waits for his own flat to come through. And he don't seem to have come to any harm yet. In fact just noticed this morning, when he grinned at me, that he seems to have started cleaning his teeth. The few he's got, that is. Since Andy isn't known for his bathroom skills this has to be Maureen's influence.

Today we're practising riding the bikes paparazzi-style. That is, two up, with the passenger facing backwards, hands free to hold a camera. Amazingly, despite the lorryloads of law concerning bikes, nobody's thought to make one about which way round you sit. They've assumed any sane person would naturally face forwards. Ha. Andy's riding now, with Damien behind him. They've graduated from straight lines – the track – to field circuits, and now to random-sized figures of eight. To make it easier one side of the bike is splashed with red paint, other side with blue. That way Andy can just shout red or blue before he turns and doesn't have to shout right or left which might be confusing to someone facing the other way. Someone like me, say, to whom left and right are toss-ups at the best of times. We haven't progressed to carrying a camcorder yet, because nobody's got one except Dale and he's refusing to lend it, but Damien's holding a brick to his eye, which is more or less the same size and weight. If we can do it over bumpy ground it must be a piss on the open road. Damien's only dropped the brick twice in the last ten minutes, and only clouted himself in the face with it once. Andy claims he wasn't to know that the lump he drove over was the top of a boulder, not a squishable molehill.

Bethan has joined Maureen on the rug. Because she's in her uniform – starts work at two – she makes the scene look amazingly responsible. Here we boys are, risking bruised bums, sprained wrists and facial self-bricking in pursuit of self-improvement and we got our very own medical staff on standby.

The other bike's clutch cable has snapped, so I'm sitting on the grass by it chatting to Sparky, asking him what happened with Eileen after I left them at the Crucible. I left early – shagged, I suddenly was, about four. Too much stress at the funeral and then too much quick booze. Got a taxi home and slumped with Floss till Bethan and Mam came in. Sparky says Eileen seems to have accepted that her twin's state of mind was nothing much to do with us. She's pointing the finger at Stu's wife, and even more so at the bloke she dumped Stu for.

"You know who it is," Sparky says, looking at me as if he's sure I must know.

"Who?" First I even heard that there was another bloke involved. Or maybe I missed it. With Stu it was rides and boozing, not heart-to-hearts.

Sparky stares at me a second longer, and then says, "Carno."

"Shit."

He don't have to say more. Sparky and I were at school together. I know Carno, though I wish I didn't. Carno is the fuck-bastard who killed my Dad. Just hearing his name makes my jaw twist and cramps my guts. What the fuck is someone like Stu's wife doing with Carno?

Sparky guesses the question. "Working for him, she was."

Carno. A man who can kill someone's dad, and another bloke too, one of his own men, and walk away. Waste disposal, that's what Carno does. Got a big depot at the edge of town. Wish someone would waste him. A heap of money in waste. Specially dangerous waste. Even more if you charge for dealing with it properly, and then just dump it. My Dad was an ambulance man. He earned his money helping people. Carno earns his money dumping shit. Three drums of Arcton 11 down a storm drain and a worker in after it. We're talking lethal volatile. Refrigerant. Someone calls an ambulance, and Carno still don't say what the stuff is. Lets Dad go down after his worker, knowing it'll kill him too. All so he doesn't have to admit he knows. Is that cold-blooded? Fucking refrigerant-blooded? And then afterwards, when it comes to court, the driver who swore Carno was in on it changes his story and the cunt gets away with it. The dead bloke gets blamed for disobeying orders, cutting corners. And Carno just takes a fine on the business, and walks away. Fucking walks away.

"She moved into his place," Sparky says. "That's how she could pay Stu off for the house. They got a kiddie too, you know that?"

Yeah, I did. Little boy. Even been told the name, but I've forgotten it.

"Says her parents complained that Stu never went to see him, but she thinks maybe he was warned off. Said he doted on the kid. You know, maybe Carno made it difficult?"

"Mmm. Could be." Like to believe it, but lots of doting dads don't get round to seeing their kids when they split. Andy's got another kid somewhere he never sees, even though Maureen wouldn't mind. The boy would be about fifteen now. Too much hassle, Andy says. And he's an OK mate.

"Can't compete with Carno," says Sparky. "When he wants something, he gets it."

"Aye, he does." You can't get back at him, either. I tried, after Dad died. I was fifteen myself then, and it nearly got me locked up. Carno lives miles away, down by the Usk, but I spotted his Jag outside Llanelly Village church. Guest at a wedding or something. Remembered the number plate, 100 TC. Thomas Carno. I was cycling back from a mate in Gilwern, no tools on me or anything, but I found a spade in the graveyard leant up against my favourite statue, the one of a dog and his master, and I used it to bash in every panel on that Jag. Even got the blade underneath and bent the exhaust, because I knew they cost two thousand quid new. Doing it was noisy but I didn't care, just got into it. A crowd of blokes come out to watch, half of them in grey tail suits and fancy hats, and when I put the spade down they jump me. The police take me away and put me in a cell and tell me I'm looking at time, because the Jag's a write-off. And then a few hours later I hear that Mr Carno's being very nice about it, understanding like, knowing what happened to my dad, and isn't going to press charges. Persuaded his insurance company likewise. I got to listen to how grateful I should be to Mr Carno. I even see him at the police station, and he's so smooth with the coppers I want to puke. The police try to make me say I'm sorry but I say no way, and tell them the only reason Carno's dropping charges is because he don't want me in court saying how he killed my Dad. Carno doesn't push it at the station. He waits till I'm out and about again, and then comes round to the small-holding asking to see me. Mam won't give him the time of day but he spots me in the field and comes over and says that if I try anything like that again he'll cut my dick off. He's a lot larger and stronger than me – late developer I was, just a wisp in those days – and he actually grabs me there and hurts me so bad I go down on my knees. He's really calm and just stands over me, watching me gagging on the grass. Says no one gets at him and walks away upright, and he's only letting me off light this time because I'm a poor fatherless boy and I don't know the rules. I gasp that I'm telling the police and he says no I'm not, not if I value my dick, and it pains me to say so but he's right. He fucking scared me. Twitchy inside for weeks. I hate him for that, too. Should have been him scared, not me. Still, I was only fifteen. And wrecking the car was good. It helped. Mind, I'd choose something different these days. No point in cars; the bastard insurance always pays.

How old would Carno be now? I'm remembering what he looked like, jowly face, business suit, close-cut thinning hair, and thinking he must be an old man now, thirteen years on, but then when you're fifteen anyone over twenty-five looks past it. May have been only thirty-ish. Make him forty five-ish now. Not so far past it.

Sparky fiddles with the top button of his shirt, looking like he's trying to fasten it. I can see two neat ironing lines down the front. Bit agitated this morning, perhaps.

"Told Eileen you had it in for Carno once," he says. "The time you totalled his Jag. She was…" – he nods his head emphatically –

"well, you should have stayed. She was kind of excited."

"Oh aye?" I never told Sparky that Carno hurt me. I never told anyone. Not even Mam. Too afraid she'd do something and Carno would hurt her too. Nobody walks away upright, he said. But I wouldn't have told Sparky anyway because we weren't friends then. Just went to the same school. The whole town, never mind the school, knew about me trashing Carno's Jag and getting away with it. So they thought. Earned me some not-stupid points, for a while.

"You tell her why?" I ask.

"Why what?"

I've jumped too far back. "Er... what he did. Why I had it in for him."

"Oh. Yeah, kind of. She said well now he'd killed two people."

He'd done that anyway. But Sparky means Dad and Stu. Not sure I like Dad and Stu lumped together. Carno didn't push Stu down those cellar steps. Didn't pour whisky in his gob. Didn't lie to him, and save his own hide by killing him, which is what he did to my dad. And Stu didn't lose his life trying to save someone else's.

"She went back with Dale," Sparky says. "After. Said she wanted somewhere more private, like. Hmm."

He's fixed wide-open eyes on the grass. Is he suggesting Dale pulled? Don't believe it. Eileen didn't look like a woman out for a shag, and Dale never makes first moves. Expect she sussed him for the most sensible there and wanted more conversation with no distractions. Somewhere Jonno wasn't, for instance.

There's a woofing behind us and we turn to see Floss galloping over the turf, pursued by the pups hell-bent on catching her and dragging her to the ground by her dugs. Watching the pups run is a treat; they fall over blades of grass, their own noses. I shout to Andy to stop the trail bike; one bump could cost us four hundred quid. Floss shoots between Bethan and Maureen and hunkers down close – protect me protect me she's saying in doggy language. Amazing how she chooses the women, as if she knows they've got dugs too and'll understand. Or maybe they smell of picnic. I snatch up a pup as it passes, lie back, and roll it across my chest. It's got a fat bare tum, skin soft as chammy. Soon we're all doing it. There's six of us and six of them, and we're all gooing and laughing at the wriggling bodies, while Floss sits smug on the rug, congratulating herself on knowing that soppy humans dote on her babies even if she don't.

No one bothers with the bikes again. Once we're flat on the grass in the sunshine it's too much effort to get up. The pups wriggle and chew at our hands and then suddenly fall asleep like they've been switched off. I hear Bethan get up and say tara and wave a hand at her, and then stare up into the sky at gauzy drifts of high cloud, polish smear against the blue. An aeroplane going to America tows a vapour trail like an out-of-focus message. I find myself thinking about Carno, and then about Carly, and notice how close their names are. Never thought that before. Carno's to blame for Carly's rages, too. Shit, when we were kids she and I used to play – we was Princess Leia and Han Solo for years. What Carno did screwed her up proper.

So then I imagine Carly bending over Carno, stubbing a fag out on his sleeping bastard face, and I think yeah, you go to it, girl, really hurt him. Not mental at all.

# 3

Waste is big in the Valleys. House junk, industrial waste, demolition trash, litter. House junk specially. We seem to have a lot to get rid of. Or maybe we break things more than most. Or maybe we buy cheap stuff and it don't last, so we get through more sofas, mattresses, carpets, tellies, cars than anywhere else. One of Mam's friends gets all her carpets second hand from Aber market, and when they're clotted with grandkid baby rusks and dog hair and your feet stick to the cola stains she just throws the lot out and gets new ones. New old ones, that is. You can't walk a hundred yards on some of the hills round here without finding a soggy armchair to sit on, and it's got worse since shops stopped taking soft furnishings part exchange. The fire regulations came in and they can't sell them on. If you can't flog them private yourself you got to ring the council, or dump them. Everyone knows that picking a phone up takes more effort than sneaking a three piece suite up the mountain and tucking it behind a hummock, so that's where they end up.

And businesses flytip too, 'cos they've got to pay to use the tips. They load the waste in a pickup or lorry and dump it. Or get some cowboy to do it for them. There's places above Pontypool where it's plastic bags as far as the eye can see. We got no pride in the landscape, that's the trouble. It's got value, but we can't see it. And the reason we can't see it is because the whole place used to be a dump. Under our feet, up on the skyline, you can't forget it. Hills of spoil, plains of landfill. Land that's been dumped on forever, from the coal and steel days. They did it grand scale, we do it small scale.

It's a tradition.

That Carno's a kind of dung beetle. Gets fat on the shit people produce. Na, that's insulting to dung beetles. Mr Attenborough says the plains of Africa'd be waist high in shit if it weren't for them. Carno's an imposter dung beetle – looks like he's cleaning up, even as he spews out the other end. His kind play it win-win. There's a lot of rubbish, and enough people who haven't got the time or transport to dump it themselves, so they look for someone to do it for them, and take the cheapest quote. The Carno-beetle quote. Waste is gregarious. Dumps grow overnight; just needs one person to seed it. A couple of armchairs, a pick-up of rubble, and a week later the Carno-beetles have moved in and you need artics to take it away. So the bastards are charging one end and ducking tip fees the other. Must do enough legit to hand in forms where they have to, but the flytipping's where the big profits lie. And fouling up the territory is nothing to them, because with the money they make they don't have to live here.

Thought nothing of rubbish when I was little. Quite interesting to kids. Scrap, specially. The other side of the mountain there's a steep escarpment below the top road. Older kids nick cars, give them a spin, strip the audio fittings, and then take them up and push them down the slope. Only a few thorn bushes to slow them so they go a hell of a way, bouncing and rolling and breaking up. Then younger kids come up from below and scavenge the remains. Got myself a set of alloys once, which the older kids hadn't bothered to nick because they wanted to see the car roll. No vehicle to put them on, but didn't stop me gloating over them. No second thoughts till the time I came across gravestones dumped in the old quarry. All with local names: Parry, Thomas, Bevan, Meredith. Smashed up, but so you could still read chunks of them. Someone must have cleared an old graveyard. From the dates on the stones, could have been someone's parents' grandparents. Knew it weren't right. Made me feel hot. Bet that was Carno. Could have been Carno, anyway. Some mutant beetle like him.

It was after Dad died and we knew what happened that I started noticing the shit everywhere. Once you see it, you're never blind again. For a while I was a one-kid crusade. If I caught flytippers up here the least they got was an earful. I used to go looking for them, walking round like the Lone Ranger, air rifle over a shoulder, the old dog behind me pretending to be Tonto. Set him on a bloke once, because he took exception to the names I called him. I put up skull and crossbones signs saying 'Flytippers will be shot.' Spelt right, too. That got in the papers. Photo of the sign and everything. Didn't own up to it, of course, but the article weren't too disapproving, so maybe I should have. Maybe I'd be Director of Dumping by now. Or maybe they'd have sent a SWAT team round to take the rifle off me and locked me up. Who knows.

I gave up my lone patrols after a while because in the end you got to let things go. Feeling stirred up isn't comfortable. Either it becomes your life's sad work, or you stop and move on. Thinking about it can still stir me up, so I try not to. And that includes thinking about Carno. I want him punished – killed, preferably, nastily, like he killed my Dad – but I don't want to swing for him, so the only way is not to think about him. Been a while since I did. Can't help it, though, when people push him at me. Dale rings early evening and he's on about Carno too. And Eileen. Warns me I might get a visit from her.

"Eh ?" I say. "What for?"

"Got it in her head he's to blame for messing Stu up. Taking his wife and kid."

"So?"

"Thinks you've got something in common. Sparky told him about your dad. You having a rough time, hating him." He sighs. "Just like, humour her. She's kind of upset. Angry upset."

"Told her where I live, did you?"

"Couldn't see reason not to."

I chew on this a moment. I know I don't want Eileen up here – an Eileen who's going to grind on about Carno – but I can't find words to make it sound reasonable. Getting stirred up doesn't seem enough. The poor cow's stirred up herself, sounds like.

"Just let her talk," says Dale. "You don't have to do nothing. Is Bethan around?"

"At work," I say. "Till ninish."

"Mmm. Well. Just don't agree to top him, that's all."

"Ha ha."

He gives a chuckle. "Just see it, like, as something you're doing for Stu."

"Right," I say. "Yeah."

I put the phone down feeling heavy. Shit shit shit, I think. And Dale thinks it's nothing. Carno's just a story to him.

Mam's back from Randolph's office and I don't want her getting stirred up too, so I tell her Stu's sister's coming round, just to say hi to his old friends, but that I'll take Floss out for a run when she does. We won't bother her. Mam says, "As you like, Jay," with a sniff like I'm eighteen again and suggesting she's an embarrassment. Too bad; no way round it.

Eileen arrives sevenish. Never know it was evening though; the sun's still hot and the midges are still fizzing in the shadows, waiting till it's cooler before they zip out and munch on us. Eileen drives up in a VW Polo. Yellow. According to the registration it's only a year old, which makes her an expensively vehicled person. She poops at the gate, as if she knows the chicks aren't friendly; or maybe she's used to having gates opened for her. I walk up with Floss and wave her through and she hardly looks at me as she drives down to the yard. I can see through the glass she's dressed smart. The small-holding isn't used to smart visitors and I feel it setting its jaw and hunching its shoulders, making itself shabbier by the second. Floss is going to jump up when Eileen gets out of the Polo, but because I'm feeling put-upon that she's here I don't call her in. I remember that the woman thinks I'm stupid. If she decides I'm too uncouth to be useful that'll be fine by me.

She gets out of the Polo and brushes Floss away. "Down dog," she says with a frown. "Shoo." She's as tall and thin and dark-eyed as she was last night, and wearing a sleeveless silky top over tan trousers. Her sandals are thin soles attached by gold plaits to her big toes.

"Hello." Her smile's just a flicker. "Did Dale tell you I might visit?"

I push my hands into my pockets. "Aye."

She stares at me and then says, "I thought you might be able to help me out."

"Don't know about that," I say. "Depends."

A small frown marks her forehead, as if she's grasping I'm not overjoyed to see her but don't understand why. Can't see Floss getting her walk, because of those sandals, but I still don't want her mixing with Mam, so I sigh and say, "You wanna come round the back?"

She shakes her head. "No. I was wondering.... You know Carno, don't you?"

"Aye. Well, been a while. But yeah."

"And you know where he lives?"

"Aye." So do the rest, mind. Carno's place, that's what it's known as. "Why d'you want to know that?"

"I don't want to know it," she says. "I got the address from Mum and Dad. I want to see it."

"So what's stopping you?" The way she's looking at me tells me she knows I've a special interest in Carno. But it don't explain why she's come here.

"I want to see him," she says. "The man himself."

"Ah, now." I feel my head shaking.

"I'm not going to do anything," she says. "Just... look at him."

I think of saying she's more chance of seeing him without me; and then wonder if that's true. Unless Carno's had his face remodelled I'd know him anywhere, even thirteen years on, and it's true, the others might not. More have heard of him than know the man himself. But would he recognise me? 'Course not. Just a fly he swatted a long time ago. A kid of fifteen. Bet I'm bigger than him now, too.

"Just want you to come with me. Identify him for me."

My head's still shaking, but I'm searching around for a reason to back it. All I know is that I won't enjoy seeing Carno, and she must know that already from chatting to Sparky and Dale. It hasn't stopped her. It's not something I could say.

"Please." She's begging. Actually dips her knees. "There's no one else."

I can't name a reason. She's said she's not going to do anything. Still feels a big deal, big hump to slide over, but she sounds desperate....

"OK," I sigh. Shit, I think, a second later. Shit.

But I get a smile. Beautiful smile.

"Thanks, thanks," she says. She tips her head at the car meaning 'so let's go now' and gets back inside. I hesitate – last moment to back out – but then walk round and climb in beside her. No one'll know, except me.

Eileen don't talk while she drives, and she holds the Polo's steering wheel so tight her hands squeak when she adjusts her grip. I concentrate on my lefts and rights, but sitting next to her I can wave my hands anyway, and each time I give her a direction she just nods and follows it. She drives like she dresses. Smart but not fast. She smells cool and piny, like Bethan's hair when she's just washed it. I'm not thinking ahead, yet.

Carno lives down by the river, west of Crickhowell. Only six, seven miles away, but it's another country, green and lush. No pylons marching across the valley, or the skyline. The sheep are fat and short-legged and nobody dumps in the lay-bys.

After we've left the A40 I push my mind on.

"What you going to do when we get there?" I ask.

She don't answer for a moment. She looks so cool and smart that I assume she's got the answer, but when I glance sideways at her I'm jolted. She's thinking about what I said, not how her face is

40

behaving, and her eyes are black and intense. She looks like Stu. Stu was neither cool nor smart.

She shakes her head and says, "It depends."

"Stu's wife might be there," I warn her. "And the kiddie."

"Yes." She sighs. "My nephew. Neil."

"You want to see them, too?"

"No way." A quick head shake.

What's this woman doing? What'm I doing? Shit. Feels like scatter-gun stuff. Not as if Carno's place is somewhere you can spy on from the road. We're going to have to drive right in. Carno might not even be here; we'd have been better off calling in at the depot.

On the other hand, now we're nearly here there's things creeping up in my own head. Like she's taken me a small way with her, more ways than one. Top layer knows this is a bad idea, but underneath I can feel a twinge of interest. Edges of hard thoughts surfacing. There's night security patrol notices up every few hundred yards. The houses we pass cost more than I'd earn in a lifetime. Looking at them fans coals in me.

"Gateway coming up," I say, waving my hand to indicate the other side of the road. "Couple of hundred yards. Big white posts."

She drops a gear and squeaks her hands on the wheel. Indicates. We pull in between double white gates, standing open. Through a line of trees we can see the house. Mansion, really, square-set and bright white too, like a chalk cliff-face.

"Must be worth a bit," Eileen murmurs.

"Aye."

She's got balls, I'll give her that. She trundles the Polo up to the front of the house where there's three vehicles parked on the gravel already. A Range Rover, a Golf, and a Jag. The Jag's a different model to the one I trashed but it's got the same numberplate. 100 TC. Losing one didn't put him off, then. We park beyond them so they screen us from the front door.

Eileen pulls on the brake and lets her hands drop to her lap.

"Will you ring the bell? In case it's Gabby or Neil."

"What do I say?"

"Just ask for Carno. He won't recognise you, will he? Dale said you were still at school...."

Ah, what the hell, I think. The woman's got a screw loose, but I gotta see what happens.

I walk over to the front door and lean on the bell. I can hear it inside. Sounds like a big, deep house. No one comes to the door. There's a tang of scorched meat in the air.

"Think they're out the back," I call over to the car. "Can smell barbecue. Hang on a tick."

I set off round the side of the house. Feel unreal. I'm listening out for dogs but I can't hear any. I go through a latched gate in a high hedge. Trespassing now, but it don't feel like it. It feels like I've got a right to walk on anything of Carno's. Who's to stop me? I hear distant voices. I step out from bushes on to close-clipped lawn, the size of a rugby pitch. The other side, up against the far corner of the house, there's a raised terrace. Knee high balustrades, even. The smell of charred meat makes a foul taste in my mouth. Shit, I hate this man.

There's a little party going on. Perhaps they've got the neighbours round. Two men by the smoke. Another unfolding a padded chair. At least three women. Three, no four kiddies. I start walking across to them.

One of the men by the smoke sees me first. Lifts a pointing hand and says something to his mate. The mate turns round, and even this far away I know it's Carno. Owner's stance. He's wearing a striped butcher's apron. Playing cook for his friends. Prat. A bullet-headed, running-to-fat, middle-aged prat. He looks shorter than I remember. Well, he would. My next thought is *I could take him, easy*. A warm thought.

Carno hands the implements he's holding to his butty and takes off his apron. He calls, "Oi, you!" and strides across the grass to meet me. I stop and watch him. Comes to me I seen him do this

42

before. Same green underfoot, same walk. But I'm a big boy now. I feel my hands curling, and force them to relax. Careful, Jay, I tell myself. Things to lose. Think Bethan.

"Mr Carno?" I say, when he's close enough to hear a quiet voice. Got a tan on him and it's hot work, cooking barbecue. Trickles of sweat on his bronzed forehead. Looks like he's been grilling himself.

"Who're you? This is a private garden."

"Rang the bell, Mr Carno. Could smell you were round here." I smile at him. Nice ambiguity. I jerk a thumb over my shoulder. "Got a lady out front wants to see you."

"I'm having a meal with my family. If you're trying to sell me something...."

He knows I'm not selling anything. No one sells wearing combats and boots.

"The lady needs to see you. 'Course, she could come round here...."

He stares at me bull-eyed, and then shouts back to his mate, "Pete! Check the steaks! Just got to sort something out."

I turn on my heel and start back the way I came. He follows. I can hear his breathing behind me. Unfit bastard.

"Do I know you?" His voice is rasping.

"I dunno." I glance back at him. "Do you?"

He don't reply. Just curiosity in those eyes. Na. He don't know me.

On the gravel at the front I wave at the Polo and flick a thumb back at Carno. Eileen gets out of the car. I stand aside. Once I stop moving I'm aware I'm pounding inside. Wound-up, ready-steady pounding.

Carno stares at Eileen, assuring himself he don't know her.

"Young lady," he says, "I think you've made a mistake."

In a voice like ice Eileen says, "Why didn't Gabby and Neil come to my brother's funeral?"

Carno's mind ticks in his eyes. *Funeral. Brother. Stu's death.*

*This woman, Stu's sister.* He opens his mouth, hesitates, then starts again.

"Gabby didn't think she'd be welcome. Neil is far too young."

"What?" cries Eileen. There's a shriek in there. "Too young for what? To lose a father?"

Carno's face closes up. His eyes drift away. "I'm very sorry about your brother. But this is a pointless conversation. It has nothing to do with me."

Eileen is trembling. But it don't hit alarms. I'm still standing back. Men trembling is dangerous; women trembling just means they're upset.

Carno isn't prepared either. Eileen steps forward, lifts her hand like a long-nailed claw, and slashes at him. Expression wild.

Carno gasps, "Jesus Christ!" and bats her arm way with his wrist. The speed of his reaction startles me. But she got him.

"Jay! Jay!" Eileen cries, jumping back. "Hit him! Hit him!"

"Bitch!" Carno spits. He's got his hand clamped to his cheek. "Fucking bitch." He steps forward, raising the other arm like a pump, hand balled to a fist.

I've no sensation of moving but here I am, an arm round Eileen's waist, yanking her away. By protecting her I'm also protecting Carno but that can't be helped. Down the tanned curve of Carno's cheek beads of red appear, like jewelled body studs. Fascinating. One of them pops and trickles. I feel the adrenalin rush. I could move in now, flatten the bastard, but I don't. This isn't my fight.

"Jay!" Eileen wails. Despairing.

I swing her round, away from him. Expose our backs. It's up to Carno. He's got no weapon, so he's not going to fell me with one blow. If he touches me he's down, I'll make sure of that, but I'm not starting nothing.

I can hear him swearing behind us. Swearing and stamping and muttering. There's no way I'm bundling Eileen into the Polo, or looking as if we're running away, so I just hold her tight, pressed into my shoulder. It should be her forehead against me but she's so tall it's probably her nose. She's crying now. I rock her. No hurry; we take as long as we like.

Carno blusters, "Get rid of her! I order you. Get off my land!"

Prick. *Get off my land. I order you.* Like he's lifted it from somewhere. He's got a handkerchief out now, dabbing at his face. He'll have marks there for weeks. Nail tracks are amazingly long-lived. Fucking ha ha. Hope it stimulates a lot of questions.

I say, "Piss off yourself, Carno. Can't you see the lady's upset?" and rest my hand on the back of Eileen's head, gentle-like, as if we know each other a lot better than we do.

Carno wags a furious forefinger at me. "You listen, you... I'm going to deal with this –" the finger flicks back to his face "– and when I come back you'd better be gone. Two minutes. Or else...." He can't think how to end so he leaves it hanging. I sneer at him and make sure he sees my face. *Or else.* Have to be him and a posse like him.

He crunches across the gravel as if he's cracking nuts and bangs inside the house. The moment she hears the door close Eileen pulls fiercely back from me.

"Bastard," she hisses. She means me. "Bastard, bastard. Why didn't you –?"

"Shut up. Get in the car.." But I say it mild. I should be angry with her, because I'm realising she planned this, set me up, wanted me to paste him for her – and for what, for fuck's sake? – but I don't feel it. Just a kind of weariness. When I was fifteen, as powerless as a woman, maybe I'd have liked a big bloke next to me, someone with their own grudge. Maybe I'd have said *hit him* too.

I push her towards the Polo, aiming her at the passenger door. She don't resist. Inside she gives me the car keys. She's still crying, but much calmer.

"Why didn't you?" she moans.

"You don't know what he's done," I say. "Maybe nothing."

"Dale said you hated him." She flops her head at me. "Hated him."

The weariness becomes an ache. I'm seeing myself through Eileen's eyes. Easy meat. Wind him up and point him. I slide the seat back. Turn the key.

Funny how it takes a while for emotions to creep up on you. Some emotions, that is. Some come in bang, on the dot, no mistaking. Others creep up. Like they've a journey to make. An ingratiating journey. Need to slide in slow, doff their cap, in case they're not welcome. I'm hurt. No need to admit it, and no one'll know, but hurt it is. Anyone else, I'd be angry. Kind of default, isn't it, anger? But how can I be angry with Eileen? She's lost her brother. Her twin. Anyone'd be off beam. There's worse than feeling hurt.

We're climbing the hill again, the back Llangattock mountain way, when Eileen says, "Pull over, Jay."

I glance at her. Slow down.

"Please." She frowns. It's a distracted order. I can't stop right here, but a few hundred yards on there's a farm gate. I yank the wheel and tuck the Polo in.

"Turn it off." She's staring straight ahead. Face a blank.

I turn the engine off.

"I want him hurt," she says. "I'll pay you."

I turn the engine on again. This woman is stretching my understanding.

"No," she says quickly. "Please. Listen."

I switch off again. There's silence for a moment. I'm watching the road up ahead. A magpie in the dusk, a young one, skipping around a squashed animal body on the tarmac. Could be a dead squirrel. Eileen's doing something beside me, I'm not registering what. Looking for something, maybe.

"Jay," she says. Low, shifting voice.

I turn my head. She's showing me her tit. Hands under the silk, inside her bra, lifting it out at me. Ah shit. The nipple, brown and solid, peeps at me from between her fingers. She pushes down, making it swell.

"For fuck's sake." I got a throat problem.

"Look at me," she says.

I shake my head. Eyes back on the magpie. "You don't know nothing," I say. "Not for sure."

"Yes I do," she says. "I've seen him. And I know Gabby. It's him. Has to be."

She takes my hand, pulls it towards her, and puts it on her tit. The hand don't resist. There's no place on a man that feels like a tit. Softer than puppy-tum, wonderstuff. I'm not going to fuck her, and I'm not going to punish Carno for her. That's what I'm telling myself.

I suddenly remember she called me Jay. When we were with Carno. Shit. That makes me yank my hand away. Did she do it deliberate? Can't tell. And did it mean anything to Carno? Dunno. But one thing's for sure: if he wanted to find me, it would make his job a lot easier. Not many of us Jays around. In fact, if he thought awhile, dug back a bit, he'd realise he knew at least one already.

Eileen starts to cry again. She's let the silky top fall back over her tits. I don't know what to do about crying women if you can't touch them. Daren't touch her.

I start the engine and say, "I'll take you home. Parents' place, is it?"

She don't say yes, she don't say no. She twists to look out the side window, shields her eyes with a hand. She's failed with me, so I've disappeared.

Takes half an hour back and she don't move. Doesn't look at me once, says not a word. Just herself in the car, with Mr Invisible. I leave her in the road outside her parents' place. Toss the keys into her lap after I've switched the engine off, and stride away. I'm three miles from home here, but Dale lives only ten minutes walk into town, and if he's in he'll give me a lift. On the way I know I should decide what I'm going to say to him, but I don't get further than thinking that. My mind's thick with fog.

Dale's got a flat above a workshop far end of a shed-lined cul-de-sac. Small business territory and storage lockups. His building's on a steep slope, so there's just a few steps up from the front pavement to the flat, and an entrance round the back to the yard and the basement workshop. His flat's not big – just one room apart from the hallway, with kitchen and bathroom off – but it's not as if he's stuck in there all day.

He opens the door to me looking surprised and I forget to say the usual things like, Hi Dale, how yer doin' mate.

I hear myself say, "Dropped Eileen off down the road. Need a lift home, Dale.'"

He looks at me and waits for me to say more, but I can't do it. Sometimes I get so tangled up I logjam. Questions, that's what I need. Someone else to start picking out the threads.

"You OK, Jay?" He's smiling, but wearing a little frown.

"Aye. Yeah."

"Eileen came round then?"

"Aye."

"And you been somewhere with her?"

I nod. "Round Carno's."

His eyes widen.

"I didn't touch him," I blurt out. "But she's given him some marks. She scrammed him. She's crazy, man."

"Shit, Jay." Dale grabs his jacket from beside the door and pushes a helmet into my arms. "I said talk to her. Just talk to her."

"She didn't want to talk. She wanted me to hurt him. Fuck, Dale. She set me up."

"But you didn't –?"

"Nope. Nope."

He shakes his head. Then says quiet, "Sorry mate. Didn't see it. Shit." He leads me out and round to the workshop, and his bike.

If I was going to tell anyone, it'd be Dale. Well, some things, maybe Bethan. But what Eileen just done to me, if I had to say it, I'd say it to Dale. No-competition Dale. You don't need a front with Dale. And you know he won't twist it to a joke, use it to get the others laughing. But I don't have to say it, so it don't get said.

He don't ask the questions that would force it. All the same, riding home behind him, visors up, warm wind in our faces, it's kind of easing. You do things together, things you got the same understanding of, and sometimes it's close to words. At the top of the drive I just nod at him after I've climbed off, and I feel calmer than when we started. Dunno who he uses. Maybe he don't need to.

I walk down to the house looking for Bethan. Just want Bethan. I tramp through the kitchen, the sitting room. I know she's here; the Subaru was outside. No sign of Mam. Good.

I find her in the bathroom. Having a shower. A towel draped over the chair. I snatch the curtain over the bath back, grab her round the ribs, and haul her out.

"Shit, Jay!" she howls. "For Christ's sake! I'm washing my bloody hair!"

Ah, she looks cute. Feels cute. Slippery with shampoo, a Tintin quiff on her head, eyes blind as a puppy. I kick the door shut, flip the shower head round. This bathroom is step-down, tiled to shoulder height with a floor drain, built for floods. I've butchered sheep in here. Dunno why I remember that. In seconds I'm as wet as she is. She likes wet clothes on a man – fuck knows why, but she does. See, I'm remembering her, too. I know I'm being rough, but I don't care. She's shouting and struggling, but I can hold her one-handed, and I'm not listening. It's only gonna take a minute, and she knows I'm not going to hurt her. Just need to do this. Please shut up, I tell her. It's just a fuck, for fuck's sake.

# 4

Bethan's telling me I got a problem. I'm not denying it. Never have denied it, I tell her. You want problems, Bethan, you come to the right place. Me, I'm a conglomeration of problems. Mr Conglomerated Problem, that's me. Fuck off, she says. Temporarily lost her nice manners. She's talking about a particular problem, she says. Last night's particular problem. The particular problem of me dragging her out of the shower, and raping her.

Calling it rape's a bit strong, I think. Not that I'm not ashamed of myself. But I didn't damage her. I didn't hit her. Shit, I'd never hit Bethan. She's not even bruised. I was loving her, not raping her. I'm sorry I was rough. But I thought that when women got raped it kind of destroyed them. Traumatised them, annihilated them. Bethan's been talking at me all night, and she don't look traumatised, and she don't look annihilated. She looks furious.

I've told her I'm sorry. I've told her that if I hurt her, I didn't do it deliberate, and she's welcome to hurt me back, if it'd help. First she says that's typical man, to suppose that if she wallops me, after I've raped her, that'd make it all right. Honour satisfied. Eye for an eye. Missing the point completely. But then she gets so worked up over this she decides that walloping me is kind of irresistible, since I've promised not to retaliate, and might help a bit, so she leaps out of bed – we're in bed, note, and how many rape victims put stupid rabbit pyjamas on and climb willingly into bed with their rapists? – grabs my belt off the chair, yanks the sheet back and cracks me one across the backside. It hurts. Shit it hurts. I bite the pillow and she does it again, and then I tell her to stop. Please Bethan, I gasp, it fucking hurts. She does, and when I turn my head to look at her I'm expecting it'll have taken some of the rage away, but it hasn't. Just turned it liquid, pouring down her cheeks.

So then I try explaining why I wanted her so bad. I tell her about going to Carno's, and Eileen setting me up. The cow even saying she'd pay me to hurt him. Not sure if I get everything in the right order, but we get there in the end. I don't tell her about Eileen flashing her tits at me, though, or ignoring me all the way home. I dunno why. I just can't say it. I kind of suspect that because I can't say it, it's the part I should be saying, but there's no way round that. I just tell her that Eileen used me, and made me feel like shit, and I wanted to feel OK again. And that fucking my woman in the bathroom fitted the bill.

"So attacking me made you feel good, did it?"

"Ah come on,' I say. 'I was just being keen."

"You put your hand over my mouth," she hisses. "You told me to shut up. You were pissed off, and you were taking it out on me. By raping me."

"No." Did I really put my hand over her mouth? Fuck me. Trouble is, it's all a bit of a blur. I mean, it was wet, she was slippery. It's true, she was making a lot of noise. Suppose I might have done.

"I don't want to get scared of you," she says. "It's not good, to be scared of your man."

"Ah Bethan," I say. "I'd never scare you."

"But you did!" she screeches.

I got no answer for this. If she was scared, she was scared. I can't argue with it. But she's never said she's been scared before, and we've been together a year. It was just a one off, I tell her, it'll never happen again....

Then we doze a while, or I do, anyway, but soon she's sitting up and off again. The argument takes a nosedive; she starts telling me there are other things about me she don't like. My friends, for a start.

"You like Dale," I object, blearily.

"He's a tart," she grumbles.

"Come on. Said yourself he was clever."

"OK. A clever tart. You never let me near him anyway."

"That's not true." Shit. I've never acted jealous, sure I haven't. Fucking mind reader. "You've ridden with him," I protest.

"Oh yeah," she sneers. "Really get to know someone riding behind them." She tosses her head. "I'm not talking about Dale. The others."

"Andy and Maureen are OK," I mutter. "Thought you liked them."

She groans, "Yeah, yeah."

She's sounding like someone different. Someone I don't know. Someone who's been hiding from me, keeping things from me. She's worrying me. Who's left? Damien, Sparky, Jonno? Stu's dead. I know she didn't think a lot of him.

"It's just the bikes, isn't it," she says. "I mean, even *you* don't like Jonno. They're all so...." She twists her mouth, making it ugly.

Yeah, I know. They're losers, why fight it? I fold my arms under my head. Shit, she belted me hours ago, and my bum's still zinging.

"It's what I like doing," I murmur. "We got things in common."

She shakes her head. "You're so, God, left behind."

"Can't all be flash."

"I don't want you flash," she snaps. "I just want you... different."

"Fuck off, then."

She turns round slowly to look at me. "You mean that?"

Oh scary woman. "No," I mumble. "'Course not."

She nods. She knows I love her. Must do. And where did all this shit come from, anyway? We were fine yesterday. Just because I make one mistake. Thinking about the mistake, I roll on my side. It's more comfortable anyway.

"Bethan," I murmur. "If I'm gentle –"

"You're joking."

Well, I wasn't, but I won't push it. I'm not that dull.

"How can you ask that?" she hisses, savage. "Like you've no clue at all. Shit, Jay, you get things so wrong."

"What d'you mean? Get what wrong?"

"Everything. Everything. You never read things right."

"Oi!" How can she say this? Implying I got no judgement. As good as saying I'm stupid.

"Look at last night!"

She sounds so nasty I shut up. She's just angry with me. I hope. I drop my head and keep quiet. She sits beside me and smoulders. I close my eyes and maybe I drop off a while. When I next open them it's light. Early daytime light. My eyes are gritty. What a shit of a night. Bethan's lying down now, but propped up, not asleep. Got her arms folded across her rabbits. I lie still, warming up my brain, working out what day it is. Saturday. Hey, Saturday. She's got the weekend free. Let's do something to take our minds off. Something Bethan likes.

Coaxingly I whisper, "Hey, Bethan. Leave it. Let's go somewhere. Do something different. How about we pay Paul a visit?"

She thinks about this, blinking. Then nods. Several times, as if the night's been one long, exhausting conversation and, at last, I've said something sensible. Something worth saying. Then closes her eyes.

I'm grateful Paul only lives twelve miles away. At least, my bum's grateful. I don't make a joke of the soreness to Bethan, because I've looked at the damage in the bathroom mirror and it isn't a joke. My Mam and Dad never more than cuffed me when I was a kid, so I've never seen strap marks before. Shit, Bethan must have been angry. Two thick red stripes, made up of thousands of tiny blood blisters. Like a tattoo where someone's gone needle crazy but forgotten the ink. Fucking Carno's fault, I think.

But twelve miles of sore bum is worth it. Riding to Paul's the sky lifts. Even forget how little sleep I've had. Going to Paul's is taking time out. Escaping. Paul lives due east, far side of Aber, not quite Raglan, rich farming territory. But it's not the geography that's the escape, it's the man himself, and his family.

Paul isn't in when we arrive but Simone is, and the older girl.

"Mum!" Franny yells, after she's said hi to us. She's got a burred English accent, her Mam's Bristol crossed with Paul's London. "Jay and Bethan are here!" Then she grins at us, flicks her chestnut hair out of her dancing eyes and disappears, 'cos she's seventeen years old and got better things to do than overexcite her parents' boring friends. Even if we're nearer her age than theirs. Ah, but she's a luscious girl.

Simone comes out of the cottage to greet us, all smiles. She's forty-five, Simone, but Paul and Simone wouldn't know middle-age if it reared up and kicked them. You know they've been the same, dressed the same, spoken the same, for ever.

"Hi strangers!" She's in jeans, slim body twisted, hands in her back pockets like she's her daughter's age. "Paul's out shopping. He'll be back soon. Come in, come in."

We follow her inside into the big kitchen, where the furniture's old and scruffy, and there's everything from WD40 to paper flowers on the chock-a-block window sills. Simone whirls around making us coffee, telling us Paul nearly rang me last night, because his bike keeps cutting out on him, and he's doing his nut trying to work out why. Well, she don't use those words, but that's the sense. She asks after some of Bethan's workmates; Simone's a physio at the same hospital and they got mutual acquaintances. I see Bethan smile for the first time since she said tara to me yesterday lunchtime.

I like Simone because she's easy, energetic and friendly, and married to Paul, who's a one-off gem, and because I know she fancies me. Put that last, see, to prove I'm not shallow. I know she fancies me because she said so, at Paul's forty-fifth birthday party a couple of years ago. She said it loud and clear, no embarrassment, at the end of the evening, in a mutual rant with Paul about growing old and crumbling away, listing all the things they'd be leaving behind, which included lusting and flirting, what with the crimplene and continence pads and walking frames and that. I even got to give her a little snog afterwards, to show my appreciation. She held my hand tight while I kissed her, and then whispered in my ear that I was a lovely boy, and I'd made an old woman very happy. OK, she was pissed, but she weren't lying, and because you know she regards fancying people as normal as nose-blowing and nothing to get steamed up about – or do anything about – it was just a funny, magic, party moment. If she remembered it the next day, it never altered nothing.

Paul returns soon with the younger girl, Boo, who's fourteen and tall as her dad already, all stick legs and shy smile. Never used to be shy with me, but that's hormones for you. Paul dumps the shopping on the table, smiling and saying I must be psychic, and drags me outside to look at his FireBlade. Bethan and Simone'll natter on for hours.

We open the shed doors and circle his machine. As you do. A ritual of respect. Scratch chins and gaze. Nice bike, OK, dream bike, but wasted on Paul. Told him this when he bought it last year. Paul learnt to ride in the days when bikes were crap and you had to ride cautious, and he's too old now to learn new tricks. He says garbage, it's just that he's got the girls to think of and being a weekend biker he don't get the practice. But maybe it's just as well he's cautious, because he's a shit mechanic. Don't use his eyes. Once tried to start a bike with the carbs off.

While we circle we prattle on. I talk easy with Paul. Could say anything to him. Well, near anything. He knows more about me than anyone except maybe Mam. He knows me so well because he once had a professional interest in our family. After Dad died and Carly got fat and started beating everyone up, he was her social worker. That's what he does, his job, social work. Looking out for teenagers who've lost the plot. Got no thanks from Carly, of course, but when he started visiting us it was only a couple of years after Dad died, and he could see she wasn't the only one with troubles. He knows all about Carno and me trashing the Jag and he never ticked me off for it, though he said I was lucky. He told me that losing a dad like we lost ours would screw up any family. He said that feeling angry was OK. He said I should be proud of myself, coping with Dad dying on top of my dyslexia shit, and not running so wild I got myself banged up. When he talked to Mam he didn't speak to her like she was a case, but like she was a normal person, just with difficult kids and too much on her plate. And he said all this incidental-like, not lecturing us, but ambling round the place, spending time with us, taking an interest. Carly called him a wanker, but everyone was a wanker to her, and he just laughed and said he'd been called worse.

And then his car was off the road and he turned up on an old SP370, and it didn't take long to discover that I knew more about bikes, even at seventeen, than he did. None of his mates rode and he didn't have the time or know-how to maintain the SP proper, and keeping it on the road was killing him. Social workers do OK, but they aren't rich. Simone wasn't working in those days and the first time I went down to his place to help out I felt quite sorry for them, the little cottage a tip and kids' washing everywhere. I was shy of Simone because I was still a mumbler then and I hated the way people acted when they couldn't understand me, either ignoring me or pretending they'd understood when they hadn't. But maybe because Simone had little kids who mumbled themselves she was good at working things out and if she had a problem she just said, 'What?' or 'Sorry?' as if getting it wrong the first time was normal, and it gave me a chance to try again, a bit clearer.

That was ten years ago, and I'm still calling in now and again to say hi. Things have shifted in the meantime. Paul thinks I've sorted my life out pretty well, considering, and I know he envies me my summers off. He's tired of his job. He says that twenty-five years in social work is too long and he'd give it up tomorrow if he could afford it but he can't with the girls still at school, and then they'll go to college, he expects, and it'll be all their fault when he keels over with a heart attack. Either that or he'll strangle a client and get himself put away. Quite fancies the idea, he says, as long as his cell don't have a phone.

So we circle the bike, scratching our chins, and it's Paul who's needing my help now, not me his. He says the bike's just cutting out, no reason at all that he can see. It cuts out, and then a minute later starts again, well, usually. Maybe after a little bump around. He's checked the fuel line and it seems OK, but he's nervous about dismantling the carbs, so he hasn't inspected the jets. I ask him if it's just the engine that cuts, or if the lights and instruments go as well, but he says he's not sure. I shake my head; can't believe he hasn't checked the electrics. I got an idea already.

I get him to wheel it out on to the hardstanding and start it up. Lovely grumble. I switch the lights on.

"OK," I say, and reach down the side of the engine. The motor cuts. And the lights.

"There!" Paul cries. "See? Just like that."

"I did that," I say. He wasn't looking, berk.

"What?" He comes round my side.

"You got a cracked earth wire," I say. "Has to be. Try it again."

He presses the starter. Nothing happens. I reach down and twitch the wire. Engine fires up.

"There," I say, directing his gaze at it. "Low tension earth wire." I squat down and peer at it. "Cracked. Right at the end. Bad connection."

"Ah, Jay," he says. "Jay, Jay." He's so pleased his eyes and mouth stay wide open. "Bloody genius, Jay."

"Twat." I fiddle through his box for tools. It's a moments' work to trim the wire and reconnect it. "OK," I say. "Should be fine now." I sit back on my haunches.

"Reckon I get a test ride for that."

He don't reply, so I glance up at him, grinning. I got him, his face is comical.

"Be covered," I assure him. "Long as I got your permission."

"Only third party, aren't you?"

"Won't drop it. Promise."

Well, he's got no choice. The price of favours. I chuckle at him and grab my helmet. Roll the bike out into the lane. Check the controls. Everything's where I expect it to be. I'd offer to take Paul pillion, but the only time he's ridden behind me he was so scared I know he won't do it again. Nothing to do with my riding; show me anyone who claims they like riding pillion and I'll show you a masochist. Or a girl. One who don't ride herself, that is.

I cruise the wide lanes a mile or so, feeling my way in. Seat's nicely padded, that's a bonus. Hey, I think, these racers are fun. They need the right curves, the right surfaces, but round here there's no shortage. Smoothy bendy B-roads, just the job.

The bike's staggeringly responsive. Think it and it's done; just got to make sure I have the right thoughts. But I know all the roads round here and I'm building speed fast. A bike like this only gets into its stride past legal limits. Paul don't know what he's missing. I throw it around a while, enjoying myself, and then, because I feel on the edge of an even better ride, I can't resist making for the Aber-Raglan dual carriageway. Eight miles of near-empty straight. Gotta try it. Just to see what it'll do.

The answer, after I've opened it up, is… dunno: the needle goes haywire past 120. Can't spare the eyes anyway, gotta keep them peeled ahead, because this is a favourite spot for cops with speed guns. But they always operated from lay-bys, and you can see the unmarked cars a mile away.

Shit, this is it. As fast as a very fast thing. Hardly any shake. What a rush. Immaculate. But it's gonna be over too quickly. Eight miles equals less than four minutes. Must have been holding it three already. I'm reaching the moment when you know you're at the beginning of the end. When next second, maybe next second, OK next second, you're gonna have to ease off. I don't want to do it. Shit, can't do it. It's so perfect it waters my eyes, even behind the visor. I'm leaving everything behind. Everyone behind. Stretching them to a blur. So easy. Who wants the world sharp again?

I can see the roundabout up ahead, rushing towards me, and I know I should be braking, but I'm not. Should be scared, but I'm not. Mesmerised, more like. Seduced.

I'm past the SLOW sign when I come to my senses. Like the scenery jumps at me. Oh shit fucking shit. Can't brake cornering, so it's gotta be now, before I hit the curve. I twist down the throttle and haul on front and back.

Oh, she's a beaut, she's a life-saver. Brakes like a VC10. I'm probably still doing 70 as I throttle up again and power through the roundabout, flipped over so far I could pick pebbles off the tarmac, but it's over in a wink, and I've made it. Did I deserve that? No way. No way. What a fucking lucky boy.

I slow right down. Hands tremble a tad. Can feel my shirt wet on my back under the jacket. Shit, I was scared, just wasn't registering it. Bit worrying, that. Is that what Bethan meant last night? About not reading things right? Fuck. Wish she hadn't said that.

I give myself a stiff talking to on the way back to the cottage. That was idiot-stuff, I tell myself. On Paul's bike, for fuck's sake. If I'd killed myself he'd never have forgiven himself. Do his head in. The second numbskull thing I've done in just over twelve hours. I'm behaving like, well, shit, like Carly. That brings me up short. Can't have that. I'm OK. Bethan thinks I'm OK too. She's here. Hasn't left me. And I didn't drop the bike, I'm still alive. Just got to get a grip.

Paul's waiting out the front for me when I get back. He sees me, pulls his hand from his face and starts walking round in small circles. Suggests a sudden release. Hell, I've only been half an hour.

"Enjoy yourself?" he says, not smiling, as I switch off and unstrap my helmet.

"Good brakes." I grin at him. "Fucking good."

He rolls his eyes and reclaims the bike. I gather he's not pleased with me but anyone would have done the same. He'll get over it. After he's tucked it away we walk round the back, where Bethan and Simone are sitting at a picnic table in the little garden. They've broken open a six-pack of beer. Boo is lying on a rug on the grass beyond them, heels kicking her backside, leafing through a magazine. Bethan catches my eye as we join them. Doesn't smile at me, but don't scowl neither.

"I was asking Bethan how Carly and Russell are," Simone tells me. "I didn't realise the wedding was just a few weeks ago. But she says she hasn't seen them."

"Haven't killed each other yet," I say. "Give 'em time."

Paul makes a snorting noise. Not humorous; weary. He don't want to talk about Carly and I don't either. Feels a raw spot, just now. Paul tosses me a can and I pop it. Trouble is, all the things that have been happening to me over the last few days, from Stu's funeral to visiting Carno, Paul wouldn't want to hear about. It's getting so there's not a lot left, except bikes. Shit. What am I saying? I don't usually think this. Lack-of-sleep glooms, that's my problem.

Franny swings out of the cottage over to us and snatches up a can. She throws me a grin that from anyone else would count as lewd, then does the same to Bethan, making clear it's not, and flounces back into the house.

"Minx," Paul says.

"She's just passed her driving test," Simone says. "Paul says it makes him feel old."

Bethan laughs. Boo pipes up with, "There's still me, Dad!," and flicks a page of the magazine over.

Paul sighs. Simone dips her mouth at him. I get a muddly feeling, like there's something going on here I don't understand. Between Paul and Simone? Or Paul and Franny? I stare at Bethan, who's put her sunglasses on and tipped her face to the sun. She looks classy, sexy, relaxed. She's not feeling anything wrong. She likes it here. If Paul and Simone were younger they'd be real friends. This is her kind of place.

I get up and go and stand over Boo. Dunno why; maybe just because she's a distance from the others. Or maybe because the picnic bench is too hard for my bum. I wonder if I'm just getting muddled because of last night. Noticing things that wouldn't bother me before. Well, if I got no judgement, like Bethan says, how can I tell?

Boo becomes aware I'm standing over her, and twists her head round to me. She's stopped looking shy now.

"Gissa ride on your bike," she says.

"No!" Paul's voice comes quick from behind me. Shit, he's on the ball. I grin down at Boo and take a swig of beer.

"Bet you're better than Dad," she complains.

"Certainly am."

"Da-ad." Boo turns over to moan at him. "You're such a hypocrite."

"And proud of it," Paul says. "The answer's no."

Boo pulls a face like a six-year-old. Thumps her magazine. A little-girlie hand, but the fingernails pearly with varnish. Shit, Paul's lucky to have daughters like these, all fresh and free and clever, who're gonna go to college and live easy, sunshine lives, and make their parents proud. I take a swig of beer. My backside's sore. Bit sore generally. Maybe I shouldn't have come here today.

I don't want to drag Bethan away though, because it's her day off and she's enjoying herself. Simone gives us lunch in the garden – just rolls and ham and greenstuff – and then suggests Bethan walk round with her and Boo to a neighbour who lets Boo ride his pony round his farm. Boo says Bethan can have a ride too if she likes. Bethan's only sat on a horse a couple of times but she's game for it and gets quite excited. I'd like to see her ride myself but Paul isn't interested, so I say I'll stay here with him.

After they've gone Paul goes inside to make a phone call and I lay myself out on Boo's rug. More comfortable than the chairs. Prop myself on an elbow and flick through her magazine. It's full of photos of bright little girls as skinny as she is, only a few years older, and wimpy-looking boys with floppy blonde hair and doe eyes. There's one makes me laugh; looks the spit of Dale, if you added a few years and pumped him up a bit. I fold the magazine over at the place and tell myself to show Bethan when she comes back.

I must have put my head down then, because the next thing I know something's prodding me in the side and there's a voice above me.

"Jay. Oi, Jay."

It's Franny, grinding a bare toe into my ribs. I grab her foot and push it away.

"God, you sleep deeply," she says.

"Nothing on my conscience."

She sniggers, tucking her foot back into a sandal. "I bet. Where's Dad?"

I blink on this a moment, and then sit up and look around. Feel a bit woozy, but it's sleeping in the sun that's done it; only had the one beer earlier.

"I dunno." I feel stupid. "What's the time?"

"After four," she says. "I need the car keys."

I been lying here nearly two hours? Where the fuck is Paul?

"Err... making a phone call...?" I can't clear the muzz.

"He's not inside," she says.

I jump up. Shake the fog away. He'll be with the bike. Weird, to work on it without me – and what needs doing to it, anyway? – but there's nowhere else. Franny follows me round the side of the cottage.

The shed door is open, and there's no bike inside. We stare at the empty concrete floor.

"Gone out somewhere," I say.

Franny groans. "Oh God. I need to be at Justin's in quarter of an hour."

I don't know who Justin is, or where he lives, and I don't care if she's late meeting him. Paul's gone out somewhere on his bike, leaving me here, and that's weird.

Franny coos at my expression. "I expect he didn't want to wake you. Or maybe he couldn't."

I nod.

"Are you awake now?" she scoffs.

"Ah fuck off," I say, a bit rougher than I intend.

"Shut up." Sounds genuinely offended.

I shake my head. Apology. I try to mind my language here.

"Now I'm going to be late."

I'm not listening. I'm offended too. Maybe I pissed Paul off, disappearing so long this morning. Maybe that's what I was picking up earlier. Could be. Could be. So now he's buggered off for a ride without me.

Franny steps back and taps the seat of my bike, leant alongside.

"You could give me a lift," she wheedles. "It's only in Raglan. Mum'd fetch me later."

"No," I say, automatic. "Paul'd skin me."

"Christ. Not scared of Dad, are you?"

"No."

She gazes at Bethan's crash helmet, propped at the back of the seat. Then licks a finger and wipes a speck of dirt from the surface.

"Well, then." She's made her voice low and intimate. She shouldn't do that. Don't know her own power.

Ah hell, she's not a little girl any more. No reason for me to feel like a dirty old man. It's not like she's flashing her tits at me. Wow, though, but that's a bad thought. Dirty old man thought. Pulls my reins in again.

"No," I say, much more firmly. "You'll have to wait."

She pouts, just like Boo did earlier. Knocks a decade off her. But she don't argue. I realise she never expected me to agree. Whew. Glad I didn't.

And then we hear the grumble of a big bike.

"Here he is now," I say. Whew again.

We watch Paul bounce up the drive and I can see he's got his eyes on us. Franny's still fiddling with the helmet. Before he's cut the engine he's flipped his visor up.

"What the hell are you two doing?"

Franny gives an exaggerated sigh. "Nothing, Dad." She flaps at him. "Turn it off."

Paul cuts the engine.

"Waiting for you," she says slow and loud, like he's thick. "I need the car keys."

"Why?"

"Justin. I'm late already."

Paul rummages in his jeans pocket and tosses them to her. She don't thank him. Turns on her heel and marches off to the car. I wait outside the shed while Paul puts the bike to bed. He's been sweating inside his helmet. Makes his hair thin so I can see his scalp through it. He looks his age, near fifty, and bad-tempered with it.

"I don't want you giving the girls rides," he says, shutting the shed up. "You know that."

"I wasn't," I say. "We was just wondering where you were. Looking out for you."

"Huh."

"Fucking wasn't, Paul."

He looks back at me quick. "OK." He nods. "Sorry. Sorry. Didn't mean to snap."

"Where you been?"

"Out."

"Shit."

"Ah Jay." He sighs. "Just needed to relax."

I follow him round to the back garden. What's he saying? He don't relax when we ride together? We done it for years. I don't mind going slow.

Bethan gets back from horse riding soon after – even cantered, she did, fearless girl – and we leave around half five. Paul's trying to persuade me to stay for a drink, but he knows I got the bike and it's easy for one to slide into four or five, so I decide to go before

I'm tempted. Seems to annoy him that I refuse. He's keener on the drink than he used to be. Simone ticks him off for bullying me and reminds him that a few years ago he was always lecturing me about mixing drink and substances with bikes, and he gets a mite tetchy with her, too.

All the ride back I'm wanting to ask Bethan if she noticed anything different about Paul, or if it were just me. She didn't look like she felt anything odd; but then she was mostly with Simone. The way he watched me with the girls, didn't forgive me for riding his bike, didn't want to ride with me, pushed me to have a drink, risk my licence. Like he got the hump with me, resented me, shit, like he was jealous. But that's crazy.

Back home we got the kitchen to ourselves, and I tell Bethan about him going off in the afternoon. Realise we've hardly spoken a word to each other all day. But her mood seems OK – her hiya to Mam out in the yard sounded chirpy enough.

She snorts at me and says Simone thinks he's bonkers, buying himself such a big bike.

"Boo calls it Crisis," she sniggers.

"Crisis?"

"As in mid-life."

"Eh?"

"God, you know. Old blokes being stupid. Says at least he hasn't found himself a bimbo."

"Boo said that?" She's only fourteen, shit.

Bethan chuckles. "She's wild."

"So why didn't he want to ride with me?"

"I dunno." She gives me a snide look, remembering she's cross with me. "Maybe thought you were going to rape him."

"Oh fuck off. Serious."

"I dunno. Having a bad day? Probably nothing to do with you. Just felt like it. He didn't ask us to go round. I'm hungry, Jay. Cook me some tea."

She starts rattling through cupboards looking for something to snack on. I think maybe she's right. But it also comes to me that she don't like hearing of problems I got with other people. Yeah, that's it, I got her. It's why she don't like hearing about me and Carly either. Dunno why, mind.

I agree to cook the tea because it'll earn me some points, which I'm obviously still owing. I'm not a natural in the kitchen but I manage sausage and beans. Mam says, "What's he done, then?" when Bethan calls her in to eat and she sees me serving out, and Bethan flashes me a look, but she don't let on anything's wrong. I'm grateful for that. No need for Mam to worry too.

We'd go out normally, Saturday night, but we don't get round to it tonight. Been a busy twenty-four hours. We watch telly with Mam instead and I'm restless, waiting for crunch time, when we go off to bed. After Mam goes, about ten-ish, I roll a couple of joints to mellow me, and Bethan shares them, which I take as a good sign.

However in the bedroom she puts on her rabbit pyjamas again, which isn't so promising. I say, "Still pissed with me, then?" and she says, "A bit." But she says it with her nose wrinkled, not delivered sharp. Like it's just the truth.

When we're in bed she lets me put my arm round her and tells me that she thinks it's going to be OK, as long as I never scare her again. I say never ever and try nuzzling the rabbits, but she pushes me away, exasperated, and says I got to listen, just once, and stop trying to hustle her. I dunno why she calls it hustling. All I want to do is show her I love her. She's got a little speech for me. She says she knows I was upset, but that's no excuse for putting my hand on her mouth and just doing what I want with her, like I'm blind and deaf and she's nothing except a screw. If someone near twice my weight and strength did the same to me I'd understand. And I kind of do, although imagining a woman twice my weight and strength holding me helpless and coming on to me isn't as frightening as maybe it should be, but that'll be a failure on my part. Anyway, she says if I ever do it again, or anything else that scares her as much, I won't get another chance. She means it. And I understand that.

# 5

A week later weird, heavy news: Carno's depot is torched. On the Friday night, it happens, though it's not till Saturday evening I get to hear about it. I'm in the Crucible – alone, Bethan's working – and everyone I meet's got different stories. Damien's the one tells me first, and he just says the depot's been torched, like it's definitely arson, and claims the place is a write-off. But then some guy interrupts and says it's just a couple of skips gone up, and not much damage except to a dog chained too close that's unfortunately been fried. Another guy says he's heard Carno's been storing catering waste overnight, which he shouldn't, and he reckons it's not arson at all, but spontaneous combustion. Get a lecture on the science of composting in hot weather. However Andy, whose brother is a part-time firefighter, says that's crap, it's ninty-nine per cent certain it's arson, and they had to bring in a relief team from Ebbw Vale to help, which may have been because they weren't sure what they were dealing with, the place being a waste depot, or maybe because the fire was bigger than everyone's saying. My mental image is expanding and contracting and expanding again, depending on who I'm talking to.

Dale comes in later than usual, and he's like me – hasn't heard about it at all. We're always last in the news chain, because he's down in Cwmbran daytimes – even occasional Saturdays, like today – and I live out of town.

He murmurs, "Strange news, eh?" in my ear but neither of us mentions Eileen while there's a crowd around. I'm glad Bethan's not here. Feel disturbed.

At closing time a group of us wander back to Andy's house. Dale and I hang back a few yards on the walk. Keep bumping shoulders because of the lack of weaving space, caused by inconsiderate vehicles parked two legs up on the pavement.

"Weren't you, then?" Dale says.

"Eh?"

"Torching Carno's."

"Shit, I'm not stupid."

We amble on, and then he says, "Carno know you, did he, when you went down with Eileen?"

"Na." Then I remember Eileen using my name. I stop dead. "Ah."

"What?"

"She shouted my name. In front of him."

"What? Jay? Nothing else?"

"Aye, but...."

We walk on a bit, digesting this. Or not. Feel it's stuck somewhere, myself.

Next thing I'm aware of is Dale saying, "Oi, Jay, leave it out."

"Eh?" Realise the side of my hand's fizzing. I just taken a swipe at a Peugeot. Maybe the car behind, too. Fuck.

Dale murmurs, "You'll be OK. Must be lots with grudges against Carno."

"Name of Jay?"

"Don't get yourself wound up. Play it cool, if the cops come asking. You'll be fine."

But I'm still chewing on it as we go into Andy's. Play it cool, Dale says. All right for him. Hate explanations. It's getting things straight as they come out, that's what's difficult. Paul always said if I was ever in serious trouble to say nothing. To sit calm and ask for a solicitor, so I could sort it out with someone who'd listen properly and who could speak to the cops for me. Good advice, if you've got something on your conscience. But maybe looks suspicious, if you haven't.

I blot it out then. Drink a few more ales, smother the lot with blow. Andy's changed the carbs on his bike now, so there's decisions about the Stu-run to make, and that keeps my mind off too. Dale's says it's got to be next weekend, or else we'll have to wait another fortnight, because he's working every other Saturday till the end of July. I got no problem with next weekend, and if Bethan's coming it should be OK with her, because she's on alternate weekends too. Dale says if we don't make it definite, now, nothing will happen, because we're all such idle bastards, so in the end he makes the decision for us. All we have to do is show we're paying attention and nod. Dunno what we'd do without the boy. Destination Cricieth, and we meet here, Andy's place, ten o'clock next Saturday morning. Leave round eleven. Twelve latest. We choose Andy's place so at least we'll be sure he'll make it to the start. Everyone's here except Jonno, and he may not be able to come anyway, with his security work. But anyone sees him, Dale says, tell him, so he don't feel left out. When people come back from Cricieth's up to them. Depends on the weather and the booze, usually. Finding a dry window when you're sober enough to ride, that's the trick.

I don't leave till four-ish and it's too late then to get a taxi. But it'll only take half an hour to walk. Hitting the fresh air sobers me back to thinking about Carno's depot. A ten minute detour would get me a glimpse of it and the thought pulls at me while I'm at the edge of town. But it's easy to be stopped by the cops when you're staggering home and getting stopped outside Carno's, even though I got a perfect right to gawp, wouldn't look good. Might have extra security in anyway, aye, bound to.

Out of town the dark's brightening in the east already and the mountain horizon's coming into focus. Backlighting does wonders for landscape – it's an uplifting sight, no other word for it. Not a single car on the road and can't have been for a while, because of all the sheep snoring on the tarmac. Couple of times they cough and make me start. Sound like phlegmy old men. I wonder what time Friday night Carno's place went up and feel dull I didn't ask. Didn't want to sound interested, I suppose. I try to list what I was doing night before last and can't remember. Fuck. Stop on the tarmac, and it's still a blank. Fuck, fuck.

It's because I'm seeing a uniform doing the asking. OK. I got it. Tea with Mam round seven, then chores – cleaned out the puppy shed, that's it, had a bonfire – then took Floss downhill a mile or so and raced the shade line back up so we could watch the sun set twice. Yeah, well. That's a detail I might not confide. Had a beer back home – must have been round ten – and was definitely clocked by Mam before she went to bed. Watched telly till Bethan came in just after midnight. Gave her a beer and helped her off with her uniform without scaring her at all. You'd think she'd be tired after an eight hour shift but she takes a while to unwind and she's often in the mood straight after work. Just a friendly roll on the cushions – nothing too memorable, but she'd remember I was there. She's forgiven me for last weekend and got her manners back – recall her squeaking, "Please, Jay!" most politely and gratifyingly, towards the end. Dunno what time we turned in, probably round one thirty. Slept solid at least eight hours, snoozed another hour, got up round eleven. No way I could have snuck out of the house after going to bed; neither Mam nor Bethan were pissed, and getting dressed again once we'd gone to bed and firing up an engine – bike or car – would definitely have woken them. Since I've never torched anywhere I dunno how long it takes, breaking in, setting a fire, and getting out again, but I reckon I'm in the clear. If you trust Mam and Bethan's word, that is.

Once I've sorted that out I feel easier. And I bet myself that because I've gone to the trouble to think things through, I won't be asked to say them. That's usually the way. When I get home I let myself into the house quiet, apologise to Floss for making her wag her stump while she's yawning and nearly causing her to fall over, and then strip off in the bedroom and snuggle in beside Bethan. She mumbles, "Get off, you're freezing," but I ignore it because she's

70

hot and cosy-feeling, and she's always warming her icy flesh on me. I lose my bet. Next morning's the most embarrassing of my life. Thank shit there's no boys here to witness it.

First thing I know I'm being woken by Mam at the door spitting at me, face like fury, saying to get up, now, this moment, because the police are here, and she's bloody well going to settle this right now and I'm not to say a word to the bastards unless she says so. She keeps shouting, "Jay, you awake? You hear me, Jay?" and gets me to say, "Aye, right," before I've grasped what I'm agreeing to. Bethan leaps out of bed like someone electrocuted the sheet, throws on her clothes, and I can hear her snapping and snarling down the corridor before I've even got my combats on.

When I go through to the kitchen I find two cops, plain clothes, showing they're taking this serious, one mid-twenties, fair and heavy-built, the other grey-haired, paunchy, about fifty. They're standing near the back door, close together, like they're safeguarding their escape route. Mam and Bethan are the other side of the table, ranting at them. It's a fine thing to have women on your side, especially women with no fear of the law, but it's noisy. Batters a brain that's half asleep. And makes me feel slow: both Mam and Bethan got gaps in their knowledge, but they hurl out questions and fill the holes so fast I'm whirling.

"Between one and two?" Mam shouts. "He was here, right, Bethan?"

Bethan nods like she's banging a post in with her forehead and when I open my mouth to confirm it Mam snaps, "Shut it, Jay, what did I tell you?"

"I got back from the hospital at midnight," Bethan tells them. "We had a beer together. Didn't go to bed till two."

The grey-haired cop says hello, Jay, he's Detective Sergeant Evans, and his mate is DC Scott. Sorry to get me up so early – ironic smile here, since it's past eleven. He fixes me with pale eyes and says maybe this would be easier down the station, just a quiet chat, like. Mam hisses over her dead body, and if they're not arresting me they can whistle. The cop says, "Jay?" ignoring her, so Mam moves between us to cut his gaze, like she's afraid he's trying to hypnotise me into agreeing.

"He was here, for God's sake," Bethan sneers. "How many times d'you need telling?"

The fair cop nods at me and says, "You don't deny threatening Mr Carno a week ago, do you?"

"I never –"

"He never," Bethan says loudly at the same time, and goes on to tell them, very fast and breathy, what happened with Eileen – as much as she knows, that is – and how I stopped her and Carno fighting, and how pissed off I was when I got back from his place. The last in general terms, 'course. And how I'm not so stupid I'd threaten him one week, face to face, with the chance he'd know me, and burn his place down the next. Mam keeps her eyes steady behind her glasses while Bethan's speaking and you'd never guess the visit to Carno's was news to her. I think Bethan's saying too much altogether, but she's got reason to feel angry with Eileen and she's not thinking of anyone except me. She even says how Dale arranged the meet.

"This would be Dale...?"

Bethan catches herself, realising she's been running on.

Mam says, "Dale Farrell," flatly, and to me, "He can look after himself."

I can see she's shocked by what Bethan's been saying, and angry, and is thinking Dale's responsible for this. Humiliating. Treating me like I got no judgement of my own. Like I can be pushed around by my mates.

"Dale wouldn't torch anywhere," Bethan says contemptuously. "Got a good job and everything. It's ridiculous. Bet Carno did it himself. Probably an insurance scam."

The Evans copper sighs.

Mam wags her finger at them and says, "You leave Jay alone now. I warn you. Carno's done enough damage round here." She looks at them fierce, checking they know what she means. They do – something of it, anyway. "He gets Jay into trouble over this, and I'll swing for him, I swear."

Evans sucks his teeth. His mate stares at Mam like she's an annoying specimen. I suddenly remember something.

"Eurotrash," I say. "Some chick painting her tits to look like faces. Tits big as balloons."

"What?" DC Scott can't help a snigger. A glance at Evans, who smiles too. Fuck them.

"The telly. I remember it. Friday night. Way after one, it was."

"There you are, then." Mam weren't pleased with the sniggering either. She makes a shooing motion with her arms. "Now get out. Out."

And, fuck me, they go. Tell me they've got enough, for the time being anyway, and leave.

First thing Mam does, after we've watched the cop car bump up on to the road from the track and disappear, is to push me twice in the chest, then grab my arm and shake me, hard. She's so wound up she's trembling.

"Hey, Mam, leave off!"

"Did you do that, Jay, you tell me now."

"Ah Mam," I groan. "'Course not. Fucking hell, Mam. Promise."

She goes on shaking me until Bethan says, "He didn't, Mam. Honest. We were telling the truth."

It's like no one listens to me. Like I'm a kid and no one trusts me, everyone says shut up, Jay, keep your mouth shut, Jay. Insulting.

I follow Bethan back to the kitchen and tell her, "You shouldn't have said all that. Not about Eileen and Dale. Stupid cow.'

Bethan whips round and shouts, "What d'you want? Get banged up for arson when it's not you? Anyway –" she tosses her head, defiant, "– they must know it already."

"How d'you work that?"

73

"Been talking to Carno, haven't they? He knows who Eileen is. She's the one scrammed him. Didn't ask about her, did they/ Because they know. Carno's living with Stu's wife, for Christ's sake. Must know Eileen, and where she lives, everything."

OK, she's got a point. Mulish, I say, "They didn't know about Dale."

"They're not going to arrest Dale, are they?"

"How d'you know?" Shit, both Mam and Bethan, they're innocents. Not wary of the law because they know the odd copper – or did, in Mam's case – and think they're all OK.

Bethan makes an exasperated noise. Fuck her. She's got no answer except to suggest I'm dull.

"I gotta ring him," I say.

"For Christ's sake."

"I'll ring him," Mam says. "I'm the one said it. And give him a piece of my mind."

I flip. "Dale didn't make me do nothing!" I shout. "Didn't arrange nothing! Just warned me Eileen knew about us and Carno, and to expect her round. Trying to be helpful." Why can't they fucking listen?

"You should know better," Mam says. "Going round to Carno's. You stupid boy." Her face twists like she's going to cry. Bethan turns on me, savage.

"See what you've done? Upset your Mam!"

"For fuck's sake!"

I slam out of the kitchen. Fucking women. Make me look two inches tall in front of policemen, then turn on me. I stomp out to the bog and sit there, resenting everyone. Fuck Carno. Fuck Eileen. I hear someone come out of the house, and then Bethan calling.

"Jay? Jay?"

She don't sound sorry. I'm not speaking to her.

"I know you're in there, Jay."

"Piss off."

"Don't know what you're so riled about. Just helping you."

"Ha ha."

"We were."

"I could have done it."

"No you couldn't. Why'd they believe you?"

"I told them about the telly programme. That's proof."

There's silence. Then Bethan hisses, "I could have told you that. Anyone could've."

I'm silent now.

"And," she says, "what were you doing anyway, watching the bloody telly then?"

What's she mean? Then? What was happening then? Oh shit, we were having our friendly roll on the cushions.

I give up. Fucking women. "Oh piss off." I say.

An hour later everyone's calmed down. Dumped the blame on the cops and Carno. Bethan's had a little weep. A shock, that – didn't realise how stressed she was. Seemed so quick and snappy with the cops. Anyway, Mam's accepted that I didn't tell her about visiting Carno because I was thinking of her and not wanting to upset her, and Bethan's agreed that dropping Dale in it just now was maybe a mistake, but she was too panicked and fired up to think straight. I've admitted that going to see Carno with Eileen wasn't a great idea, and that Mam and Bethan were trying to help me just now and not deliberately trying to humiliate me, and that the cops would have known about Eileen already. Happy families again. Well. Not raging, anyway. I've tried ringing Dale but he's not in, or not answering. Could be in his workshop. Bethan's got to go to work now – says she's OK, really, it'll be a relief – so I've decided to ride over to see him, just to check.

On the way I can't resist riding past Carno's depot. Gotta take a look. No one'll recognise me in a helmet. Anyway, now the police have visited and haven't dragged me off, who cares if they do.

I can smell the place a street away. Burnt rubber, burnt oil. Disgusting. I cruise past the high chain fence as slow as I can without falling over, but I can't see much. A couple of steel artic-containers looking scorched, that's about it. Sheds have still got their roofs. Can't see round the back, of course, and these containers might have been moved. Could be more damage elsewhere. Hope so.

I reach the big double gates and see they're open. Expect they're still clearing up, working overtime. There's a big uniformed lad standing in the entrance. Shit. Jonno! Playing security. Can't stop a grin.

No one else around so I swing into the culvert and pull up in front of him. Can tell him about the Stu-run next weekend. I cut the engine and lift my visor.

"Called in the experts, then," I say.

Jonno blinks at me, and folds his arms across his chest. The uniform's blue and straining. Got a walkie-talkie on his belt.

"You've got a nerve," he says.

"Why's that?"

"This your work, is it?"

"I wish."

"Carno thinks it is." He taps the walkie-talkie. "One call on this, could have the dogs on you."

"Go on then."

"Don't want to disturb them. They're pining. You heard one of them roasted?"

"Shame."

"Yeah." Jonno sounds genuinely regretful.

"Much damage, then?"

"Just these two –" he jerks a thumb at the containers, "– and the office round the back."

"The office?"

"Yeah. Three sites, they reckon. Nothing fancy. Petrol sloshed in the tanks, and broke a window and tipped a dribble through the grill. Building's OK but made a mess. Carno's really pissed."

"How'd he get past the dogs?" I ask.

"Chained up. Kept getting in the waste, Carno says. Don't store it proper, more like. No point having dogs if they're not running loose."

Conversation's difficult in a helmet so I loosen the strap and take it off. Jonno watches me, odd expression on his face. Can't read it.

"You free next weekend?" I say. 'Only we're doing the Cricieth run. Decided last night."

"Ah, shit." He clears his face and thinks a moment.

"Andy's place, Saturday morning. Ten-ish."

"OK. I'll see. Everyone going?"

"Looks like it."

"You got a tent? Burnt a big hole in mine."

"Oh aye." The dangers of lighting gas stoves when you're pissed. "Na. I'm taking Bethan. Wouldn't share with you, anyway."

"Wanker. Call Mr Carno for that."

"He here then?"

"Clearing out the office. Call him now, shall I?" He unclips the walkie-talkie. "You can tell him you didn't torch the place."

I stare at him. "Shit, Jonno."

He presses something on the machine and it crackles. "Mr Carno? Main gate. Got a friend of yours here. Says it weren't him, honest."

Is he kidding me? "That thing on?" I hiss.

"You wanna speak to him? I gotta call him anyway, you taken your helmet off. Had a video installed already. It's in the office." He nods up to the top of the gatepost. There's a camera on a bracket.

The line crackles with a voice. I slip my arm through the helmet and reach for the ignition key.

"Stay put," Jonno says. He actually pushes my hand away.

"For fuck's sake."

"' S'OK. Won't let him do nothing. You gotta stay."

I don't believe this. No, I do believe it. This is Jonno, mixing for the whim of it. Not even a hundred per cent confident whose side he'll be on. But why argue? I got things I could say to Carno. He's coming round the side of the burnt-out containers now. I got to decide whether to get off the bike, so I'm free to move around, or stay here, relaxed like. I decide to sit tight.

"You!" Carno's pointing a finger at me from ten yards away. He's blotchy in the face, seething. Well, he's trying to sort out a burnt-out office, must have done wonders for his temper. And hey, he's still got pink worm-tracks down his face where Eileen scratched him.

He's coming straight at me and I suddenly realise he's not going to stop. Staying on the bike was a bad decision. Shit.

At the last minute Jonno steps in front of him.

"Now Mr Carno," he says. "Hold on, Mr Carno."

"Get out of my way, you fat ape."

I can't see Jonno's face but I reckon Carno's lucky to survive that. Helps my confidence.

"Says he didn't do it, Mr Carno," Jonno says.

"He can tell that to the fucking police," Carno snaps. He whips out a mobile.

"Have already," I say, peering round Jonno's chest. "They just been round. In all night with my Mam. You check."

"Your Mam," Carno scoffs. "Fucking liar." But saying I've already seen the police has stalled him. And having eighteen stone of uniform between us. He changes his mind about the phone and pockets it. Jonno moves aside an inch or two.

"They've arrested your crazy woman." Carno wags his finger at me again. This man is rude. "And they know she got someone to do it. They know, you hear that? She's fucking admitted it."

"So?"

"She won't stay stum for ever. You'll see. Jesus Christ, it's gonna cost me thousands and thousands...."

"Glad to hear it, Mr Carno," I say. "But I was asleep and snoring."

He glares at me like he'd enjoy dismembering me.

"Then you got someone else to do it,' he says. 'I know you're behind it. All over that bitch, I saw you. You burn my place and then come round here smirking about it. They don't nail you, I will, and that's a promise."

"I'm quaking."

His eyes become slits. "Your Daddy was a stupid cunt, too."

That does it. I was cool till then. Now I'm gonna dismember him. But I got to leap off the bike first and prop it, which takes several seconds, long enough for Carno to jog backwards, shouting for someone called Seeger, and for Jonno to turn round and block me.

"Get out the way!" I push at him but it's like trying to shift a building. "Fucking move!" I shout.

"Can't hit the boss," he says. "You try, have to deck you. I got no choice, Jay."

I don't want to fucking fight Jonno. And now there's another man far end of the yard. Uniform like Jonno's.

Carno's waving his arms around. Looks excited. Three against one. I take this further, I'm gonna get hammered. Shit. Shit. Without the bike maybe I'd risk it. Be worth it, for the chance of one sweet fist in Carno's face. But a kick at the bike could have it over, could cost me hundreds. Takes effort, but I lift my palms and back off.

"That's him!" Carno urges the man Seeger, pointing at me. Fuck, he don't want to leave it. "Hold him!" he shouts to Jonno.

Jonno twitches towards me, then pulls back. He's not so dull he don't know what Carno's after. Jonno'd scrap with a mate, one to one – even expect no hard feelings – but a beating's different.

"See you, Jonno," I murmur. I keep my eyes on his as I swing astride the bike. Feel like I'm training a dangerous dog to stay. "Saturday," I say. "Might even get you a tent."

And shit, his eyes light up, like a minute ago he wasn't threatening to deck me. I fire the bike up and he swings round, just in time to block the others. I roar back out on to the road.

A couple of streets away I stop to put on my helmet. Heart's thumping and I'm near shitting myself. Close one, close one. But crowing too. Elated, even. Going for him, watching him retreat – that felt good. A big release. Sort of repeat of last time, only no Eileen to foul things up here, just Jonno, making it interestingly hairy, and this time, fuck me, I think I won.

"There's no way it's one of us," Dale says. "No way."

I've caught Dale in, and the cops haven't been round to see him yet, or, if they have, didn't find him in. Says he only got back from visiting Helen, one of his women friends, half an hour ago. I know Helen; she's a razorfaced blonde, thirty-rising-fifty, who's been around since I was a kid. Dale's claiming he only visited to score, but either she's excessively paranoid about short-stay callers or he finds her rewarding company, because he's been there all morning. Since she's known for dealing in her underwear weekends and only opening the door to boys she fancies, you can take your pick. I've told him about Evans and Scott visiting our place this morning and Bethan letting his name out, heat of the moment, and about me visiting Carno and learning that Eileen's been arrested.

He's not bothered by Bethan's slip-up, though he does take the blow he's just bought out of his jacket and clump across the boards to tuck it away in his bedside locker. We're going through the boys, one by one, trying to imagine them burning Carno's place for Eileen.

"It's never Sparky," I say. "If Sparky torched a place, he'd need weeks to plan it. Fuses and that. Not just slosh petrol about. Anyway, why'd he do it? Got nothing against Carno."

"She'll have paid," Dale says. "There's only you'd have done it for free."

"Sparky don't need money. Still gets pocket money from his Mam and Nan, on top of his invalidity. What about Jonno? He's always short."

"Shit, Jay, he's guarding the place."

"So?"

"If Jonno was going to hurt someone, he'd just wade in and hurt them, face to face. Not creep around setting poxy fires."

"Aye. Can't be him anyway," I say, thinking. "Dog got killed. Jonno'd never light a fire near a chained dog."

"Well, it's not Damien, is it?" We both chuckle, imagining it. Dunno why, really. Just Damien never does anything on his own. Always needs someone to tell him what to do. Can't see him taking a woman out for a pint solo, never mind planning an arson attack with one.

"And it can't be Andy," Dale says. "Saw him Saturday night, didn't we?"

"Aye."

"Didn't smell of petrol, did he?"

"Na."

"Right. Not him."

"Weren't you, then?" I ask.

"Not that I remember."

"Between one and two, the cops say. You got an alibi?"

Dale thinks about this, then says, "Nope."

"And she came back here. Night of the funeral."

"They don't know that."

"They know you arranged the meet."

Dale's dismissive. "I got no motive. What'd she be offering? Few hundred? A thousand? Don't need it. And I've nothing against Carno."

"Maybe it's no one round here. Where's she from? Eileen. She tell you?"

"Birmingham, I think she said."

"Must be boys there you could hire. Not as if it needed local knowledge. Or maybe someone here we don't know… with her parents around, must know other people."

Dale's shaking his head. "They've only been here since round the time Stu's wife left. Couple of years, no longer than that. And she hasn't been here once. Think that's part of why she's so angry."

"Eh?"

"Hadn't seen Stu for a while. I mean, all this shit's coming down on him, wife leaving and taking the kid, and then his job, and she's off in Birmingham, not bothering to come and see him. And then he's dead."

"Right. Talked a lot, did you?"

"Na." Dale smiles. "Less than an hour. And mostly about you. After what Sparky told her. She was just latched on to that."

"Mmm. You don't reckon she could have done it herself?"

"So why say she used someone? Only makes it look worse."

"Yeah." I'm remembering those gold sandals. Can't see Eileen climbing fences. All the same, young fit woman, it's possible. "So why say anything?"

"Ah, must be rough when they go at you. Or maybe she wants Carno to know."

Yeah. Can see that. If you're angry enough you don't care about yourself. More important you get your point across. Like me with his Jag.

"Bet the cops know she didn't do it herself. Maybe back in Birmingham Friday night. That's why they're chasing us."

"Mmm." That moment we hear a motor chugging outside. I walk over to the front window. Talk about chasing. Recognise the car, and the blokes getting out of it. From here I can see that the fair one, Scott, has got a bald spot top of his head.

"Hey Dale, they're here now."

Dale comes alongside and stares down. Sighs.

"You wanna be here?"

"Don't mind. No crime in it. They'd expect I'd make contact."

"Where's your bike?"

"Tucked in the yard."

"You split. Don't let 'em have another go at you. I'll say you been round, any case. Nothing to hide, eh? Back door."

I only hesitate a moment. If it's what Dale wants. Wouldn't have wanted him round our place this morning. Not that he's got two helpful women here busting to speak up for him.

At the back stairs I say, "You look out now." ˙

"Be fine. I'll ring you after. You're the one should look out. Serious, now. Lock up tight for a while. And tell your Mam and Bethan. Just in case."


Riding home, I'm not anxious about him. OK, he's got no alibi and the cops know he spent time with Eileen, but he's never been in trouble, ever – not even a caution, he says – which, if it's true, makes him near saint-like for these parts. Got a high-skill job and that always impresses coppers. It's the wasters they push around. And he don't fire up easily, so no danger of him overreacting and them turning nasty out of spite. And there's something about the boy himself. Dale's a coaster. Life's easy, placid, effortless. Things don't go wrong for Dale. They don't go too right either, as in him finding some purpose outside work, say, or meeting the right woman, but they don't go wrong. Can't imagine it any other way.

When I get home I stroll around the yard after locking the bike up, checking everything's secure. Though I can't see Carno getting back at me by damaging the property, and I'm certainly not worrying Mam or Bethan by mentioning the possibility to them. There's a difference between attacking an empty depot and someone's home. Saying you're gonna nail someone, like he did, sounds to me like either he's out to prove his case, with or without the cops, or have a go at me personally. First option's out, because he's not going to find proof of something I didn't do, and second option don't scare me neither.

I go inside and find a nice surprise: little sister Carly in the kitchen, swinging her legs on the table as usual, nattering with Mam. Just what I need. Russell's dropped her off to have Sunday tea with us while he goes with a mate to look at a pickup he fancies. Given his track record with motors, I look forward to admiring another heap of mechanical shit. But Carly's remarkably cheerful, though this don't make her any more charming. She's excited about Carno's depot going up, and wishes she'd been here this morning when the police visited. Says she's disappointed I wasn't banged up. Says she'd enjoy visiting me in prison, and if it weren't me torched the place, it should have been, matter of family honour.

"Oh, shut it," I say.

"Don't tease,' Mam says. "You wouldn't really like Jay in trouble."

"Least it'd show he could do something." Carly sniffs. "'Stead of sitting round on his fat arse all day."

"Talking of fat arses –"

"Oh, you two," sighs Mam.

"Well," sneers Carly. "Don't do anything, does he? Did you burn it, Jay, go on, you can tell your little sister, I'd be proud of you."

"No he didn't," Mam says. "He was here with Bethan."

"Bethan?" Carly cackles. "Did you, Jay?"

"No."

"But she asked you to? The Eileen woman?"

"No."

"Not what Mam says. She says –"

"No one said anything about burning anywhere." I turn complaining to Mam. "Why d'you tell her?"

Mam groans and starts banging around with pots and pans. I know I'm whining. When Carly's here it's like she's thirteen and I'm fifteen forever. We can't seem to help it.

"So why didn't you do it?" Carly lifts her lip at me. "You scared of Carno?"

"'Course not."

"Used to be shit scared."

"I never –"

"Liar."

What's she on about? Trashed his Jag, didn't I? What did she ever do? I never told her about Carno hurting me. Never never ever.

Mam murmurs, "Hush up, Carly. If Jay was scared of Carno maybe he had reason."

"I wasn't!" I roar. "Fucking cow!"

"Temper temper," says Carly. "Just wondering why you turned down the chance."

"That's enough." Mam stops clattering and sticks her chin at Carly. "You stop baiting Jay, and Jay –" she does the same to me, "– you stop rising."

Carly puffs out. "I'd have done it."

"More fool you, then," Mam retorts.

I was going to tell Mam about Carno still thinking I'm involved – not say I went to the depot, but that I got it from Jonno – but I'm not saying it in front of Carly. Probably accuse me of trying to steal the credit. Pigface. And how does she know I was once scared of Carno? Mam too. I never told them nothing. Like they've been spying on me from inside my brain.

"So who did it then?" Carly turns off the aggression and switches so fast to normal I want to pummel her. Winds you up, then leave you flailing. Like she always has to control the mood. But for Mam's sake I wind down too.

"Search me. The cops are with Dale now. Just left him."

"Dale?" She whoops. "Dreamy Dale? Ah shit. If he did it I'll go round now and screw him senseless."

"Carly!" Mam's tolerant of swearing, not of lewd talk.

"Wouldn't have you," I sneer. Probably untrue, mind. Grim thought. "Wasn't him, anyway."

"Ah." Carly pretends she's disappointed. "So wasn't one of you boys?"

"Nope." I say over to Mam, "The cops got Eileen though. Admitted she's paid someone. Saw Jonno. He's working at Carno's place.'"

Mam sighs, "Stupid girl."

Carly says, "And you got no idea?"

"Nope."

She grins to herself, jiggling her legs. "That's OK, then, Mam, isn't it? Carno taught a lesson, and Jay and the boys in the clear."

"So far," mutters Mam.

Carly drivels on a while, enjoying herself. She's got no tact. She's happy, talking about bad things happening to Carno. It's like she's separated the man from what he did. Mam hates hearing about Carno. Even bad things happening to him. It's all reminders. I can see this, anyone could see it, but not Carly. It's just her her her all the way.

I finally change the subject by asking about Russell, and enquire whether she's stopped picking his spots for him. Mam just thinks I'm being disgusting, but Carly knows what I mean. Gives me the finger and says married life's fine, thanks, not that it's any of my business. I tell Mam I'm taking Bethan away next weekend with some of the boys and I'm looking for a spare tent for Jonno. Used to have a few light-duty tents when we were kids, all shapes and sizes, for sleeping out on summer nights. Mam says she's pretty sure there's at least one, bike-rack sized, up in the roof space, if the mice haven't had it. I get the ladder out from the utility and Carly leaps off the table and says if I'm going up she wants to come too. Carly loves looking through sheds and storerooms, eyeing up what she can nick for her and Russell. I tell her she's too fat to get through the trap, but we're out of Mam's hearing by the time I say it, down the far end of the corridor, and she don't take offence. Just sneers and scampers up first, proving I'm wrong.

There's room to stand in the attic where the trap opens, but you got to watch where you put your feet, because the boarding's patchy. Dad kept saying he was going to convert it into a games room for Carly and me, but he hadn't done it by the time he died, and no one was interested after. There's a centre light bulb that gives off a lot more light once Carly's wiped it, and the inside of the roof's lined with neat tongue and groove, like they used to do in the days when they built houses proper. Nothing's stored tidy up here, because me and Carly've been through it too many times, but not for a long while. Five, six years, maybe.

One side there's boxes of all our old toys. Well, mine mostly. Carly was never into dollies and that. Wanted clothes and hi fi and grown-up things by the time she was ten. There's a box of radio control stuff, and the monster truck and speedboat that went with it. Probably still work if I got new batteries. Shit, even now I could fancy a tinker. Behind the boxes is a stack of baby stuff, paddling pool, buggy, crib. Dunno why Mam keeps this lot. Carly swears she's never having children – doing social services a favour, I reckon – and even if she changed her mind she'd only go for new stuff. Never talked kiddies with Bethan but I expect she would too. No one wants second-hand baby gear. Beyond that's a pile no one touches because it's all Dad's old stuff. Work books, manuals and that, and clothes. Uniforms, and a few suits Mam reckoned I might wear when I got bigger, only I never had a need for suits when I was eighteen, and after that I shot up another few inches and got too big anyway. She could chuck this lot, too.

"Here it is." Carly's just the other side of Dad's stuff. "Least, looks like it." She holds up an orange drawstring bag, shaped like a small lumpy bolster.

I'm still distracted with exploring so I say, "Triffic. Drop it down the trap," over my shoulder but the next thing I know something hits me, bam, back of the head. Stupid cow's thrown it at me.

"For fuck's sake, Carly."

"And hey, sleeping bags too," she says. She tosses one of them at me.

"Don't mess things up."

"And wow." Her voice slows. "Hey, wow. Look at this." She's gazing at something at her feet, expression of wonder. "So that's where Mam hid them."

I step back out of the toys and boxes to come alongside her. She's looking down at a pile of metal implements, lying loose on the floor: fire tongs, heavy poker – old Cortina gearstick, make brilliant pokers – and a dinky kindling hatchet.

"Shit," I say. We stare down together. Don't need to say anything. Contemplating a moment of shared history. The weapons of our last fight. Our last, most deadly-serious fight.

"You started it," Carly murmurs.

She could be right. Probably called her Pigface once too often. But she's the one who picked up a weapon. The poker, it was. Because for the first time she realised she might not win. Fifteen and seventeen, we were. Remember that clear. Can't recall what the fight was about, though. About hating each other, expect, like it always was. She was heavier than me then, a lot heavier, and had been for a while, but I was taller and getting stronger, and I'd taken all I could of her rages and being her punchbag. For once I went as mad as her. She'd already smashed a fist in my nose and made it bleed and I'd got her down on the sitting room carpet and pushed her face into the armchair seat hoping she'd smother, but she'd elbowed me in the groin and struggled free, and next thing I know she's leapt up with the poker in her hand and she's swishing it through the air at me. I leap up too and think this is it, she's lost it, this time she's really gonna kill me. She whacks me across the left wrist with the metal and my hand goes dead and I can't see anything to fight back with except the little hatchet, and that's too small to reach her but I pick it up anyway and slash around with it. I'm so mad I'd have butchered her, if I could have got at her. And then Mam comes in, and sees her two kids trying to murder each other, blood everywhere from my nose, and definitely looking like one's going to succeed. She screams in between us, and Randolph's round and charges in behind her – just neighbourly, Mam and he were, in those days – and it takes the two of them to stop us. Carly collapses weeping and Mam takes her into the kitchen to sit her down, and Randolph holds me against the wall talking into my face until I hear him and start blubbing too, and then he takes me down the hospital to have my wrist and nose checked. Bones cracked in both. We tell them I've fallen down the stairs. Don't let on it's a bungalow. Paul speaks to us a few days later and says it's never to happen again, but we know it already – terrified both of us – and it never does. And since we never had grate fires anyway, with Randolph supplying the boiler fuel so cheap, Mam takes the fire tools away and hides them. Here.

"Christ, we were shit." Carly's shaking her head.

"You were," I say. "I were a battered brother."

"Only 'cos you were so useless." But she's not sounding angry, more upset. "You trashed that car, and then it's like it's all over for you. Pally with wanker Paul, even, yes sir, no sir, be a good boy sir. Pathetic."

I don't understand.

"See?" she says. "Haven't a clue, have you?"

She's making me feel stupid. What she's saying? That I didn't care about Dad? That trying to sort myself out, trying not to upset Mam, means I didn't care?

"It's not right," she says. "Mr Fucking Happy. You shouldn't have been."

Mr Fucking Happy? Maybe she's got a loose definition of happy. Mr Not Fucking Raging All the Time, that would be more like it.

"You don't understand anything," she sighs.

"Might," I say. "You never tell me nothing."

She looks at me hard. "So why were you so scared of Carno?"

"Wasn't."

"You were. After you smashed up the Jag. Like you did it, big shot action, and then after, you get cold feet…."

Oh shit. OK, I'm going to give something to her. Tell her something. Dunno why, because I know she'll abuse it, but I'll do it. It don't matter now. Not a big deal.

I say, "He said he'd cut my dick off."

Her mouth drops open. "Carno did? When?"

"After the Jag. He came round here. Mam sent him away and

he found me in the field. He said he'd cut my dick off, and then he grabbed me."

She's looking at me eyes wide, mouth still open.

"What'd he do?"

"Just... grabbed me. There." I indicate. "Made me fall down."

"He touched you up?"

"No," I say, wearily. "He was trying to hurt me. Did, too."

"What did Mam say?"

"Didn't tell her. Didn't tell no one."

Her eyes narrow. "This true?"

"No," I sigh. "Made it up."

"And that's why you were scared?"

"Only for a while. Shit, Carly, you pull everything out. I'd done what I wanted to do. Wasn't scared *off* anything. Just... he freaked me, for a little while."

She turns for the trap. "I'm gonna tell Mam."

"No, fucking hell, Carly, what's she gonna do? Why'd she want to know? Always pushing stuff on her."

She turns round startled, like no one's said this to her before. Maybe they haven't. We never talk, that's the trouble. Just bicker and shout.

"Who'm I gonna tell then?"

"Why've you got to tell anyone?"

She gawps at me. Then shakes her head fast. Out of the question. She starts climbing down the ladder. "Mam!" she shouts.

So Mam has to hear about something that happened thirteen years ago, just because Carly's got to evacuate her brain of any shit she doesn't like. It was nothing, I tell Mam, don't listen to her. It's not important. I dunno why Carly's so steamed up about it anyway; she's done worse than grab someone's balls herself. Mam says she guessed at the time that Carno had threatened me, which wasn't surprising given what I'd done to his car, and that, all in all, she's glad if I was scared off trying anything else. Carly says she's taking it all too light, and rants on about it being a serious sexual assault, and I can see that by the time she gets home with Russell she'll be telling him that Carno dragged me out in the fields when I was fifteen and raped me. Probably be all over town by tonight. It's like everything happened yesterday to Carly. Still seething about it, right on top. In the middle of me shouting at her to shut up the telephone rings and it's Dale.

"You got a problem there?" he says, hearing Carly roaring on in the background.

"Nope." I turn round and yell, "Shut it, will you! It's Dale!" and Mam says, "Hush, love." Carly stamps off into the sitting room.

"OK," I say. "How'd it go?"

He's quiet a moment. "Fine. Well. Think they believed me when I said I didn't know Carno. Personal-like. Said they'd check with him, but they didn't argue. Got a bit nasty at the end, wanted to search the place, and I said not without a warrant. Looking for money, petrol can, I dunno. I couldn't risk it. They didn't like that. Said they'd be back, but I doubt it. Not to search, anyway, no point. I told them it was only you Eileen was interested in, and I knew for certain you'd turned her down. Told them I'd seen you straight after you left her, and you were definitely pissed with her for asking. They got nothing, Jay."

Well, knew Dale would sort it. The rest of the afternoon and evening I spend putting the old tent up in the field and playing with it. Anything to keep out of the house while Carly's still here. Quite enjoy myself. Seal a few little holes with tape. It's a nice tent, easily big enough for Jonno and his gear. Wonder if I could sell it to him. Even wonder, idle like, whether to sleep out tonight. Maybe a bit much to spring on Bethan at midnight but you never know. Could make a camp fire, heap all the bedding in, get it looking inviting. Should be her day off tomorrow, might be game for it. Only thing puts me off is waking early, like you always do when you're camping. At tea time Carly comes out to call me in and sneer at me for being such a kid, and I tell her I'm thinking of getting the radio control stuff down after and playing with that. She believes me. Gullible cow.

# 6

I'm trying to fill in three forms this morning and it's defeating me. The trouble with getting up early is it gives you too much empty time. You think, right, this is the day to deal with things that are nagging at you – and people nagging at you, like Mam, before she goes into town with Randolph – so you settle down, telling yourself a quick hour and it'll all be over, but then an hour's gone by and Bethan's pacing around hissing, "God's sake, Jay, just do them," and I'm not even half way through the first. Keep seeing other things I gotta do, put the pups out for a pee, have a slash myself, kick the cupboard door that don't shut proper, straighten the sheep-dip calendar, wait for the kettle to boil again, anything. Bethan refuses to help me because Mam told her not to; Mam says if I never write anything I'll forget how to do it altogether, and then where will I be. Same place I am now, I say, only one less mind-grinding chore to contemplate.

There's a short form from the DSS, just previous-employer stuff, a longer one from the bike insurance, because the poxy broker's changed my company and they want a proposal form filled, and a fucking enormous one from the tax people. Had a quick flick through this, mind, and reckon that most of it don't apply, so I'm planning to fill in just two pages and sign it. I don't even know why I'm making such a fuss, because most of what they want is figures, not words, and most of the words are ones I can copy from pays slips and old forms. But it still does my head in. In the end Bethan comes into the kitchen and stands over me, points at each box, tells me to speak the answer, and then makes me write it down. Print it, she says, when they want words, don't join the letters up. Says it looks stupid when half are capitals and half are little ones. I don't intend it like that. Just how they come out my hand.

But it's a great feeling after. Two brown envelopes, one white, sealed and put in the box on the gate for the postman. Bethan says there, wasn't so bad, was it, and Mam'll be proud of me. Patronising cow.

I could do with another little sleep now. This is because we did kip out last night. Not that I'm regretting it; very romantic it was. Good move too, in reassuring Bethan after yesterday's cop visit – she leaves me roaring off to see Dale about it, and comes back to campfire games in the garden. We sat round the glowing embers drinking tea and smoking spliffs listening to the sheep cough and then lay back pretending we're space-wrecked on a deserted planet, and all those little dots in the sky are spaceships racing down to rescue us. Bethan actually sees one fall, and when we start looking out for them we see several more. Useless pilots can't handle re-entry. Get quite excited, in case one does make it, and then start giggling and decide to give up on them and do our duty by re-populating the planet. It's not too warm at two in the morning but the cold stiffens Bethan's tits into rocks, which is compensation. Crawl into the tent after and kick what's left of our clothes out the flap. Trouble is, it's like a sauna six o'clock this morning, have to heave ourselves out of the swamp by seven, and I can't cope with only four hours sleep.

I'm just thinking maybe Bethan won't complain if I take a quick snooze on the sofa when the phone rings. Bethan shouts that it's Paul, wants to speak to me. I haul myself into the kitchen.

"Just seen the Echo," Paul's voice says. "Is Carly all right?"

"Eh?"

"The paper. Arson at Carno's works? Said they're holding a woman. Hinting at a grudge attack."

"Errr." I open my eyes wide, hoping it'll let more into my brain. "Err. Ah, Paul, that's not Carly."

"It's not? Oh, well, that's...that's... I just thought, you know...." He sounds part embarrassed, but mostly relieved.

"She's all for it, mind," I say. "But it weren't her. Woman name of Eileen. Long story. Didn't do it herself, paid someone else to do it."

"Ah." A cautious note creeps in. "No one we know?"

"Nope. Dale and I had the cops round, but they went away again. Weren't me, Paul, straight up. Nor Dale. Mystery to us too. Just visited us because we knew Eileen. Sister of a mate who died."

"Right. Does sound a long story. Well. I'm relieved to hear it."

"I'll tell Carly you thought of her. She'll be chuffed."

Paul laughs. "You do that." He pauses. "Listen, sorry about me being antisocial when you were over. Just... get these moods. You want to go for a run at the weekend? Make up for the one we didn't take?"

He *was* in a mood. I read some things right.

"Ah, shit, Paul," I say. "Can't this weekend. Going to Cricieth with the boys. Camping over."

"Cricieth? Up North? You lucky sod. Fantastic scenery."

"Come too. More the merrier."

"Mmm." He's amused by the idea, not taking it serious.

"Or come over one evening. Light till near ten. Could get a fair run in."

He picks up enthusiasm.

"Might do that. Yeah. Not tonight though. I'll have a word with Simone."

The call puts paid to sneaky snoozes, and being as it's Bethan's day off she gets to decide what we do the rest of the day. Go to Cardiff shopping, she says. Clothes shopping. Got two hundred quid in her purse desperate to meet new friends. Mam doesn't charge her enough keep, obviously. The prospect of girlie shopping don't fill me with glee, but I'm stuck with it. Means going in the Subaru because I won't risk the bike in Cardiff – not for the hours we'll be trailing around shops – and if she's going on a real bender we'll need the load space anyway.

It's a good thing we do go in the car because fifty minutes later, just turned off Gabalfa roundabout into Cardiff, the sky goes black and it starts spitting raindrops like some giant up there's gobbing on us. Parking the car in the multi-storey there's a crack of thunder so loud it makes Bethan stop her ears and while it's rolling over we turn to each other and grin like kiddies. I'm hoping the storms stay around long enough to watch them when we get home, but it's not likely. Shame.

What can you say about shopping? What can you say about shopping in a two-hour thunder storm? It's hot and wet and occasionally noisy. Since I got no taste in women's clothes, according to Bethan, I got no function except as pack horse. My opinion's only asked when she wants to confirm something isn't right. Like I say, hey, that's nice, and she says, right, too tarty then, and puts it away. And what's so wrong with tarty, I've tried complaining, maybe tarts know a thing or two, but she just snorts, as if exciting me with what she wears is way down her list. Mind, she does dress nice. Just not tarty, more's the pity. Still, there's always her uniform.

By the tenth or eleventh shop I'm loaded up like a mule and starting to feel grumpy. She's sympathetic and leaves me in the Glendower with a late afternoon pint surrounded by coloured bags. Look like a Christmas tree where someone's nicked the tree. She comes back half an hour later with a bag from River Island containing a midnight blue shirt covered in tiny stars which she says is a present for me. Says she chose it because it reminded her of last night. I say, "Aah," and we kiss. Couple of squishy love-birds.

I'm starving by now and we don't want to drive out of Cardiff in the rush hour, specially since it's still raining – light but steady now – so we stash the goodies in the Subaru and go to a pub opposite the multi-storey to eat. Bethan rings Mam to tell her not to cook for us – thoughtful girl, it never crossed my mind – and we treat ourselves to steak and chips. Leave prompt at seven, because Bethan wants to round off the day with some sloppy film on the telly when we get home. She drives because she knows that watching someone shop is more exhausting than being the shopper, and what with my four hours sleep and three recent pints she don't want me nodding off at the wheel.

The motorway's awash with rain water and when we turn up Risca way it's just as bad. We run into trouble in Cwmcarn. Bethan's worrying she's going to miss the start of the film and may be going a bit fast. Hits a duckpond puddle with her nearside wheels which makes the car swerve, and although she corrects it without hitting anything, she overdoes the correction and we bang the front tyre up against the kerb. Makes a horrible screech. She gasps, "Oh shit," and we listen, and sure enough there's a thump thump starting and then the steering goes wonky and she has to pull over with a puncture.

"Great," I say, seeing as how she's wrecked the tyre but I'm gonna be the one to get wet changing it.

"Oh Jay," she wails. "I'm sorry. Really sorry."

I don't mind too much. Been useless all afternoon doing girlie things. Now's my chance to get stuck in to something manly, show Bethan how indispensable I am. While I'm loosening the wheel nuts she leans out the window and says, "Jay? There's a phone box just up there."

"So there is," I say. Less than fifty yards away.

"I'm going to ring Mam. Get her to start the video." She climbs out of the car and hoods her jacket over her head.

"Fine." Think she's potty myself. This'll be done in a couple of minutes and we're only fifteen miles from home. If she misses the start what's she gonna do? Watch it at the end?

The car's still jacked up but the spare's on and I'm squatting beside it twiddling the nuts fingertight when I hear her tripping back. More than tripping, running.

"Jay! Jay!" she gasps. "Mam's had a funny phone call!"

I yank on the jack handle and the tyre sinks to the tarmac.

"Funny as in...?"

She's leaning over me, twisting her hands.

"Nasty. A man. Jay, listen."

"I'm listening."

"Said to tell you they'd nailed your friend."

"Eh?"

"Says that's all he said. Tell Jay we've nailed his friend. Then put the phone down ...."

"Shit." I get the brace on the wheel nuts and jerk them tight, fast as I can. Jumping inside. "Means Dale. Must do. Shit."

"That's what I thought. Was only half an hour ago."

"Not the police, was it?"

"I don't know." Bethan's moaning. "Doesn't sound like it, does it?"

Can't tell, hearing it second hand. Well, probably couldn't tell first hand. Coppers been known to make off-the-record snide calls. But it's the word 'nails' that makes me think me it isn't. Same way Carno put it to me. His expression. Could mean he's found something he thinks proves something against Dale, or could be they've had a go at him.

"We'll call in now," I say, throwing the tools in the back of the Subaru. "Just check he's OK. Can't be long back from work."

"If he's not there we go straight back to Mam's," Bethan says. "We can ring people from there. She's on her own. Pretending she wasn't worried, but...."

"OK, OK."

It's automatic that I jump in the driver's seat. Wish Bethan still had her mobile. Sold it on because she never used it, working in a hospital, and then moved in with me. Could use it now.

"Dale didn't do anything for Eileen, did he?" Bethan asks, outskirts of Crumlin. "I mean, I know he wouldn't have burnt the place himself, but passed her on to someone. Besides you."

"Says not. She did take the names of a few boys. But that was earlier, in the Crucible. Nothing to do with Dale. When she went back with him he says she just talked about me. 'Cos of what Sparky had said."

Bethan nods at the windscreen. We're rising up through Abertillery and the hills that loom over us are shrouded in fog. Where they're wooded the canopies poke out through the swirls like floating bush-forests. Gorillas-in-the-mist landscape, that's what Bethan calls it. The rain's keeping the traffic slow and dithery. Keep coming up behind idiots who don't know what they're doing and having to punch the brakes.

"Take it easy," Bethan hisses.

"Stupid bastards," I mutter.

Nip the back way through Brynmawr and out on to the Beaufort road. We'll be there in two minutes. I swing into Dale's cul-de-sac and wind the Subaru through the parked cars. There's no Guzzi propped down the end but if he's in for the evening there wouldn't be, it'd be round the back. I swing the Subaru up on to the pavement.

"Lock up," I tell Bethan, as we leap out. "You got all your gear in the back."

I clatter up the steps to the flat. Bethan's just behind. Bang on the door hard. It swings open.

"Dale!" I shout. If the door's open he must be here.

"Dale!" I call again. No answer. I cross the little hall and push open the door. "Dale? You here? Oh. Fucking hell."

I missed him first because I was looking at the wrong height. He's lying on the floor. On his back, arms as wide as they'll go, palms up. Not moving. Think he's got his eyes closed. I take a step towards him, and that's as far as I get. Can't absorb it. His hands are lying in pools of red. Shiny sticky goo across the painted boards.

I hear Bethan gasp, "Jesus Christ!" and for a moment I think she's being really tasteless but of course she's not, she don't know what she's saying. She swoops past me, and is down on her knees beside him.

"Dale!" she cries, "Can you hear me, Dale?"

Can't see his face now. Just those leaking hands. Centre of his palms are black and messy. I know that's where the problem is. I got to do something about them. I come up behind Bethan and squat down next to his arm.

"Don't touch him!" Bethan hisses. "Leave him!"

Dale's legs shift. He moans.

"Lie still, lie still," Bethan says quickly. "Jay. Ring for an ambulance. Now. Now!"

Dale's alive. Moaning and moving. Can see his chest heaving. Makes something heave in my own chest. Bethan's hands are flicking over him, lifting his T-shirt, checking his hips, legs. Then she rests her hand light on his breastbone and says, "It's OK, Dale. Lie still. Be over soon. Lie still. Phone, Jay."

I stumble back to near the door, where the phone is. It's still connected. Press nine nine nine.

'Ask for ambulance service,' Bethan orders. 'Tell them there's a man been attacked and he's nailed to the floor by his hands and he's bleeding. Don't try and explain. They'll send the police anyway. Probably fire service too. Just answer their questions.'

I do what she says. I don't know the name or number of Dale's flat but I tell the phone woman it's right down the end of the cul-de-sac and above a workshop, and she says not to worry, they already got it on screen. She asks if it's safe for us to stay there and if anyone else is hurt and I say it is and no they're not. She tells me to stay on the line. My thighs go weak so I sit down on the chair next to the phone with the receiver propped on my shoulder, and watch Bethan being a nurse on the floor beside Dale. She's grown up and I'm useless. One of Dale's legs is trembling, jittering and vibrating. Like he's cold. I'm cold too. I got nothing to do except sit here, feeling cold and useless, waiting for the world to arrive.

# 7

When I get back from a crack-of-dawn coffee down the hospital canteen there's a different copper on the door outside Dale's room. Don't know why the fuck they've got a copper there anyway – damage been done, hasn't it? As I pass him and lay a hand on the door he says, "Hang on mate, can't go in there."

"Watch me," I say.

He's up like a shot. I'm so pissed with the uniform I'd clout him if it weren't for him thinking he's protecting Dale.

"I'm his friend," I say. "Been here all night. Ask the nurses."

One of them trots past just that moment and trills, "Hi, Jay, trying to get yourself arrested again?" with a snickering laugh. Thinks she's funny. Tart. The copper blinks after her.

"You sure you're allowed in?" he asks.

"I am. Works like this, see. You there –" I point at his chair, "– me in there. OK?"

Might spend hours getting it through his bone skull, except Sister can see us from her glass cubicle across the lino tiles and her eyebrows have risen like bristling catkins at the sound of voices. She pokes her head out to hiss, "Patients are sleeping. It's all right, officer. He's sitting with his friend. You can let him in."

The copper mutters, "OK. Just asking," and lets me pass.

Inside the room Dale's still asleep. Not a natural sleeping position, propped up on his back, arms resting straight outside the covers, but looks peaceful. Pale, but peaceful. His hands are wrapped in thick white bandages and one of them's stained already, but his fingers are poking out and the damage don't look half what it did when they brought him in. Three nails in each palm, the bastards. But only one bone chipped, and that's in his left hand. And they weren't huge nails – maybe why they used three each side. Or maybe they just liked squeezing the trigger. Definitely a nail gun, not a hammer job. Dale says there were three of them. Well, he moaned *three* when the cops asked how many men there were. Before the nurses told them to eff off, that is, and not speak to a boy who'd still got lumps of floorboard attached to his hands. I knew there had to be more than one because he isn't too hurt anywhere else, and although he's not a muscle boy he could fight if he had to. But it don't look like he did, so probably he wasn't allowed to, which means at least two.

I'm waiting here because I'm not leaving him with only the fucking pigs for company – and I'd call them worse if I could think of worse, since it's obviously them who dropped his name to Carno – and no one can raise any family even to tell them what's happened, never mind get them over here. I know Dale's Mam lives in Swansea, but I also know she won't be a Farrell because she's remarried, and there's a lot of married women in Swansea. Dale was taken away to get the nails out as soon as we got here, and what with the anaesthetic and pain killers they say no talking till this morning. However it's five now and hospital mornings start a couple of hours before normal mornings, so this could be in an hour or so. And that's another reason I'm hanging on here, because I'm expecting Evans and Scott back to do the talking, and if I get the chance I intend to give them more of what I gave them last night. Which was the least they deserved, the big-mouth bastards, though they won't admit it. The dispute over this explains the little nurse's quip just now.

The easy chair by the bed's not too uncomfortable and I managed a few hours sleep myself earlier, before the birds woke me. Dawn chorus – more a screeching match. Need to axe those roosting trees. And then the room caught the sun. Got the blind slats angled the wrong way, but I don't want to pull the cord and alter them in case it's noisy. It's not bothering Dale so let him sleep. I get a strange feeling when I look at him. Like I got a blockage middle of my chest. Shit, it was only yesterday I was saying to myself: things don't go wrong for Dale. No need to try imagining it now.

A nurse sticks her head round the door and whispers, "Jay? Message from Bethan. Says it's OK, Randolph stayed over, and he's hanging on today with your Mam, so there's no need to rush back. Says she'll pop in when she gets a break, OK?"

I lift a hand at her and she leaves, snapping the door shut. So why'd she bother to whisper, silly cow. The noise makes Dale stir. I watch his face get less peaceful, specially when he tries shifting an arm. His eyes open. I see his brain slowly opening too.

"Hi," he murmurs. Tries a little smile. "You look like shit."

"Aye. Thanks."

He closes his eyes again for a minute, then opens them and says, "Kill for some water."

"'Course." I slosh water from the jug by his bed into the plastic mug. The nurses have thoughtfully provided some bendy straws. Plonk two in and hold the mug while he sucks.

"Ah." He pulls back, nods he's had enough, and I put the glass away. He looks down at himself. "Is it just me hands? Nothing else?"

"Nothing else. Fit as a flea, wrists inwards." Not quite the truth, since he's got a few bruises here and there. Smudgy purple one over his ribs, like someone kicked him or knelt on him hard, but didn't worry anyone enough to X-ray.

"Are they gonna be all right?"

"Your hands? 'Course they are." Don't know this for sure – doctors going on about checking tendons last night – but I seen enough hospital programmes on the telly to know not to agitate the patient.

He nods and closes his eyes again. I sit back.

We're woken again quarter to seven when a woman in a purple uniform comes in with a tray of breakfast. No one's told her this is a patient who can't use his hands and she clucks over the toast and cereal wondering how she's going to find someone to help him. I tell her we'll do a deal. Give me the cereal and in return I'll feed Dale the toast. She says I drive a hard bargain but it's OK with her, and gets him a mug with a spout for the tea. After the toast Dale says he needs a piss. There's cardboard bottles down the side of the bed which I say I could hold for him, I suppose, but Dale says fuck that, and staggers out of bed to piss in the basin. Don't need help because he's got no clothes on. From the back he's not marked at all.

I rinse the basin out after and help him get the covers back up. He's trying to grip them with his fingers but the action's making him hiss.

"You want more drugs?" I ask.

"Oh aye, roll us a spliff, Jay."

"Painkillers, tit."

We have a little cackle, as if it's funny, and I go off and ask the nurses. But getting drugs out of nurses is like squeezing the last gob of toothpaste out of the plastic tube: lots of hopeful air and the promise of goodies sometime, but when it's coming, fuck knows. They say they can only offer paracetamol anyway, at least till the doctor's visited.

I'm just back telling Dale it might be a while when DS Evans and his belly sidles into the room. Baldy Scott follows, escorted by Sister.

"Jay," Sister says. "These gentlemen want a chat with Dale. They'd like you to wait in the dayroom."

Evans and Scott are refusing to catch my eye and look as if their mouths been zipped. "Lost their tongues, have they?" I say.

"Out." She's got a commanding manner, this Sister. "Dayroom. And wait there, because they want a word with you afterwards."

This is her solution to the aggro problem: insist on acting as go-between. It's her territory, so what she says goes.

Dale murmurs, "'S'OK, Jay," and since this Sister isn't so dragon-like one to one, and last night was the kind lady who let me stay overnight in his room rather than down the corridor, as the cops suggested, I don't argue.

Waiting in the dayroom gives me a chance for a ciggie, propped against the window sill and puffing the smoke through the nine-inch slit. Can see a soggy splattering of dog-ends down below, so I know I'm not the first. I'm just dropping my own stub down to join them when Bethan comes in. I swing round. She's in her uniform, and pale with it.

"How's Mam?" I ask.

"Left too early this morning to see her," she says. "OK last night. Happier with you here than home."

"Aye." The cops were too, I suspect. Saved them having to make a decision whether to spend money protecting me. Baldy Scott got close to slinging me out several times – temper on him, that one – but was always persuaded to back off by Evans.

Bethan asks after Dale and I tell her he seems OK, just sore-handed. And because I didn't get the chance to say it last night, but've thought about it a lot since, I tell her I think she was brilliant at Dale's flat, when we found him. Brilliant. Tell her I'd have freaked without her.

"No you wouldn't," she murmurs. But then looks bleak. "I keep seeing it. Don't know how anyone could do that. Sick. Suppose we hadn't gone round –"

"Aye." A killer, that one. I've not dwelt on it.

"Not going to be able to ride for a bit, is he."

"Nope."

"And with the Criccieth run coming up."

"Ah shit." I'd forgotten about that.

"You told any of the others?"

"Not yet. Probably know already. Had a few hours to get around town."

She tries a smile. Then gives a shaky sigh, like what she really wants to say has got to come out. "I been thinking. D'you suppose, if we hadn't been away yesterday –?"

I say quickly, "No way of knowing." I've been brushing it aside all night. The thought that Dale might have got himself crucified on his floor because they couldn't find me. It's a shit thought. I'm not entertaining it.

"We've got to think about it," Bethan says.

I turn away. "I'll have a word with the pigs. See if they got Carno banged up."

She nods. "It's not just you, you know. There's Mam and –"

"I know."

"Sorry, only I'm a bit –"

"Bethan. I'll sort it. I know."

"OK then."

I give her a quick kiss and a squeeze and she grips me tight. 'Course she's scared.

She goes off back to her Obs and Gynae ward and while I'm having another ciggie out the window Evans and Scott come in. I don't hurry to finish it.

"Not meant to do that in here," Scott says.

I ignore him. I don't like Baldy Scott. Didn't even wince when he first saw Dale.

"Ah, forgot." Scott smiles at the NO SMOKING sign beside the window. "Let's see… N..n… noo.. Sm.. sm…?"

"Go fuck yourself." Bastard. Could stamp on his head and enjoy it.

Evans sighs. Rocks on his toes. "OK, OK. Jay. Truce, OK?"

Truce? Who started this? Just because Bethan wrote stuff for me last night.

"Please." He sounds tired, conciliatory. "We need to talk."

I pull fast on the ciggie. "Done too much talking already, you have. You got Carno banged up?"

"Umm." He hesitates. "Mr Carno had an engagement yesterday afternoon. Went on till evening. A dozen witnesses."

"Ah, come on."

"Like you had your Mam and girlfriend when his place went up."

I stub the ciggie out. "For fuck's sake. He said it to me. Nail me, that's what he said. He's got men. Line 'em up."

"Dale didn't see them, Jay. They were wearing stocking masks. Two big, one smaller, that's all he says. But yes, we know he's got men. We're talking to him again. We're not pussyfooting. Whatever your friend did, he didn't deserve nailing down."

"He didn't do nothing! Like I didn't!"

"Don't shout. Sit down." He taps the back of an armchair. Sits down himself in the one beside it. Baldy Scott crosses his arms over his chest and leans back against a big book cupboard. Sneer on his face suggests he's distancing himself.

"Sit," Evans says again. "Please."

I know I'm being soft-soaped but I find myself stomping over.

"Sit," repeats Evans. I sit.

"Right," he says. "Now. Do you know anyone with a nail gun?"

"Carno," I say.

His eyes flicker. "Besides Carno."

I know it's Carno, so I don't want to think about it. But he carries on staring at me, so I force myself.

"No. Well. Know a few builders...."

"Have you seen them with nail guns?"

"Nope."

"D'you know what a nail gun looks like?"

"Barrel and big hand grips. Kind of square-shape."

"Right. Yeah. Know what you mean. The one that nailed your friend, it must have been quite big." He holds his hands apart, describes a lap-sized rectangle. "Maybe green, or orange."

"Haven't seen one."

"OK. Thing is, it was probably used touching him. You know, pushing at him." He screws a knuckle into the palm of his left hand.

"So?"

"There were three nails each side. His hands would've been bloody for some of the shots. If we found a gun in someone's possession, it might be interesting to examine."

"Aye. Can see that."

"So what I'm saying is, we're looking for the gun, as well as the men. It hasn't turned up so far, and there's a good chance whoever used it has still got it. I'm just telling you this in case you come across it."

"Why should I come across a nail gun?"

"Well, there's two ways. One, you might go looking, and if you do, which I don't recommend, but you could be foolish enough, then if you find it, don't tamper with it. Just bring it to us. Or even better, tell us where it is so we can find it. Two, if it's still with its owners, they might take it to you, and I think you should know what they look like. Just in case."

"I see three men in stockings carrying a nail gun I'll give you a buzz."

"I'm not joking, Jay."

I can see he's not.

"You don't live alone, and maybe that's good. Or maybe it's not."

"They wouldn't do nothing to Mam or Bethan."

"Probably not."

"And we got a Doberman."

"That's Floss, is it? Very fierce."

I just stop myself saying, "And there's the guard-chickens." He's rattling me.

"They've probably done all they want," he says. "Be very risky to go for you now. But I want you all to be careful."

"Aye," I say. "We'll be careful."

"Right." He puts his hands on the chair arms, ready to get up, then ticks. "Ah, message from the ward Sister. Any chance of you persuading Dale to go stay with his Mam? She says they'll let him out soon, maybe even today, assuming the doctors give him the OK and he's got someone to look after him. I don't want him too far away, in case we want to speak to him again, but Swansea'd be fair."

"He don't want to go, then?"

"Won't even give us her name. Says he'll tell her himself when he's fit. Seems to think she's a worrier. Could go through his things again and probably track her down, but it might come better from you."

I don't like the idea of Dale down in Swansea, but I can see he's not going to manage on his own. Hmm. Might be more than one answer to that.

"And," says Evans, "you can tell him we made a little confiscation while we were checking things out."

"Ah shit," I sigh.

"Too little to bother with. But just to save him looking."

"Ah. Right. So police benefit fund, is it?"

"Don't be smart. You'll speak to him?"

"I'll have a word."

We take Dale home with us at the end of Bethan's shift. It's easy. The hospital wants the bed, Dale don't want to go to Swansea but knows he can't manage on his own, and when I sound Mam out she's almost gooey with the prospect. Not like Mam to be gooey, but maybe she's thinking it could be me with my hands bandaged, grace of God, and is gushingly grateful it isn't. 'Course I ask Dale if there's anywhere else he'd prefer – a workmate's place, say – but he says no way. Vehement, like we're the only choice. Don't know what Evans'll make of it, two targets, one already hit, one potential, under one roof, but haven't told him. Sister said she'd inform him when he made contact – which he's bound to have done by now – and we haven't had any cop cars screaming over the mountain to object, so I assume he's accepted it.

We've put Dale in Carly's old room. Given what he knows

about her he expected it to be papered in Arnie Schwarzneggar and Van Damm posters, and he was surprised to see it's quite girlie really. In fact more girlie than it was when she was last here, a year or so back, because she's taken the Trainspotting and Pulp Fiction posters with her, and all that's left are old pics of Kurt Cobain who she had a heavy crush on till he copped out and blew his head off. He's tired and subdued, Dale. Said he'd just have a short rest when we got home, but he's been in bed and asleep ever since, and it's near eight now.

Bethan and I've had an argument about duties regarding him. I know I'm being a tit. Comes of wanting something and working towards it, without thinking things through. I'm having a little panic. There's jobs I'm happy to do for Dale, but also jobs I've reservations about, and these are things that've got to be done, but which I don't want Bethan doing. Like bathing him, for instance. It's one thing the doctors said, not to get his bandages wet. He goes back to the hospital in a week and they said to keep them intact and dry till then. Considering they're stained with blood and getting grubby already this seems unhygienic to me, but Bethan says it's normal and she's got the qualifications to back it. She's really exasperated with me; like she's anxious about the whole situation but being brave and not uttering a word of objection to Dale being here, while I'm fussing on about stupid stuff like this. She's groaned that she's seen enough male genitals in her time not to get lewd-eyed at the sight of Dale's, that someone's got to do it, and Mam's eyesight'd make it hard enough finding Dale never mind his genitals through steamed-up glasses in a hot bathroom. So where's the argument? Nowhere, is the answer, and I'll be backing down soon, because I know I'm just twittering and there's no way I'm soaping his balls for him.

We've had a couple of phone calls already from people who've heard something's up – Andy heard today via his fire service brother, and he says he'll tell Damien, save us been bothered again. Sparky rang to offer his condolences and ask our postcode as he's gonna send Dale a card. Wouldn't have been surprised if it had been a bouquet of flowers. I couldn't tell either of them much about what happened, because although I sat with Dale all morning at the hospital and he was awake most of the time, he still hasn't told me nothing. Dunno if this is odd or not. He must realise I'd want to know. Maybe there's not much to tell. Three men rushing in, holding you down and firing a nail gun into you could all be over in a few seconds. Maybe that's all that happened. Maybe no one said anything. Just did the job quick, and got out again. Shit. I don't like thinking about it. Dunno if it'd be worse when the men were there, or after they'd gone. Makes things squirm inside me.

It's not just me being sensitive about this, because Carly rang Mam early evening, not knowing anything about it, and Mam says that when she told her Carly was struck dumb. Couldn't speak for several seconds. Carly. I told Mam that she was probably having an ecstatic moment at the violence of it, and it would only give her ideas – had a flash-thought of Russell and his spot problem here – but I didn't mean it. Had to admit I didn't, too, with both Bethan and Mam turning savage on me, calling the remark vicious and mean. Carly said she wanted to come over and see Dale but Mam put her off, tactfully saying he'd had enough excitement for one day, and maybe she could call in later in the week, if she was still keen.

When Dale wakes, me and Bethan are going to make a list of things he wants from the flat – well, Bethan is – and go round and fetch them. I expect he'll want the Guzzi brought round too. It's locked in the workshop, but everyone living close by will know the flat's empty by now and there's always some thieving bastard with a crowbar who'll take advantage. As for clothes, Bethan says big T-shirts are easiest – no way he'd get his bandages through shirt sleeves – and loose tracksuit bottoms that can be hoiked up and down even with feeble fingers, so he can use the toilet on his own. Thank shit for that, anyway, is what I say.

Randolph and I are just taking a stroll round the place now, with our minds on security. Been a while since we rubbed shoulders, exchanged more than greetings and head tips. He's a big heavy guy, Randolph, slow speaking, sort of grizzled plod of the earth. Wasn't too fond of him straight after Dad died, always round here poking his nose in, but maybe back then I resented any bloke who was alive when Dad wasn't. Got a lot of respect for him these days. Sixty-six last birthday but you see him swinging a sledgehammer or tossing sheep around and you'd never believe he's a pensioner. He's like all the farmers round here – never in a hurry, always got time for a two-hour jaw with a neighbour, dogs yapping 'come on, come on' round his feet till they give up in disgust and expire on the grass, but because he does nothing except work, all the daylight hours there are, he gets everything done in the end. He's got his coal merchant business as well, of course, but his drivers and Mam and the answerphone do most of that.

"I've had a word with your Mam 'bout the pups," he says, as we pass the dog shed. "You want to think about getting rid of them soon. Easily old enough, aren't they? Worth a bit."

"Aye. Could do. You think –?"

"I don't think nothing," he says. "Just considering your Mam. One less thing to worry about."

That's the only thing that's riling about Randolph: him assuming he got the monopoly on caring about Mam. Can't see anyone deliberately harming the pups or stealing them; be a financial disaster if they did, as well as breaking Mam's heart, but Carno can't know we got them. All the same, I feel I got to show equal consideration, and it's only Mam who likes ten weeks before pups leave home, so I say, "I'll ring the buyers tomorrow. See if they'll take 'em early."

Randolph nods. "You might leave Floss out too, overnight. Gone soft, that bitch. Meant to be a guard dog. Won't do her no harm."

I say, "Mmm," non-committal. Would mean chaining her. Be off rabbiting at dawn, else, and there's farmers round here – not

Randolph, mind – who'd shoot any dog they saw wandering free. Don't like chaining dogs anyway. Nothing wrong with her hearing from inside the house.

"You still got your Dad's twelve bore?" he asks, as we linger near the bike shed door. Heavy hardware and padlock the size of a tea plate on that.

"Nope. Sold it long time ago."

He nods again. Get the feeling he was hoping I'd say that. Paul told Mam to get rid of the gun as soon as he discovered we had it, before one of us kids used in anger. Not sure if he was imagining us blasting Carno with it, or each other.

"You don't want escalation," Randolph says. "That's all guns are good for."

"Aye."

There's something weird about all this: Randolph advising me, in his steady, ponderous tones, about taking care of the place. As if he's got old tribal embers in his bones, from the days of feuding and fighting and looking after your own. He told me once that when his own daddy was a lad he used to go fighting most Saturday nights on the hill over Ebbw Vale. None of the boys had cars in those days, and it was a long hike from one valley community to another, so to save breath they met up half way and set about each other with fists and sticks. No reason to it, except mutual loathing and liking for a dust-up. So nothing's changed much, except the boys have got softer and less keen on fresh air, and the aggro's moved into town.

I can't work up any sense of anxiety over the place, or myself, and I'm not sure whether this is Randolph's influence, making trouble seem boringly normal and about as terrifying as dipping reluctant sheep, or whether I'm just too tired to bother. Two nights with only a few hours sleep and several high-stress moments between has got me beat. And I've still got the run over to Dale's flat to come. Any other time I'd be drooling at the chance of riding his Guzzi. But I can't work up the enthusiasm tonight.

"You think anything's amiss," Randolph says, "or you and Bethan got to go out for more than a short while, you give us a ring, OK?"

"Yep," I say.

"Can always get one of my boys over if I can't manage it myself. You don't want your Mam and that sick lad left alone."

"Aye, OK. Thanks." Randolph's 'boys' are all over thirty-five. But there are a lot of them. Six, maybe seven. All solid as sheds.

"It's nasty-minded, what they did to the lad. If we could help out, it'd be a pleasure."

He talks about Dale as if he's a kid. Well, he talks to me like I'm a kid. And talks about 'helping out' as if he could still fancy a set-to himself, if the need arose. Maybe we got Mam to thank for keeping him young-thinking and lusty.

We end up standing in the yard, gazing around the buildings like cowboys inspecting a wagon-train ring. I'm left with the feeling Randolph'll be slightly disappointed if no whooping Indians come over the hill. Seems the wrong way round, somehow. Him raring for action – well, stolidly prepared – and me with my heart sagging at the thought.

# 8

Middle of the night Bethan kicks me awake. Heel smart on my shin.

"Eh?"

"Sorry."

Sorry? She just kicked me. I lift my head up quick. "You hear something?"

She sighs, weary. "No."

Maybe she got cramp. I shift over and start to drift off again.

"Jay?" It's just a whisper.

I snap my eyes open."What?"

She sighs again. Little whimper in it. "I'm frightened."

Right. I turn over, put my arms round her. She clings onto me, face pushing into my chest. I hug her tight.

"Nothing's going to happen," I murmur into her hair.

Her face stops pushing. Little silence. Then, "You promise?"

"'Course." Hey, easy. I'm Mr Fix-the Future.

"I mean, you won't do anything. Because of Dale...."

Oh right. I got her.

"It's nothing to do with us, is it?" she pleads. "I mean, Carno made a mistake, didn't he?"

"Certainly did."

"Don't say it like that."

"Hey," I jiggle her. "It's OK. The cops have got it. I'm not planning nothing."

"You mean that?"

"Promise."

I've said it definite but her head's still tense on my chest. I whisper, "Dale being here don't make things riskier."

"No. I know."

"He needs looking after."

Her head's agreeing.

"And they won't try again. They'd be stupid to."

"I know. I know."

"So what is it, then?"

There's a long pause. Then she squeezes out, little and breathy, "Nothing. Just. Bit scared."

I hold her tight again. No remedy to that. But I can make the bed feel safe.

The phone ringing wakes me in the morning. I hear it being answered. Empty bed beside me. Look at the clock. Shit, eleven thirty, Bethan'll have been at work hours. I shoot out of bed, wondering if Dale's lying in Carly's room starving to death on account of having no one to help him dress, but when I barge into the room next door I find it's empty. Discover him in the kitchen with Mam and Floss and the pups. Got himself dressed, or Mam helped him. Two of the pups are trying to unravel his bandages.

"I shouldn't pet them too much, love," Mam's saying. "You don't know where they've been. Ah –" She turns to me. "You got a call from Paul. Says he's coming round this evening. Ring him back if there's a problem. I got the number."

"Right." Well, there could be a problem, if he's coming round for his ride. Depends who's here, and who doesn't want to be left on their own. But there might be other callers. I'll leave it a while. Dale looks perkier this morning. Shifting around, playing footsie with the pups. Bit unkempt – a two-day beard on him, though it's hardly noticeable, him being a blondie, and his hair's a tangle – but definitely more his usual self.

"You had breakfast?" I ask.

"Yup. That's Paul Paul, is it? Down Raglan way?"

"Aye. Meant to be going for a ride. Got himself a FireBlade now."

'Shit. Leave you for dust, then?"

"Not so you'd notice. How's your hands?"

He holds them out and waggles the fingers. They're plumper than they should be and mauvish round the knuckles, where the bandage starts, but you can see he's pleased.

"Pretty good, eh? Maybe manage a spoon, day or two."

Mam is bustling round picking up bags. "I'm off to Randolph's now. We're going into town. You boys need anything?"

Neither of us got requests. "You want me to walk you?" I say.

"Don't be soft." She checks she's holding everything she needs and clicks out the back door. Dale looks at me puzzled.

"Evans just said to be careful," I say.

"Eh?"

I realise we've been talking among ourselves about precautions, and reasons for them, but no one's told Dale. He's been asleep. I say, "The afternoon they came round for you, we were out, Bethan and me." Well, he's got to know sometime. Whatever, him getting nailed weren't our fault. I tell him about the phone call that Mam took, and how we were in Cwmcarn when we heard about it. "It's maybe that you weren't their first choice. That's what Evans is thinking. Doesn't think they'd try again, but…."

Dale stares at me. Pulls his hands from the table on to his lap.

"Should have told you earlier. You don't have to be stay. Honest. You want to go to your Mam's?"

He's looking stunned. Blinks and shakes his head. "No. Shit. No."

"OK."

Didn't mean to scare him. If I did. Find it hard to imagine Dale scared. Like I'm being disloyal, just considering it. But shit, after what happened, who wouldn't be? It's only because it's him – I'd have no problem if it were Sparky or Damien. Even Andy. Even me. I'm having to make adjustments. Not used to having to think what

I'm saying to Dale. Frustrating, though, because it's stopping me asking what happened in the flat, and I really want to know if the men said or did anything that might link them to Carno. But I suppose he's told the cops.

After I've had breakfast I ring a few puppy buyers and tell them they can have their babies as soon as they want, and a couple say they'll be over tomorrow. Mam'll grieve over losing them but the cash'll compensate. Afterwards we sit out the back. Thunderstorm weather's well gone – it's fresh and breezy today. I bring the trail bike round, the one that broke its clutch cable when we were fooling around in the field, and start tinkering with it. The little tent Bethan and I slept out in is still pitched – got soaked Monday and we're letting it dry out – and I tell Dale that's the tent I was planning to lend Jonno for the run. Looks like it won't happen now, I say, with him and me and Bethan not going. Doubt the others will fancy a run on their own.

It's a good ten minutes later that Dale says, "You really not going on the run?"

"'Course not. Can't leave you here with Mam and Floss. Be bored out your skull."

I carry on tinkering and a few minutes later Dale says, "Why d'you have to leave me?"

"You're not going to be riding a bike by Saturday, tell you that for free."

"Could go pillion."

"You serious? Reckon you could manage camping?"

"Why not? Only for a night. Long as I got straws for the ale."

He's serious. The idea makes me grin, it's so stupid. But there'd be no shortage of helpers for putting up his tent, feeding him. "Who'd you go pillion with?"

He grunts. "Aye, well."

Hope he's not suggesting I leave Bethan behind. Certainly not letting her ride behind anyone else. She wouldn't anyway. Dale and me, we're the only ones she trusts.

"Expect any of the boys would take you," I say. "Could be a tight fit behind Jonno, mind."

"Not riding with him," Dale says. "Fucking maniac."

He ponders who he could trust with his body. Not one of them, I'd say. Andy's a good rider but his bikes are crap. Never once made a run without grinding to a halt somewhere. Failing machinery is dangerous. Damien and Sparky's bikes are light-weight and riding two-up'd make them handle different. Specially with all the camping gear. Some riders adapt easy; not sure Damien would, and dead certain Sparky wouldn't. Rides very mechanically, Sparky does.

"You trust Andy to ride your bike?" I say. "That's an idea."

Dale pulls a sour face. "Not keen."

Can't blame him. We once had a fantasy about Andy, based on everything he touches going into a decline. Imagined him winning the lottery, buying himself a spanking new house, glittering new bike, huge 4x4 for Maureen. Took bets on how long it would take him to reduce the lot to scrap. No one said longer than a month. Can see why Dale might not want his gloves on the Guzzi.

"He's hoping to take Maureen, anyway, if they can dump the kids," Dale says.

"Perhaps Bethan'd drive you in the car." Be expensive and I'd miss her behind me, but we could load it with the gear, free up the bikes.

"Don't wanna go in a car." Dale sounds stubborn. Makes me laugh. This idea is so crazy we just got to do it.

I leave him to ponder more while I take the trail bike round the field to test the cable. A thought occurs to me while I'm bumping back.

"You'd never get a jacket on!" I shout. "You thought of that?"

He has. "Got an old waxed jacket," he calls back. "Don't mind cutting a slice up the sleeves. Pin them tight after. Be OK."

"Right." I chuckle to myself and go off for another circuit. Next time I come round I shout, "Might mean sleeping in your boots!"

Even Bethan's not so Florence Nightingale when she's had a skinful.

"So what's new?" he shouts back.

We're both grinning. Idea's really got hold. Next time I come round he gets up and flags me down. "Give us a ride."

I chug nearer and he swings his leg over. Not a big saddle on this bike, but room enough. You don't need hands riding pillion. Well, not unless you're female and just got to molest the rider.

I make a slow circuit, careful to avoid bumps. Feel a tit if I had him off and damaged in our own field.

"I'm OK," he calls in my ear. "Take it up a bit."

Shit, if the boys can do it backwards, 'course he can do it forwards. Dunno why I'm fussing. Soon we're roaring round the field. Best thing about field riding is not having to wear helmets. Makes it feel twice as fast, and a zillion times more free.

All good things gotta come to an end, though, like that drip of petrol I put in earlier turns to vapour and we have to limp and jig back to the house.

As Dale gets off he says, "Your mate Paul, he a good rider?"

Not difficult to guess his line of thought. "Asked him already," I say. "Said no. That's why he's coming round tonight."

"No as in can't, or as in doesn't want to?"

"Fancy a ride on a FireBlade, would you?"

"If he's not a crap rider, maybe."

"He's not crap. Been riding thirty years, off and on. Just too slow for the bike."

"Well, never go too fast on runs, do we? Not like it's a race."

True. Speed of the slowest bike, usually. Not saying the odd rider don't make a dash for it now and then, few miles from a stop maybe, but it's not obligatory.

"I dunno," I say. "No harm asking, I suppose."

"Would he be OK? Mix in, like?"

"Oh aye. Get pissed, fall over, no problem."

"How about you suggest he gives me a ride this evening. So I can see what he's like. Then if he's OK, I give you the nod."

"Sort of test ride? Shit, Dale."

"My skin."

It's agreed. We don't tell Mam when Randolph drops her back from town, because we don't want her squishing the idea before it's got wings. Once it's flying – if it gets flying – be much harder to squish. I tell her about the two pups leaving tomorrow and she sighs and makes a big fuss of them, like they're going off to their doom, which at the price buyers are paying I very much doubt. Never remember Mam so sloppy over me and Carly when we were little, but then we couldn't get shut in a shed every time we got under her feet.

Bethan returns from work and nabs the sheltered sunny bit round the side for some serious toasting – go mad for sun, these working women, given a glimpse of it. I go out after a while, remembering her waking me last night. She's face down on the canvas bed.

I bend over her. "Hey, Bethan," I say quiet. "You OK?"

"Fine," she mumbles into the pillow.

I squat down next to her head. "You sure?"

She turns her head so I can see her face proper. She knows what I'm asking about. She nearly says something flip, but changes her mind. Her hand comes up and pinches my knee.

"I'm fine. Honest. Thanks."

"OK," I murmur. I kiss her on the eyebrow and she smiles and pushes me away. Tells me I'm in her sun. So I leave her to it.

We get a visit from Evans soon after. He wants Dale to read his statement through – had to be written for him, obviously – and sign it. Perhaps he'll hold the pen in his teeth. I park them both in the sitting room and close the door. Only takes a few minutes. When they come out Dale looks tight and Evans over-cheery, as if he's been trying to buck the boy up. Evans gives me a copy of the two-line statement he took off me first night at the hospital and I wait for him to read it out to me, but he don't, so he saves himself a smacking. He asks what I've been doing since he last saw me and I say zilch. He says they're still pursuing their enquiries but admits they haven't got anyone new locked up yet, either for the arson or the attack on Dale. It's the type of crimes, he says, makes them tricky. All these inconsiderate criminals, you can see him thinking, paying other people to do their creepy work for them. Funny: without sidekick Scott beside him he seems more human. He pats Floss and tells her she's a clever bitch, having such fine pups. Even his belly looks larger, like he's relaxed enough to let it flop. He insists on giving us his mobile number and says if we see or hear anything he should know, to ring him. Day or night.

After he's gone I wonder if I should be doing something. Bethan's worrying I might and Evans seems to expect it. Perhaps Dale thinks I should be rampaging about, revenging him? But I don't feel no impulse. I been enjoying myself today. Shit, maybe Bethan's right, I am weird. Or maybe I just burnt out at the hospital, aiming flak at the cops.

When I've made us mugs of tea and Dale's got his wedged between his bandages I say, "Dale, you think I should be doing something about Carno?"

He don't have to think about it. Just shakes his head and says, "No," very firmly. No elaboration. But seems clear enough. So that's him and Bethan, rock solid. Well, that's a relief, I think.

Paul gets here around half six. I see him bumping very cautious down the track – shit place to drop a bike and it happens easy on loose surfaces so I'm not criticising – and go out to meet him. I told Dale to let me have a word with him first.

He props the bike in the yard and takes his helmet off. A while since he was here – couple of years, maybe.

He smiles, gazing around. "Doesn't change, does it?"

"Think it should?"

"No. Of course not. It's kind of –" he searches for the word, "– reassuring. How's your Mam?"

"OK. Can't drive no more, but we manage. She'll be out to see you now. You decided where we're going?"

"I was thinking of Sennybridge. Pub there with a garden. Could have a quick pint."

"Aye, sounds great. Need to ask you a favour though. I got a mate here. Dale."

"Dale? Ah, met him once, didn't I? The race engine wizz? He wants to come too? No problem."

"Aye, well, it's him who's got the problem. With his hands."
"What?"

I take a big breath and explain. Get it more or less straight. Leastways, Paul's expression changes from struggling frown to comprehending gape. Feel a bit underhand because I'm telling him this not because he's a friend and I'm just sharing news, but because I want him feeling sorry for Dale. Still, he's got to know.

Paul hisses, "Shit," a few times, and, "Fucking hell," a few more, but it's not like he's got delicate sensibilities. Just the choice of weapon that shocks him.

"The thing is," I end up, "he'd fancy a pint too, means us taking him."

He doesn't say, "With bandaged hands!" because he knows Dale won't need them. And he knows how a ride cheers a man.

"We can share it," he says, magnanimous. "You one way, me the other. No problem."

"Great," I say. "You're a mate, Paul."

Taking Dale with us turns out an even more brilliant idea than it started, because Carly rings just then and announces she's coming over. I speak to her and ask her why she thinks Dale'd want to see her pig-ugly mug when he's never shown interest before, and she says she isn't coming to see him, she's coming to see Mam. So I don't tell her we're going out. Ha ha.

Next we got to find a jacket for Dale, and in fact Carly does come in useful here, or rather her teenage-years fat bum does, because there's several huge jackets still hanging behind piles of other coats, women's size 18, which we can't see anyone using again, so no one's going to mind a couple of slashes up the arms to make them loose enough to get the bandages through. Looks freaky, Dale does, in boots, tracksuit trousers, ladies hip-length leatherette jacket, sleeves slashed to the elbows, helmet and bandages. Paul and I get the giggles. Mam and Bethan just roll their eyes at each other – don't know what they'll roll when we tell them what else we're planning – and Mam checks Dale's got his drinking straws and tells him not to wave his bandages around and frighten no one.

Paul don't quibble when Dale says he'd like to ride out with him – think he's flattered, actually. Well, you got a FireBlade, course you're first choice. I know Dale'll be OK. The bike's lightweight for its power, but still heavy enough not to handle funny, and Paul's used to pillion passengers – takes Simone and the girls around when he can. I let them lead; that way I won't be setting the pace and Paul can ride as relaxed as he wants. On the straights he'll be shooting off for the horizon anyway.

It's a cut-glass evening and the hills either side up to Brecon look so close and crisp you want to reach out and pinch them. Not even many insects, because of the breeze. I can see Dale's tracksuit bottoms flapping and I bet his legs are getting cold. If we do the run to Cricieth he'll need over-trousers, definitely. And maybe something behind him to wedge him tight on the pillion, save him having to watch the road all the time. No hands and acceleration like a rocket – could shoot off the back if you weren't paying attention.

I get left behind on the dual carriageway round Brecon, but catch them up a couple of miles on, where the roads get bendy. He don't trust the bike enough, Paul, that's his weakness, can't give himself up to it. It's a popular road with bikers, this A40. Bendy twisty smoothy. Even tonight we see half as many as cars, and weekends they'd probably outnumber them. Builth Bike Show weekend it's a racetrack. Feels good, riding with a mate in front, other bikers whipping past. Some lift their hands. Some nod. Comradely.

At the pub car park I help Dale off with his coat – says he's not stepping a foot from the bike looking such a nutter – and Paul goes inside to buy a round.

Walking over to one of the garden tables, Paul well out of earshot, I say, "Well? What d'you think?"

"He's OK," Dale says. "Felt hundred percent safe. An' the bike's brilliant. Let's persuade him."

So when Paul returns with the pints that's what we do. No working round to it, just hit him straight. Tell him he remembers I was going to Cricieth this weekend? Well, he's got to come too. Got to, no arguments, because else Dale won't be able to go, and if he can't go, neither can Bethan and I. And if we three don't go, the whole trip'll get called off, and the life of one prematurely cut-down young man, a much-missed mate, won't get celebrated. And it'll all be on his conscience. When Paul's finished choking into his beer we go on to list the advantages to him. He'll have a cracking time, in grateful and fun-loving company. He'll get a buzz from using his bike as the distance machine it is, rather than the piddling run-about he mostly uses it for. He'll find that all the chicks love a FireBlade and there are lots of chicks in Cricieth, guaranteed, so as long as he keeps his helmet on he should be well in. And a point I make separately, remembering his little girl's name for the bike, that it's important for a man his age to have a hobby, and spend time on it, save him getting restless in other ways.

"Fucking cheek!" Paul is laughing so much he can hardly hold his glass. I know he's going to agree. His face is wearing an expression I haven't seen for a long time. Delighted. Like a mask's loosened right up and dropped away.

"So why d'you wait till now to ask me?" he says. "Test driving me, were you? Bastards."

"You passed, Paul," I say.

"Flying colours," Dale says. "Be an honour riding with you."

"What crap. Shut up. I've got to think."

We sit quiet while he thinks. Can see him mentally checking things out. Gives a little frown.

"Would it be OK with the others? How many are there?"

"'Course," I say. "Only four, besides us. Might ogle your bike a bit, maybe push you to lend it. But just say no. They'll understand."

"Hmm." He eyes me hard, reminding me I pushed him not so long ago. "When till when?"

"Saturday morning till whenever you fancy Sunday."

"Right. So. If I did… what would I need?"

Got him. No way he's backing out now. Nothing to do except list the gear he's to take with him: tent, sleeping bag, torch, stove if he wants a brew-up, waterproofs and beer money. Tell him we'll spread Dale's load around the other bikes, so he don't have to carry more than his own stuff.

"How long have you got to have those bandages on?" Paul asks Dale. "You going to manage in a tent? Be a lot simpler with something smaller."

"Next week I go back," Dale says. "Said to leave them till then."

"Bet you could get Bethan to change them," I say. "Spill something disgusting on them. Then tell her to make a smaller job."

We speculate on disgusting substances – dog shit's the obvious choice, except don't want him going septic. Paul suggests jam; dunno why Dale and I find this funny. Depends on your definition of disgusting, I suppose. Homemade or shop we want to know. Paul looks a tad miffed, like we've caught him out being soft, but he gets over it.

We don't stay long, because Paul wants to get back to Raglan before dark. I tell him to ring me Friday some time, in case there are last minute details to give him, otherwise we'll see him ten-ish Saturday morning at my place and go on together to Andy's. We whip back along the A40 to Brecon. Outside Crickhowell Dale and

I peel off up the mountain road, and Paul heads for home.

The Escort's parked in the yard when we get back. Means Carly's still here. Fuck. She must hear the bike arriving because she comes out to greet us. Her eyes light on the jacket Dale's wearing.

"Who said you could have that?" she cries at me, indignant, before I've even got my helmet off. Then she registers Dale's bandages and forgets she's got a grievance. "Shit, Dale," she says. "Jay told me. Terrible. Deserve shooting, the bastards."

She seems genuinely upset. Developing a softer side, maybe. Na.

Dale says, "Aye, well," looking uncomfortable.

"You doing anything, Jay?" Carly demands. "Shouldn't be allowed to get away with it."

"Leave it, Carly," I say. "It's none of your business."

"Who says?"

Anyone with half a brain, I think of saying, but don't want a shouting match in front of Dale.

Inside the kitchen I help him off with the coat. He's wincing a bit. Mam comes through from the sitting room where she's been watching telly with Bethan and peers at him. Says, "God's sake. Was that wise? You all right Dale?"

"I'm great," he says.

"Dale?" Bethan calls from the sitting room. "You want that shave now? Or you want to leave it till tomorrow?"

"I'll shave you," Carly offers, bright and girly.

"No you won't," I say. Terrifying thought, Carly wielding a razor.

"Think I'll leave it till tomorrow," calls Dale. "Thanks anyway."

Bethan pokes her head in. "Tell us when you want to go to bed." She's smiling. Always gets on better with Carly when I'm not around. As her eyes catch Dale she gets the giggles. Wearing a helmet hasn't improved his tangles.

"Shit, Dale. You really need your hair brushed."

Carly's looking from one to the other, belligerent, like she's thinking how come Bethan gets to put Dale to bed.

"I'll do it," she says quick. She snatches up a brush from the sideboard. "Sit down."

"For fuck's sake," I say.

"It's OK," mumbles Dale. "Could do with a brush."

So he has to sit there having his head pulled around while Carly drags the brush through it. Suppose he's lucky it isn't a comb. There's something about mauling a man's head about that makes women silly – once Carly's got the tangles out she and Bethan get hilarious trying out different styles and making him look stupid. Dale is patient, but then he can't see what they're doing. Looks too knackered to object anyway.

"Needs a wash, really," Bethan says. "You want to get Jay to do it tomorrow." She scrutinises what Carly's doing. "You fancy a quiff, Dale? Hey, not bad." She titters into the back of her hand.

"Good, isn't it?" Carly stands back to admire her handiwork. Put a quiff on him like a rhino horn.

"Tell them to fuck off," I say.

"You got lovely hair," Carly coos. "Ought to look after it. Amazingly shiny."

I can't stand no more of this. "Paul's coming to Cricieth with us," I say. "Just fixed it up with him."

"What?" says Bethan.

"Cricieth?" says Carly. "Who's going to Cricieth?"

"We are." I'm trying not to sneer. "Saturday over Sunday. Told you. A run for Stu. Paul says he'll take Dale pillion."

"What!" cries Bethan again. She's not against the idea though; her eyes have lit up.

"Wanker Paul?" scoffs Carly.

"You sure about this?" Bethan bends over Dale.

"Aye," says Dale.

Bethan thinks a moment, then calls back into the sitting room, "Mam? You hear that?" She turns back. "Mean leaving her alone, Jay."

128

She's just being responsible. I know she wants to go. It'll be an escape.

"Randolph'll come over," I say. "Anyway, we'll be out the way. Get her to stick a note on the gate. Dale and Jay gone away."

Carly's got a frowning pout on her face like she's trying to think up reasons to object and coming up blank. But then she surprises me.

"I think you should go," she says. "Show Carno it don't change nothing. One in his eye."

"Not that he'll know," Bethan murmurs.

Carly ignores this. "You go. Definitely."

I nearly thank her sarky – Carly says we go, Dale, that's the clincher – but stop myself. Carly being positive is a novelty. Mustn't discourage her.

Mam comes in again. She's heard what we're planning and she's not going to object, but she's not pleased either. Her mouth's in a tight stupid-boys line.

She says snappily, "I think you ought to go to bed, Dale."

"Aye, think I will." Dale gets up.

"Any chance he could have his bandages made smaller?" I ask Bethan.

She shakes her head. "They're pressure bandages. He'll be sorer without them. Got a bone chipped, remember."

"Right." To Dale I say, "Better forget the dog shit, then."

"Aye."

Bethan bounces out after him and I hear her saying, sounding aggressively nursy, "Forget what about dog shit?"

When they're out of hearing Carly hisses at me, "You ought to be doing something."

"No he shouldn't," Mam snaps. "Don't you dare encourage him."

"I am doing something," I say. "I'm taking Dale to Cricieth. That's what he wants. He don't want nothing else."

"So you're letting it go? You got no balls. If it were my mate –"

"Now you just shut up." Mam wags a fierce finger in Carly's face. "I mean it. And Jay, don't you listen to her."

"No danger," I say.

# 9

Well, we got here, and we're all agreed: as far as landscape goes, crossing the mountains outside Dolgellau's the highlight of the run up. It's the scale that does it. Mountains down south got nothing on these lumpy giants. Riding up through the pass felt like cracking open the sky. Stopped at the highest point to have a look round and Sparky said it were a religious experience. What, like entering heaven, Dale asked, grinning, and Sparky nodded. Starting to wonder about Sparky. Neatness and an interest in religion – definite danger signs. From up the top we could see the peaks northward, much sharper, patches of white on them even, looking like the Alps or somewhere – gotta do a run round Snowdon tomorrow, see them close to. The southern Rhayader to Llangurig stretch came a close second, talking landscape, just because it's the first off home territory that hits you as different and wild-looking. Saw some fine bikes on that stretch too – born-again bikers up from Cardiff, all day-glo machines and matching leathers, doing wide Saturday morning circuits. Waiting two hours between the two stretches for Andy's bike to get mended after his chain broke – at a little village called Clatter, fittingly – knocked the gloss off that section, but it could have been worse. Turns out Paul's a member of the AA, and since all Andy needed was a new connector link he got them to turn out with one. The bloke fitted it too. Brilliant. Doubt he believed Paul was Andy's pillion and Maureen was really riding the FireBlade – Paul refused to say Andy's heap were his bike, pride wouldn't let him – but by the time he got out to us it was too late to quibble. Weird thing, next village up from Clatter was called

Carno. No kidding. Just an ordinary little place, but we all went dead slow through it, like we were marvelling at the spooky coincidence, or expecting something nasty to jump out at us. And then belted off the other side like kids who've pulled a fast one. No other incidents with the bikes; maybe lucky Paul was leading that middle section and knows the route, because there's a couple of very surprising bends that come at you from nowhere, but we had his brake light to warn us and nobody lost it and overshot. And we got Dale so well wedged in on the back of the FireBlade he could have taken a kip through the hairpins.

It was near five before we got to Cricieth. We've ended up west of town so we can pitch our tents on the edge of the beach without anyone complaining. Just farmland and a little track behind us that we bumped the bikes down, magic view over to Harlech and the mountains across the bay, and only a half mile stroll into town. Plenty of scrub for the women to piss behind and if anyone fancies a dip the sea's lapping in front. Weather's middling. Not hot. Hazy sunny. Clouds inland, but Paul says there always are, because of the mountains, and it don't mean they're planning to soak us.

At home we left everything quiet. Quieter than it's been for weeks, in fact, since all but one of the pups have gone to their new owners. Randolph's staying over with Mam, but this is more to take her mind off losing her babies than to protect her. Evans knows we're going to Cricieth – been round to chat with Dale again – and anyone who knows any of the boys would know it too, and since that's a sizeable chunk of the local population we're not expecting nailgunners to turn up at the small-holding looking for targets. I've been round with Andy to Dale's place to reboard the holes in his floor – well, I did the boarding, save Dale going through first time he sets foot in the place, Andy just scrubbed stains away – and we even found matching paint in the workshop, so now you can hardly see the joins. I was glad I'd been round earlier with Bethan getting Dale's stuff; entering the flat weren't as churning as the first time. Andy'd got no pictures to recall so he just whistled at the holes and we got stuck in.

Everyone's pitched their tent now – Bethan did Dale's – though Andy and Maureen have had a spot of bother with theirs. Looks like they've forgotten an important pole. It don't worry them though; Maureen's got a rug and packet of biscuits out in front of it already. Jonno's delighted with our old tent and keeps climbing in and out to demonstrate how amazingly well it fits. Sparky spent a long time finding the perfect site for his, and it's the neatest-erected little two-man you ever saw. Lined up on compass points, he says. Takes all sorts. Damien's squashed his right up to Andy and Maureen's lopsided heap so he can chat to them lying in his bag; we've suggested they stop kidding themselves he's a mate and just adopt him. Paul put his igloo tent up in seconds and he's been building a stone ring for the fire we'll have later and collecting driftwood. Fizzing with energy, Paul is. That break at Clatter got him easy with the others, specially since he was the one to save Andy's bacon, and he's agitating to go off to the pub soon. I seen him already taking sneaky swigs from a half bottle of scotch.

But we got to call in at a chippie first, get ballast for all that ale. Dale's says he's starving, first time he's felt chip-hungry all week. Got some colour back, Dale has. Still quiet but that's normal. Bethan insists he's not to touch anything he eats from a chippie with his hands, because they'll make his bandages greasy and he'll stink forever. But chippie food is easy to finger-feed and he's got volunteers keen to help.

We chain the bikes together with the heavy duty chain Jonno wore slung round him on the journey and trudge into town. Not a busy place, Cricieth, six thirty in the evening. Pretty though. Unassuming pretty. No beach attractions and nothing raucous; quiet houses and Bed and Breakfasts looking out over the bay. Got a little tumbled-down castle on a mound sticking out into the sea that's going to make a spectacular silhouette when the sun goes down. Expect most of the local talent's gone somewhere more exciting for their Saturday night.

We buy sausage and chips and sit on the front munching. Dale holds his mouth open like a baby bird and anyone who's got a spare hand pops something in. Except Sparky, who does it carefully, with reverence. First time most of the boys saw Dale's bandages was this morning and Sparky's in serious awe of them. Catch him gazing at them like they're cocoons and he's expecting something miraculous to burst out. Damien came over white when he first saw us. Allergic to the sight of blood, he's confessed, even imagining it. But he seems recovered now.

Jonno reckons that if we bought another bag of chips as bait we could catch a few sea gulls and roast them later on the fire. Not sentimental about sea birds, Jonno. Says they've got evil eyes. We try luring them close with scraps but they're too fast to catch. Wise up very quickly, and those yellow beads get even more evil. We tell Jonno not to fall asleep outside his tent tonight or they'll peck his eyes out at first light. Maureen tells us some long enthralling tale about walking on a beach near where gulls were nesting and getting pecked round the head by them.

Jonno says, "That's not true, Maureen, is it?" and she says, "On my life Jonno, you look out now." Difficult to tell when Maureen's being serious.

Think Paul's quite pissed by the time we get to the first pub, thanks to the whisky he's been supping. Though he holds his drink well; just a glint in his eye and a flush on his neck. The pub's near empty and the staff are intrigued by Dale's drinking straws and bandages. No one wants to say what really happened to him, so while Dale's at the bar we just touch our noses and say, "Ah, sorry mate, he don't want to talk about it." When he's sitting down out of hearing they get a variety of stories. They don't go for the scorched hands rescuing kiddies from the flaming orphanage, nor the rope burns abseiling down Snowdon, but narrow their eyes looking half-convinced by the trail bike not quite squeezing between two hard tree trunks.

Paul's enjoying himself. Elated. Sitting between me and Dale saying, "This is it, boys," and beaming round the room. Got a definite glaze on him. Find his sneaky tots a bit irritating, myself. Like he thinks we haven't noticed. Hope he's got the stamina to keep upright for another four hours.

We drink several ales to Stu. That's what we come for, after all. Mostly drinking a dark brew that's new to us called Black Widow, which seems fitting. Still hard to think of great things to say about Stu, but he was at his best boozing – or at least boozing was what he was best at – so we agree that just pouring the ale down counts as tribute. Bethan's kind of elated too – escape euphoria, I reckon – and so keen on the brew she gets serious hiccups after downing it too quick and has to have crisp packets banged in her ear. Noise level rises. When Jonno gets pissed he gets loud. Well, we all do, but he gets loudest of all. Annoying loud. After a while of him laughing and swearing top of his voice the bar staff are still tolerant but their teeth are gritting. Out for a good time tonight, not a punch-up, so we decide it's time to move on. Outside the evening air's so fresh and invigorating Paul decides he's going for a walk along the front. Just realised how pissed he is, I think. He asks if I want to come but Bethan's got a taste for the ale and not interested, so I make sure he knows which pub we're going to, and leave him to it. He strides off jaunty. No cliffs for him to fall off, anyway.

Next pub have got a little terrace outside with fairy lights. Beautiful view of the sea, dusk rising like mist from the water, faraway mountains pinky grey, and a quarter moon hanging over the lot. Get quite dreamy gazing out at it. Just wish Jonno would stop barging around knocking chairs over. He don't mean to damage things but he can't sit down when he's drinking, his feet don't stay planted where he puts them, and the chairs get in his way. Bethan and Maureen shout at him to stop bulldozing around and after a while the rest of us have had enough too. He bangs into Dale's back once too often and Dale snaps at him to fuck off. Jonno gets the hump, saying he will too, he's going back to the chippie and then to the off licence to get more ale and he'll meet us back at the camp. Makes it sound like he's punishing us.

Him going off reminds me that Paul hasn't returned from his walk. It's only ten, early enough, but by half past I'm wondering where he is. Everyone wants to catch the offie before it closes at eleven. At quarter two I give Bethan some cash and tell her I'll go retrieve Paul and meet her back at the camp. She moans about having to carry my cans as well as Dale's, but Dale says no worries, he can carry a fourpack easy as long as someone shoves it against his chest.

I stroll along the front and spot Paul in a couple of minutes, sitting on one of the benches staring out to sea. He don't get up when I reach him, just gives me a dopey smile, so I sit down next to him. I can see how he's got stuck here. Mesmerizing view of moonlight and water.

We sit for a moment communing with the night and then he nods and says, "I've come to a decision, Jay." He nods again. Up and down, up and down. I'm pissed, but he's more pissed. Whisky pissed. The bottle's empty on the concrete. "I need to get away," he says.

"Aye. Nothing like getting away."

"I mean, long term away."

Nor sure what he's rambling about, so I just say, "Aye," again.

"It's the only thing,' he says. "Going mad at home. Here –" he gestures at the sea like he's creating it "– it's as if I'm reborn."

"Oh aye?" I say. "Well, happy birthday."

He turns to me. Excited light in his eyes. "Best thing you could have done, asking me to come along. Best thing. Ah –" He sighs. "You've got it sorted, Jay. You know what's important. Me –" shakes his head, tragic "– the people I work with... it's just a slog. Everything's a slog. Shitty people, shitty work. Day in, day out. Week in, week out. Year in, year out."

"Shitty people all over, Paul," I say.

"No. No." He's urgent. "It's different for you. You can choose." He nods again, as if he's hit a bullseye. "That's it. You've got choice."

I snort. "Like fuck I have."

"You have. While me...." He sits up straight, points his face out to sea. "I'm going to leave Simone."

"Oh aye."

"I'm going to leave the whole fucking lot of them. Millstones, that's what they are."

"Right. An' you're pissed."

"Of course I'm pissed. Should be pissed more often. Christ, I need a break."

There's some nights I'd listen to this. Maybe even sympathetic. But tonight it sounds like crap. He thinks I got it cushy, he's got the hard grind. He don't know nothing.

I say, "You leave Simone and the girls, you're a nutter."

"Maybe I need to be a nutter."

"For fuck's sake, Paul," I sigh. "I'm going back. Come on."

He turns round and bangs me hard on the arm. Aggressive.

"Hey!" I say.

"You're not listening. Don't believe me, do you?"

"Don't need this," I say. "Let's leave it."

"Till when?" he shouts.

"I'm going," I say. I come here to have a good time. And Paul's saying he's got problems. Don't want to hear them. Paul can do what he likes, and he knows it. Only needs bottle. No one's nailed him to a floor.

"You know how long it is since I had another woman?" he asks.

That holds me. Just curiosity, like.

"Twenty-eight years," he says. "Been faithful to Simone for twenty-eight fucking years."

"Shit," I say. Can't imagine it, actually. Same woman for as long as I been alive.

"You faithful to Bethan?" he asks.

"One hundred per cent," I say. True, but then I'm not

overloaded with offers.

"If you got the chance," he asks. "Would you?"

"Ah, tricky question."

"Would you? Be honest."

"Not if it would fuck things up with Bethan."

"I want to. I want to be unfaithful."

I let this drift around a moment. "Anyone particular in mind?"

"No. Well, yes, but she wouldn't have me. Woman at work. So no."

"You come for tips, you come to the wrong place. Try Dale."

"Dale?"

"Aye. Don't have to lift a finger, the bastard. Even Carly fancies him."

"Carly? Really? Always saw her as a hardman fan. Shit. Weird lot, aren't they?"

I assume he means women. But could just as easily be Sparky, Jonno, Andy....

"I want something to happen," he says. "Want to *make* something happen."

"Do it then." I get up. I want to be with the others, talking about nothing round a blazing fire.

Paul rises reluctantly. Sways, looking out to sea. "It'd kill Simone," he says.

"So don't do it," I say.

"Shit." He's exasperated. "It's so bloody easy for you."

"Ah fuck off, Paul," I say.

We amble back along the front, and then across the beach. Fire's already well lit – Jonno must have been back a while. Can see black shapes sitting round the flames in a spaced-out circle. Strong smell of chips, sea, wood smoke, burning plastic. Ah, nothing like a beach fire. Paul goes down to the waterfront to have a piss and I work out which shape is Bethan and sit down beside her. Feel suddenly soppy and pull her against me. She slumps on to my chest. Not weird at all, Bethan, even if just now her eyes are rolling.

Definitely overdone the Black Widow. Now I'm in the circle the firelight makes us bright. Andy and Damien are both rolling spliffs on their laps. Sparky's sitting cross-legged, straight-backed, staring into the fire like he's meditating. Jonno throws another plastic container on to the fire and it melts and goes pop, showering little gobs of burning debris on to the sand.

"Shit, Jonno." Dale lifts his wrists from his knees and pulls his legs further back. He's between Jonno and Damien, other side of the fire from us, face white in the firelight. His voice is slack from the ale. "Lay off, will you."

"You want another chip?" Jonno sounds like he's bored, wants something to do besides choking us with toxic fumes.

"Go on then." Dale opens his mouth.

Jonno moves closer to him and rams one in. "An' another?"

Dale shakes his head. Says, "Fucking cold," through his mouthful.

"Yeah you do," says Jonno.

Dale shakes his head again, but Jonno ignores him. Tries to push it in. Dale twists his head away. Jonno puts a hand on his chest and pushes him backwards on to the sand. Says, "Need feeding up, boy. Open wide." Damien and Andy look up and chuckle. Sparky frowns into the flames like the scuffling on his right's an annoying distraction. Paul wanders back dragging a plank of driftwood and tips it on end over the fire. All I can see of Dale now is his knees and feet, and Jonno leaning over him. Hear him spluttering, "Fuck off, Jonno." The sparks fly upwards as Paul lets the plank drop on to the fire. Bethan's got her head buried in my chest. Not sure she's still awake.

Start to feel dreamy myself. I'm watching the fire, and the things lit by it, Andy's hands working at his spliff, the cans of beer glinting, Dale's legs and boots the far side, and the dark shape of Jonno, wrestling over him. For some reason I get stuck on Dale's legs. They've turned over. And then I hear a yelp, and Jonno's pulling away saying, "Hey, look what you done, gone and banged yourself, yer tit."

It don't really register. The fire's hissing and cracking and I can't hear nothing else over it. Can just see Jonno's not on top of Dale any more, and Dale looks like he's curled up facing away.

Damien leans sideways and stares down at Dale. He puts his spliff aside and pulls himself closer on his elbows.

He says, "Hey, mate, you OK?" and then lifts his head and calls to the rest of us, "Think he's hurt himself."

Jonno complains, "Was only fooling around."

It's Dale's stillness that gets me going.

"What you done?" I push Bethan away, making her groan and slump sideways, and stumble round the outside of the circle. I kneel beside Dale.

"Hurt his hand," Jonno says. "Only giving him chips. Freaked out a bit, and tried to punch me."

"You OK?" I peer into Dale's face. It's screwed up, eyes tight closed, like he's waiting for sensation to pass. There's chip grease smeared over his mouth and chin. He suddenly coughs, and spits a mess of potato out. Then starts gagging.

"Stupid fucker," I hiss, meaning Jonno. How much has he forced into Dale's mouth? For a moment I think he's choking, but then I hear his breathing – see it too – and recognise the movements. He's going to spew.

Paul comes up behind me and grasps straight off what's happening. He says quickly, "Get his hair out the way."

Dale's body is heaving like Floss does after eating grass. I pull the hair off his face, as much as I can get hold of, with him lying on his side. He's trying to hold his hands clear and they're trembling. He says very weakly, "Ah shit," and vomits on to the sand. Got a stomach-load of ale and chips. Vomits again, another load. We wait until his body stops heaving and then Paul and I pull him away from the mess. Jonno's standing over us, scratching the back of his neck, expression of injured innocence.

"Didn't do nothing," he says.

Dale lurches up on an elbow. He's shaking with feeling. "You want to be held down then? Have fucking things pushed in your mouth? Cunt."

I never heard him so savage. I see Damien flinch, like he'd done it. Dale sags down again and moans, "I hurt me hand, Jay. It fucking hurts."

"OK." Dunno what to do about a hurting hand. Looks like it's his right one. I glance over to Bethan but she's out of it. He can't have broken it. Not wrapped in all that bandage. Must have just disturbed the wound.

"Ah Dale," I say. I'm really sorry for him. I should have been looking out for him. "Expect it'll fade off. You want to rest it on something?"

"I've got a blow-up pillow." Paul's pushing sand about with his boots, burying the vomit. "Girls put it in for me. Silly fluorescent thing. Wasn't planning to use it anyway. I'll get it."

He gets it and half-inflates it, and lays it on the sand so Dale can rest his hand on it. I'm not sure through the ale, but by the time we get Dale sorted out I think he's more sorry for himself than really hurt. Jonno goes off to kick at waves and complain to them that it weren't his fault, since no one else will listen, but comes stomping back when the spliffs start circulating. Dale can't be that injured because he sits up and takes a few puffs with Damien holding the roach for him. Shoots baleful looks at Jonno while he's doing it. I wake Bethan but she's not interested in staying conscious and crawls off to our tent groaning about poisonous spider brews. Maureen's got amazing stamina. Must have drunk almost as much as Bethan but takes over the rolling from Andy and turns out a succession of neat little spliffs as quick and dextrous as if she were making fairy cakes. Dale shakes his head to the third or fourth and lays back on the sand. Damien gets closer to Maureen and more and more collapsed till he ends up with his head pillowed on her thigh. She coos and pats his ear and carries on rolling up on the other thigh. Don't seem to bother Andy. Bet that plump flesh is comfortable, too.

Time stretches out and the fire burns low. Sparky gets up, eyes huge and glowing as if he's had a two hour revelation, and announces he's going to bed. He's said and done nothing except play Buddha since we came back to camp. Looks like Dale and Damien are already asleep. My back's beginning to feel cold. I think of asking Jonno to give me a hand getting Dale in his tent, because he's still awake and the strongest here, but then decide maybe it wouldn't be such a good idea. Probably trip over him and accidentally stamp him to death.

Maureen sees me stirring and pushes at Damien's shoulder to tell him to wake up 'cos it's bedtime. Expect she's brought a storybook to read him when he's tucked up. Paul says he's going for another stroll and then turning in too. He ambles off along the beach. Before Andy disappears as well I go over to Dale to see how unconscious he is. But he lifts his head the moment I touch him and gives a little jerk.

"Gonna freeze out here, mate," I say. "You want a hand into your tent?"

"Oh aye."

He pushes himself up on his elbows. He's slow and fuddled but who isn't. Seems to have forgotten about the hurt hand. Think we'll manage without Andy.

I get him up on his feet and together we lurch down the beach to have a slash. He manages his tracksuit trousers OK himself. Back at the fire I unpin the sleeves of his jacket in what's left of the firelight and help him off with it. Drop two of the safety pins in the sand but Bethan's got spares somewhere for tomorrow. Jonno's in his tent already – it's nearest to the fire and I can see the dark silhouette bulging and shivering as he's crawling around. Could be he sleeps in a circle, like a dog.

Dale and I pick our way through the scrub to his tent. He sits down at the door and squatting the far side of him I can get enough light on his feet to start unlacing his boots.

"Jay," he murmurs, after a moment. "I gotta tell you something."

"Mmm?"

"By the fire there, I been thinking." His voice has a little shudder in it, like he's cold.

"Oh aye?"

He drops his voice further. "Those men who came in my flat. Think one of them was Jonno."

"Eh?" I stop fiddling with the laces. My head swims. "Fucking hell," I say. "No. No way."

"You think?"

"Shit," I hiss. "You'd have recognised him. Even with a stocking. Hey, man. Where d'you get this?"

"He smelt right." Dale's voice is just a shake. "And what he did, earlier –"

"Jonno's a pillock," I say. "But there's no way he'd nail down a mate."

"He's not a mate." Dale's suddenly savage again.

I catch up with what he's been saying and realise I missed something. I peer into his face and say, "What d'you mean, what he did earlier?"

"That's what they did."

"Eh?" What's he saying? They pushed chips into him?

"The gun. They put it in my mouth."

All I can hear is sea. At least, I think it's sea. Kind of white-noise roar. Can't speak, can't move. Dale drops his head, as if he's ashamed of paralysing me.

"Couldn't do nothing about it. They'd already done me hands."

"Ah shit. Shit."

"Thought they were going to pull the trigger. Pissed meself, thinking it."

"Ah fuck." The picture's horrible. I don't want to think it either. "Dale. You told this to Evans?"

He nods.

"Shit, man. Why didn't you tell us before?"

His shoulders lift. Like he's run out of words. Finally says, "You didn't ask."

I only didn't ask because he didn't seem to want to tell me. That's what I thought. I can't do nothing right. But why didn't Evans say it? He wanted to scare me into being careful, all he had to do was tell me.

"Did they say anything? The men."

"Only one of them. The one with the nail gun. Used a sort of growly voice. Put on maybe. But he weren't Jonno, definitely."

"None of them were. Bet my life on it. What did the bloke say?"

He starts shaking his head, then hesitates. "Well. Nothing sensible. Told me to shut up. Bit blurry, think I was trying to yell. When they were forcing me down one of them got his glove across me mouth. That's the bloke I smelt. Then when I was down and nailed the one with the gun says he'd shut me up permanent. Gets his mate to hold my head still and pinch my nose. Kneels on me and pushes the gun in." He stops and I think he's swallowing. "Thought I was gonna die."

"Fucking hell." I find my hand on his calf, squeezing it. Silly part of him to comfort, but he's not objecting. "They didn't say nothing else?"

"Don't think so. Wasn't concentrating too well."

"Nothing about why, or warning you off?"

He shakes his head.

"Shit."

"The one who pulled me down, he smelt like Jonno."

"Smelt like what, exactly?"

He thinks about this a moment, then nods and says, "OK, might not be Jonno. He smelt like plastic. Burning plastic."

We both know what he's saying but I say it aloud anyway.

"You mean like he'd come from somewhere there was a fire?"

"Aye. That's it."

"You tell Evans this?"

"Nope. Only just came to me."

"Maybe you'd better tell him."

"Aye."

It has to be Carno's place, and it's not much, but it's something. After I've checked Dale's sleeping bag's laid out and ready for him I walk back down to the sea for another piss. Paul's still mooching about further down the beach but I don't want a chat. I feel like someone just opened a door in my head, a nasty-looking door I been hanging back from, and kicked me through. My brain's pounding. I want to lay hands on those bastards who pushed the gun into Dale's mouth. Can't see it, Dale nailed down helpless, them terrifying him, without lifting closed eyes upwards and hissing into the sky. Fuck. Fuck. I'd fix them to the ground proper, somewhere public and humiliating so anyone who fancies it could take a pop at them. Nailgun their balls. A row of dung beetles, that's it, speared through their balls with giant pins, like specimens in a museum. Put Carno in the centre: king dung beetle. I saw a scarab beetle in Cyfartha Castle museum once, spread-eagled on its pin; enormous evil-looking thing. Or maybe they could be pegged out on a hot beach and gnawed by flesh-eating crabs. Or rats. Or ants. Or Black Widow spiders.

Shit, I think, and turn round quick. Black Widows reminds me of Bethan's unhealthy state when she crawled off to bed. Get an attack of anxiety. Like anything could happen to a mate when my back's turned. I run up the beach and poke my head in our tent, find the torch, and shine it on her. It's OK. She's OK. But the poor cow didn't have the strength to get her boots off, or zip the bag up. Can't face another set of twenty-eyelet boots so I just hoick the bag up around her. She's on her side and snoring like a chainsaw. I'm not going to be sleeping for a while so I grab my own bag out, wrap it around me and sit back down by the dying fire.

Comes to me Carno's to blame for everything. I'd have a dad, without him. A sister who wasn't a maniac. Killed the kid Carly

145

used to be. Fucked her proper. And I'd have a mam who wasn't going blind. Dad would've spotted the signs. He was a paramedic.

Like Carno made it his life's work, hurting us. And now he's hurt Dale, as nasty as you can imagine.

I grind my heels into the embers. Stay with Dale. Some point to it.

I tell myself there's no way Jonno was one of his attackers. No way. Can't follow orders, can't work as a team. Be as likely to damage a fellow nailgunner as the target. Might as well take along a rutting bull-elephant.

But I bet Jonno knows Dale's attackers. Without knowing he knows them, that is. There's two lots of men could smell of burnt plastic. Carno's own men, drivers and that, and Jonno's security boys, the ones who've been at the depot all week. Get some nasty types in security, as well as the brain-dead muscle like Jonno. Wonder if he's still working there next week? Never tell with Jonno; the work moves around, and so does he. Always getting fired and taken on again. Longest job he ever had was two months nightwatching a factory, and that was only because they never checked up on him. I'll have a word with him tomorrow.

"Bethan kick you out of bed?" Paul says, coming up behind me. He sounds sober.

"Nope."

He squats down beside me. "You all right?"

"Aye."

He waits a moment, and then says, "Don't sound it."

I don't reply. If I say "I got a lot on my mind," he'll say "what?" and I might tell him. Sometimes when you run on you mess your options up.

"You pissed off with me?"

"Ah go to bed."

"You are. Because of me rambling on earlier?"

He always wants to talk. Niggle away at things. Like nothing exists until it's words.

He says, "It's just how I feel sometimes."

"Aye."

"Is Dale all right?"

I kick at the sand in front of me. "Asleep."

"I'm not going to leave Simone."

"Didn't think you were."

Paul laughs quietly. "And I don't really think you've got more choices than me."

"You were pissed, Paul. I weren't listening."

"Very wise." I can hear the smile in his voice. Gives a little sigh. "Wish I was your age again, though."

"Can't have everything."

"No. So true."

He says goodnight and goes off to his igloo. There's nothing of the fire left now except glowing squiggles in the black, like the beach is having a little volcanic eruption a few feet in front of me. When the breeze lifts the squiggles brighten to fierce red, and when it passes they sink back to dull again.

Don't think this run to Cricieth is turning out a good one. There's runs and runs. A few classics I can remember, but they're usually meeting up with other groups, or organised like, with music and show stands. But even when it's just us there have been memorable times. Getting so pissed at Angle that Jonno fell off the front into the sea. One minute he was sitting there on the parapet, shouting and swigging an ale down, next he wasn't. Must have been a good ten foot drop. Jonno can't swim so it was lucky the water was only chest deep. Couldn't find the steps back up so we threw him down a few more cans to keep him going until we could stop laughing and find a local to point the way.

Not sure what this run is meant to be, either: celebration or commemoration. Feels more like a fermentation. There's things happening in people's heads. Paul's weird – like a human yo-yo, one minute excited and wild-thinking – leaving Simone, for fuck's sake – next sensible as usual. Dale's fragile and maybe shouldn't be around Jonno, who can't touch anything delicate without breaking it. I never seen Dale freak out before. Makes me feel bad, like while he's here he's my responsibility. On the other hand if he hadn't come he wouldn't have remembered the smell of burning, and maybe I wouldn't have got to hear about what happened. Aah, got to push myself on from that; cripples me inside. Andy and Maureen are same as usual, except luckier, because they made it here the same time as the rest of us. And Damien's OK. And Bethan, if the ale hasn't rotted her brain. But Sparky's gone weird too. Could be he's losing his grip. Then it comes to me that maybe a run for Stu should be a mess. The man was a mess. So it's kind of apt. Yeah. I drift on that a while.

I'm distracted by a chorus of snoring behind me. Loudest must be Jonno. No, maybe Andy. Whichever, it's not as peaceful as it could be. I get up, thinking maybe I'll sleep now and it's time to get into the tent, and then I wonder if Dale's OK. He tells me something horrible and then I go off and leave him with his mind on it, in the dark. I walk over to his tent and stand outside the open flap, listening, hoping I'll hear him snoring too, but I don't.

I squat down and say very quietly, "Dale?"

There's a moment of nothing and then his voice says, "Jay?"

He weren't asleep. That decides me. "Aye, it's me." I wriggle inside and pull the bag in after me.

"What you doing?" Dale says. It's black as pitch in here.

"Bedding down. Bethan's pissed herself." Bethan'd not be pleased to hear me slandering her and she never has pissed herself after boozing, which is more than you can say for some, but if she does hear it from Dale tomorrow it's simpler to get out of than saying she's thrown up. Could have spilt a can, and it's easy to get wet beery puddles confused.

I hear Dale give a hissing sigh and turn over. Imagine he's untensing. I feel my way around. There's plenty of room in here. Just think we'll both sleep better with company.

# 10

I sleep like the dead till day break, then drift in and out of a doze. Remember what Dale told me last night, which snaps my eyes open and becomes a dazzling blue thought, because the top of the tent is brilliant blue. Close my eyes and force it to the back of my mind. Too heavy, too heavy. I lie still. I need a Niagara piss but my head feels OK lying here, just fuzzy, and I don't want to start a hammer off by disturbing it. Been quiet outside except for sea gulls wailing, but now I can hear a rustling and muttering like someone else's bladder has pushed them out. Shit, it's hot in here. Hot and blue. Dale's pushed his bag down to his hips and his clumps of fair hair and khaki shoulders are motionless. He spewed most of his beer last night, so I expect his bladder's hardly flexing itself, lucky sod.

I'm just thinking I've got to get up or I'll piss myself, when the front flap of the tent's pulled aside and Sparky pokes his head in. Not sure who's more surprised. We stare at each other.

"What you doing here?" he whispers.

Could ask the same myself, but don't. Decide not to repeat my lie about Bethan wetting herself because I can't face the ear-battering I'll get if she finds out.

I say, "Long story."

He blinks. "Need to talk to Dale."

"Shit, Sparky," I groan. "Can't it wait?" I push my own bag down to my socks. Got to have that piss.

Dale shifts beside me and lifts his head. A delighted smile spreads across Sparky's face. Almost tender. The man looks batty.

I say, "Let me out," and to Dale, "Sparky wants a word." Try not to say it with a sigh. Dale's head falls back. I wriggle out and Sparky dives in after me. Can't imagine what he needs to share with Dale at the crack of dawn but then I can't imagine anything except how relieving it's going to be when I get my zip open.

The sea's too far away so I just pad over to the remains of the fire and piss on the ashes. Still hot enough to sizzle. Steam rises. Ah, gallons of relief. And, amazingly, even by the end the hammer hasn't started banging. Just feel a mite wobbly and disembodied. I stretch and look around. Funny thing, Harlech and the mountains across the bay have disappeared. Could be sea forever. Surprisingly chilly out here, too, given how stuffy it was in the tent. Decide to go back. All the other tents are dead-looking. Ah, except for Damien's. The canvas is twitching and rustling. Wonder what he's doing? Just decided I'm being dull, because he's obviously having a wank, when I notice a bare foot in the open doorway. There's no way that's Damien's. Bright scarlet toenails.

I can't help staring. It's not Bethan's foot, so it has to be Maureen's. Just thinking it's a very pretty, wriggling, naughty little foot, and I'm gobsmacked by what it's up to, when I see another foot. Bigger, and other way up. Got a grimy sole, at least thirty years old. Course, Andy and Damien have swapped tents, what with the missing pole cutting the space down. Lucky Andy, the woman really does have stamina. I half think about investigating my tent, see if I can get Bethan's toes wriggling too, but decide it's a non-starter. If she's asleep she won't thank me for waking her, and if she's awake it's probably because she's in pain.

Sparky's emerging from Dale's tent as I get back. Gives me a quick smile and scoots off to his own. I crawl inside. Dale's lying on his back, staring up at the blue lining.

"Well?" I say, when a moment's passed and he hasn't said anything.

He makes a trembling noise which could be a laugh. "Ah, 'tisn't funny. You're not going to believe this. He thinks I'm Jesus."

"Eh?"

"As in Jesus Christ. This is straight up. Said to call him Judas. Kept saying he was sorry, and he shouldn't have betrayed me. Ah shit."

"You serious?" But I know he is. I'm not even that surprised. Thought something was up with Sparky. Fuck. That's all we need. Him losing it completely, two hundred miles from his Mam.

Dale rolls on to his side. "It's me hands that have done it. Thought he was looking at me funny yesterday."

"Shit," I say. "Shit shit shit."

"Seems OK otherwise, mind," Dale says. "I mean, if I were really Jesus, he'd seem OK." He buries his face in the floor mat and convulses weakly into it.

"Maybe he was sleep walking," I say. "That possible?"

Think Dale says dunno. His hair shakes anyway.

"What did you say to him?"

"Ah." He lifts up and pulls himself together. "Go back to your tent. That's what I said. And I told him I was Dale, not Jesus. He said yes, Jesus, and not to worry, he won't let on. Said he just needed to confess, but that he wouldn't betray me again."

I'm so awake now I think I might as well put my boots on.

"So he'll call you Dale, but you got to call him Judas. That'll sound very natural. What's he supposed to have done?"

"Dunno," Dale says. "Don't think he does either. Just in a muddle."

"Right. Bloody hell. So what do we do?"

"Get him home. Quick, in case he gets worse. If he weren't sleep walking, that is."

"You think he could ride?"

"If he hadn't come in here just now we'd let him, wouldn't we?"

"Well, if he seemed OK, but…." Can't ignore the fact that he did come in. I'm already trying to work out permutations. The only person capable of riding a bike who isn't already riding one is Maureen. Not sure she's got a licence, but I know she can do it. Seen her off road. And she can drive a car, so she knows road craft.

But would Sparky hand his bike over to her? And would she agree even if he did? Ah, this run really is turning out a mess.

First things first. "You got a stove?" I ask Dale. Too early in the morning for all this. My brain needs a boost. Have a brew-up.

Nothing like a mug of tea. Two things settle out. First, doing something about Sparky isn't necessarily our responsibility. There's two people here better qualified to make decisions about him. Paul and Bethan, that is. Social workers must have to deal with nutters sometimes, and nurses certainly do. So looks like we got a cast-iron excuse to pass the buck.

Second thing is there's no rush. If we do let Sparky ride himself home then it's best we're all in a group and not trickling back in ones and twos. This means waiting till everyone's capable after last night, so it has to be an afternoon start at the earliest. If Maureen rides his bike and Sparky goes behind Andy, the same applies. Can't risk Andy getting stranded somewhere in mid-Wales with only a religious maniac for company, and Maureen's bound to feel happier riding a strange bike all that way with friendly escort. Of course, if Sparky was sleep walking, or playing a weird joke on us, it don't matter either way. Somehow doubt we're going to be let off so easy though. Haven't heard a whisper from him since he went back to his tent.

I feel much more relaxed when I've thought this through and Dale's agreed it. Comes to me that other times it'd be Dale doing the thinking and me the nodding, but Dale seems happy this way. In fact he looks easy altogether; taking being the new Messiah very casually. Seems to find it funny more than anything. But then how else could he take it? He's had a tough week. Reckon he either finds a hard wall and beats his brains out against it, or says OK, Jesus it is, I can live with that.

We're keeping our voices low and sitting down by the fireplace, and no one else shows signs of stirring. Neither of us got watches so eventually I creep into my tent, hoping Bethan's close to waking and I can offer her a mug of tea and get to look at her wrist. Got an idea unfolding: if it's still early, and seeing as how body-wise I feel surprisingly good this morning, could take a run round Snowdon with Dale and be back before any decisions got to be taken here.

Bethan's awake enough to show me her wrist, but not looking for tea unless I got a drip rigged up so she can take it lying flat. Tells me I should have stopped her drinking so much Black Widow last night and is peeved I'm not catatonic too. She's noticed I weren't in the tent with her; I tell her she was snoring horrible and lying across the groundsheet so I kipped down with Dale. Her wrist says seven thirty-one, which comes as a shock – can't remember the last time I saw seven thirty of a Sunday morning – but gives us hours for a run. I tell her no one's up except Dale and me, and if we're not here when she eventually crawls out we'll be off admiring the scenery. She nods with her eyes closed. I rootle in her rucksack for safety pins for Dale's jacket and go off to tell him the good news. He's keen too; all we got to do now is find the key to the bike chain. Can't remember who took responsibility for it last night – wouldn't be Jonno, for sure – and while trying to stimulate memory I walk over to look at the chain, and blow me, we left it in the padlock. Fucking incompetents, we are.

After we've released the bike I push it a little way up the track so we don't wake the others when I fire up. Sweating under the leathers when I finally fasten Dale's helmet, then mine, and climb on. But pushing the starter I'm smiling. Like we're making our little escape from the mess here, and doing what runs are all about. And no slow bikes to think about.

I've haven't looked at a map but I reckon that if I take the Caernarfon road out of Porthmadog, which is just down the road, and keep the mountains on my off-side, then if we take major rights from there we have to end up going through the mountains. And I know Llanberis Pass is where the Snowdon train goes up, so if I catch it on road signs that has to be the place to aim for.

Only five minutes back to Porthmadog and then out on the Caernarfon road. Fuzzy sun trying to break through a high mist. This place is beautiful. Dead poor, it looks, crappy pebbledashed houses, but who looks at buildings when you got horizon peaks like these? And early morning roads are great. Early empty Sunday morning roads even better. Don't see a soul for the first four miles or so, giving me the chance to open the bike up for a good throat-clear. Then slow down for a village called Nasareth. Fuck me. Clatter, Carno and Nasareth. Like this run knew we was coming. Yeah yeah, I nod, as Dale shouts something in my ear. Maybe pick up some wine and fish from the village shop and go tell it proper on the mountain.

The village name has put Sparky in my brain. He sits there, just aerating, till we've by-passed Caernarfon and picked up signs for Llanberis, and then I wonder again why he should be calling himself Judas. Has to have a reason. Even potty people got logic. Maybe just not logical logic.

We streak through Llanberis, not stopping because it seems day-trippy, all empty carparks and attraction signs, and roar up past a long thin lake. Can't tell which of the mountains either side is Snowdon, but it don't matter. Majestic, this landscape. Towering. Slopes so steep if you rolled a pebble from the top it'd bounce right the way down. Peaks in the mist. And it all looks kind of broken. Lumps of bare rock everywhere, like the landscape's unstable and it can't stay still long enough to green. I imagine the mountains as jagged teeth, and we're whipping through the gap before they crunch shut.

It comes to me, somewhere up the narrow twisty top of the pass, that maybe Dale should have taken Sparky a bit more serious. Not a bible reader myself but everyone knows Judas was the bloke who got Jesus crucified. Caused him to get the holes in his hands. Has to be a connection. What did Judas actually do? I'm so ignorant. Something to do with a garden? Kissing? Cocks crowing? Na, that was definitely someone else.

We've come through the pass and now we're dropping down fast. Made it through the teeth. T-junction up ahead. Got to be offside turn back to Porthmadog, and yeah, that's what the sign says. A few hundred yards on there's a pull-in and I slow down enough to see that it's a viewing spot for Snowdon, but since the peaks are all clouded we don't bother.

Have to stop at the bottom though. There's a lake appearing beside us so beautiful I worry I'll drop the bike staring at it. Rhododendron bushes bursting with blooms either side of the road. The water laps right up close, almost to the edge of the tarmac. I pull over, stop the bike, and we get off.

"Hey," I say, taking off my helmet. "Couldn't have missed this."

I unstrap Dale's helmet so he can ease it off between his forearms and we stroll across a few yards of grass and sit down on rocks at the water's edge. It's a long, oval lake and the far side's a wall of mountain rising sheer out of the water. Either side of us trees and rhododendron bushes overhang the banks. The water's so still the mountain opposite's mirrored in the surface. Makes you think it must be the deepest lake in the world.

"Bet it's cold," Dale says. "Looks it."

We sit a while contemplating the coldest, deepest, most beautiful lake in the world, and then I come back to Sparky.

"He thinks he's responsible," I say. "Has to be that. It was him told Eileen to ask you about me and Carno."

"So why'd that make him responsible?" Dale asks.

"Because we haven't told him about Evans checking you out with Carno. So he thinks it has to be down to him. Thinks he's the connection. Even if he don't know why."

"You think so? Shit."

"I'll tell him," I say. "Try and make it natural, like. You tell him, he might think you're just being saintly."

Dale smiles. We contemplate the lake and its underwater mountain a while longer. Then he looks down at his bandaged hands.

"You think I'm always gonna have marks?"

"Aye," I say. "Expect so. Stigmata. Have Sparkys worshipping you forever."

"Stig what?"

"Stigmata. That's what they call them. Marks of the cross."

He sighs. "Hope they're gonna be alright."

"Ask the doctors tomorrow. And make sure you tell 'em you work with your hands. Tell 'em you do skilled work. Guitarists and that, they get class treatment. Don't settle for wait and see. You ask Bethan. You got to push, make a noise."

Dale nods. We stare out over the water. Can't be more than eight thirty in the morning. Sunday, eight thirty. Amazing. Feel like I filled my eyes with more than I usually see in a week. Head too, maybe.

Dale says, soft, "What I told you last night. You gonna tell Bethan?"

I glance back at him. His eyes are still on the water. "You don't want me to?"

"Not sure. She know I pissed myself?"

"Ah fuck. Who cares? It didn't show. She never said."

"If it goes to court, I'm not saying they put it in me mouth. And I don't want you saying it, either."

"Thought you told the cops."

"Only because Scott kept nagging at me. What next, what next. Like I got to account for every second. Or he was getting off on it. Pushing me before I got time to think. But it's not in me statement. When Evans came round I made him take it out."

"I don't know nothing. Whatever you say. They got enough, with your hands."

He nods, relieved. I mark it as another reason to get those bastards. Scaring Dale so bad he's ashamed to say it. Nothing shameful about being scared. Just are, or aren't. I pick up a stone and lob it at the water. Ripples fan out like radar. The underwater mountain wobbles.

"I'm gonna tell Bethan," I say. Be a lie to say otherwise. "But I won't blabber it around. I'll tell her not to, either."

"OK," he says. "And, Jay?"

"Aye?"

"Tell her she was great. Really glad it was you two found me. When I heard your voices... and then her talking to me. All I could lock on to."

"Aye? Thought you were out of it. Looked it."

His face twists, as if he's imagining himself as we seen him, and not liking the picture.

I lob another stone in. Take that, mountain. How dare you be so pretty. "I'm gonna have a word with Jonno. See if he knows who was around at the depot Monday. Who got themselves stinking of fire."

"You be careful," Dale says.

"They wouldn't go for you again."

"Didn't mean that." He frowns away.

Shit, I've offended him. Not sure I mean it but I say, "'Course I'll be careful."

"I'll tell Evans. He's OK. He'll do the asking."

"You think he'll get sense out of Jonno?"

Dale don't answer. He gets up and walks a little way along the lake shore. Kicks at stones. Can't find anything to do with his hands, so he swings them in front of him, then behind. A few days ago him wanting to push what happened away was relieving. Felt let off a hook. Lack of imagination, that's my problem. I let him wander and kick and swing his hands a couple of minutes, looking like the loneliest person in the world beside the deepest, coldest, most beautiful lake, till I can't stand it no more.

I pick up the helmets and call, "Better go back now, eh?"

He swings round and says, "Aye."

I don't get the chance to speak to any of the boys for the first half hour we're back, because there's others to talk to first. Or shout at.

Or get shouted at by. Unbelievable. And I been on top of things till then; good times never last. I see the first cop car as we're bumping back down the track and think, eh, local constabulary come to tell us this isn't a camp site and move us on, see the second, with a crowd beyond it, six uniforms plus our boys, voices strident, and rethink, fuck, heart stepping up to several million beats a minute, what the fuck's going on?

They're waiting for us. Me and Dale, that is. A big copper with sergeant stripes and a pockmarked face strides up to us the moment I stop the bike. Shouts behind him to keep the others away. Actually prods me in the chest as I dismount, pushing me away from the machine.

"Where've you two come from? Oi, you –" He catches at Dale. "Stand there. Right there." He's got an ugly face, ugly accent.

"What's happening?" I'm in a daze. Like to be cool and wry, saying to myself, right Stu, never do messes by halves, let's have the full shebang, but the truth is my head's spinning.

"Just ridden up, have you boys?"

"Eh?"

He's getting impatient. "Listen to me. Listen. Where the fuck have you two just come from?"

"Snowdon," Dale says. "Been to see Snowdon."

Andy's voice shouts from way back, "They been here all night, for fuck's sake!"

The copper ignores him. Holds his hand out. "Licence."

I got anxiety rising. Where do they think we've been? Just ridden up from where?

"What's happened?" They mean down south. Something's happened down south.

The Sergeant's beckoning another of the coppers up, like they mean business.

"Jay," a voice says close behind me. Paul. He's snuck up the rear. "Licence. Give it to them."

Something's happened. Why can't they fucking answer?

"Jay!" Paul's voice is fierce.

I dig in my jacket quick. The pig halts his mate and snatches the licence off me. Gazes at it. Then switches his attention to Dale.

"Name?"

"Dale Farrell."

His eyes are on Dale's bandages. Interest there, but no surprise.

Paul's voice, over my shoulder, says, "You've seen their gear. They were both here last night. Ask in Cricieth. We told you. Went to two pubs, the chippie and the off licence."

"Get over with the others," the copper says.

"They'll all remember," Paul says, mild.

"What the fuck's happened!" I shout. Mam's down there, in the small-holding.

"If you don't shut up I'll put you in the car," the Sergeant snaps.

"It's OK," Paul says soothingly. "Hey. Can't be your Mam. It's you they're checking up on."

"We been here," Dale says. "Ask anyone."

The copper gazes at Dale's hands. "You're the boy with hurt hands. You claim. Easy enough to wrap a few bandages round. You want to show me?"

I'm going for him. Except I'm not, because Paul's clamped hold of my wrist. He's strong, Paul is. Fuck him.

"For God's sake," he hisses at the copper. "This is Jay, that's Dale. You touch his hands there'll be a riot."

The Sergeant flicks me *just-try-it* look. Then says snide to Dale, "That how you hurt them, is it? Rioting?"

The man don't know, you can see it in his pig-ignorant face. Dale says quiet, "I got ID. Photo an' all." He touches his chest. "In here."

The Sergeant cocks an eyebrow, then nods at the other copper to take a look. Paul yanks me back. Dale holds his arms wide while the man unzips his jacket and goes through the pockets. He's carrying his work ID, plastic card with a sealed photo. There's not many people look like Dale. In Scandinavia maybe, not in Wales.

Still takes the cops a while to gaze at the card, stare into Dale's face, gaze back at it again.

"And there was an AA man," Paul says. "On the way up. You can check with him, too."

The Sergeant pretends he didn't hear. He steps forward and rams the ID back into Dale's jacket.

"OK," he says. "So you can get off the beach now. Piss off back where you came from."

And that's it; parting shot. Doors slam, wheels spin. Two carloads of cops, just to check a couple of IDs; obviously haven't enough to do crimewise, north Wales pigs, or they in-breed so fast they're seriously overmanned. Anyone would think we'd committed a capital crime, coming up from the grubby mongrel valleys, polluting their pure North Walian air.

It's not just me shitbrained – the others were all roused from their tents by unfriendly uniforms. We sit around the fireplace mute, like someone banged us on the heads with mallets and we got to take time remembering how to speak. Only Paul and Maureen seem unfazed, but they're respecting the damage to the rest of us and set about a two-stove brew-up to get us back into shape. Doesn't help Bethan, who takes one sip of tea, says, "Excuse me," and staggers off to be sick behind a bush. Then lurches back to our tent. Even Jonno looks pasty. He gulps his tea down and goes off to lie on the sand down the beach and point warning fingers at seagulls. Andy sups his tea and then gets up saying he's got a major crap coming and he's going off and may be some time.

Paul's still flitting around with mugs of tea. Know I should be thanking him, keeping me out of a cop car, but wouldn't mind smacking him too. OK he handled things right, but it's never him being jumped on, is it? Resent owing him. Fuck, he got away with a lot. Ordered to leave us but ignored it, interrupted, hauled me around, and no one even raised their voice at him. Looks no different from the rest of us, except in years. Why do they go for some and not others? Fucking injustice.

He's being old-hand philosophic now; tells us incidents like this are always happening because communication between police forces isn't all it could be, and cops naturally believe the worst. The shit thing is that even now I don't know what's happened down south except that, like Paul said, if it were anything effecting Mam they wouldn't be pointing fingers at me and Dale, so it has to be something against Carno. Must be. And whatever it is happened yesterday evening, not during the night, because it was only then they were interested in. Could use Paul's mobile, but who'd I ring? Not Mam, that's for sure. Just have to live with not knowing till we're home.

When I'm thinking straight and less sour again it comes to me that now's not a bad time to speak to Sparky, given that the unreasonableness and stupidity of coppers is fresh in our minds. While the cop cars were pulling away he was marching around like a lunatic goldfish, eyes wide and mouth popping. I wait until Dale and Damien wander off too, leaving us alone, and then decide I'm steady enough and say, "Evans got a lot to answer for."

Sparky don't respond for a moment. Then says, like it's a big effort. "Evans?"

"The copper investigating Carno's fire. The one that thought me and Dale were in on it. The one that got Dale hurt."

Sparky's silent, but I imagine his brain logging it. I got to make sure he understands so I add, "Said he was checking Dale out with Carno, asking if they'd got history. Carno thought I'd got someone doing the job for me, so when he hears Evans saying Dale, that's who he goes for."

Sparky's quiet a little longer, then says in a whisper. "Was me put Eileen on to Dale –"

"So? It's Evans who told Carno."

Sparky shakes his head, hasn't finished his sentence, "– and it should have been Russell."

"Russell? Russell?" Where'd he come from? "What d'you mean?"

"Russell. That night. After you'd gone. Before I suggested Dale. She's talking to me and I'm saying about what Carno did to your dad, telling her we was at school and everyone knew that you and Carly got grudges against him, and then I see Russell, and say who he is, and she goes over to talk to him."

"Eileen talking with Russell?" I'm not getting my head round this. Or rather I am, slowly, but it's making it whirl.

"Not for too long. She comes back looking fierce and saying he's a wanker, and he's smirking over his glass at her. So then I say that if she wants to know more she should chat with Dale, like you're best mates and that."

"Russell," I say. "Russell." I must sound dumb, repeating his name, but I'm having a brain upheaval. Dale didn't say nothing about Russell being at the Crucible. But why should he? Hardly knows him. Met Carly often, but only in passing, at our place. Not like they ever spent quality time together. Russell. Fuck me.

"D'you know what he and Eileen talked about?" I ask.

"'Course not. Other side of the room. But it must have been about Carno. That's why she went over."

"Right. And she came back pissed off?"

"Aye. Nose high. Like he was a bad smell."

I wonder what happened. Something to put her off. Well, could be a million things, you only got to look at him. So she goes back to Dale, and then to me, but I won't play ball. So what does she do then?

"Sparky," I say. "Glad you told me that. And you don't have to worry about Dale. It's not your fault."

He sighs so deep he sounds like he might crack. "Think I was a bit stupid this morning."

"Aye, well."

He grinds his heels into the sand in front of him. "Getting some funny thoughts. Bit better after, but then the cops arrive...."

"Not the only one feeling funny this morning."

"Mmm." He turns to me sudden. "Is Dale Dale?" Then shakes

his head furious, like he's just heard himself. "Ah shit."

"You OK?"

"Need to go home. Just...." He closes his eyes and screws his face up so tight it looks like it hurts. Something's squeezing out, he can't stop it. "He's so beautiful."

I'm glad his eyes are closed. Just manage to stifle a snort. Can see it as funny because I know he'll get himself sorted soon. A few weeks, month maybe, and he'll be OK. A bit stiff to begin with, but that's just the medication and the effects ease. You take it too tragic and you write him off. He can't help the tricks his brain gets up to.

I force my own brain to focus on him. Half of it's still with the cops visiting and what the hell Russell and Carly – yeah, fucking Carly, I know it, so keen we come up here – have been up to back home. Got to push that aside.

"The ride home," I say. "Think you can manage?"

He opens his eyes. "I dunno." His chin drops to his drawn-up knees. His eyes come over dreamy. "Keep seeing that bit up the top of the mountains. I was talking to Dale there –"

"You prefer to travel pillion?" Got to interrupt. Can't take more rhapsodizing.

He tugs at his shirt collar and agitates his head. "There's no one...."

He's already thought about it. Realised he's shaky, and considered the journey home. Shows he can't be that bad.

"We can sort something," I say. "Don't want you coming off and damaging yourself."

He shakes his head sadly, as if getting damaged might be what he deserves.

Stupid to risk it. "Sparky," I say. "You got the bike key on you?"

He feels the outside of his trouser pocket, frowning and checking. "Yeah."

"Can I have it?"

He hesitates.

"I got an idea. You'll get it back."

He digs in and hands it over, trusting.

I say, "Ta, mate," and pocket it. Slap him on the back and go off to have a word with Dale. Well, he'll get it back when he's home.

We leave two-ish. I'm agitating to be off earlier but you can't rush hangovers. There's lots of too-ing and fro-ing along the beach and slowly the tents come down and bikes get stacked. Everyone's had to be told that Sparky's feeling frail and isn't going to ride, but only Paul and Bethan have heard that Dale's Jesus. Not that either's got anything more sensible to offer than what Dale and I agreed. Paul just winced and smiled, and Bethan groaned, "Ah, you deal with it, Jay." Real pros, yeah.

Maureen's been practising on Sparky's Yam up and down the track. Amazing woman; when Andy and I put it to her that she ride she just grinned wide, as if she'd been waiting all her life for the chance, and has been bounding over the bumps ever since. Good thing Sparky's bike is little or we'd probably have trouble keeping up with her. She's not worried about lack of documents – says if we get stopped she'll bat her lashes and pretend she thought her car licence covers smaller bikes. At least she's not actually banned, like Jonno. Dale's cast a critical eye over Andy's bike to anticipate problems, got him to check what can be checked and tighten up everything that should be tight. Sparky seems OK about matters being taken out of his hands. Maybe even relieved. Spent half an hour folding up his tent to matchbox-size and another half hour packing his rucksack. Bethan's been delegated to keep an eye on him – chose her not because she's a nurse but because she can do it sitting on the sand only having to exercise her eyes, which is all she's capable of. Poor cow's thrown up again since the tea; really did poison herself last night. I've packed her rucksack for her and she's arranged to swap her full-face helmet for Maureen's open one for the journey because she's terrified of being sick again and not getting the helmet off in time. Biker's nightmare, drowning in your own vomit inside a helmet. The switch makes sense anyway; if Maureen's riding she'll need a visor.

We decide that Paul and I should take turns to lead and tail. Two nice legal bikes either end, hope no one notices the dodgy stuff between. When we finally set off I take the front, in case Bethan comes over sick and we have to stop, but after a break south of Dolgellau to fill the tanks she says the wind-battering's done her good, and we switch about for the surprising-bends section. Maureen's doing fine. She was hesitant about overtaking longer vehicles at first but Andy moved up to ride just in front and wink his rear light at her when it was safe for them both to go and she soon got the hang.

Just as well I'm riding at the back, because I can't say my mind's fully on the job – it's busy taking journeys of its own, and in conflicting directions. Chasing off after nailgunners one minute, listing starting points – speaking to Jonno about fire-scented suspects, confronting Carno even – shit, when I get on this tack I see myself thumping it out of him, could do it, too – and then a minute later I'm stamping on the mental brakes, shaking free, and swinging off down the murk road of Carly and Russell. Carly and Russell; if all this mess is down to them it throws a tool-box in the works. Can't get my head round it, can't see daylight, except I know they're in there, and I got to know what they been up to before I shoot off elsewhere.

So I don't notice much of the real journey till we hit home territory. Well, the scenery's never as exciting wending home as it is exploring out. First stop when we get home is Sparky's place, to drop him and the Yam off and warn his Mam about his state of mind. Bethan goes in on the pretext of having a piss and comes out saying she didn't have to say much. His Mam guessed he wasn't well just looking at him. There's an aunt and his physics teacher brother there as well, round for Sunday tea, and since that's a combined IQ of several million points, and all sensible and kind-hearted with it, we reckon he's in safe hands.

Then it's back to Andy's to see him and Maureen and Damien home and to restrap Dale's camping gear that's been scattered around the bikes on to the tanks of our two for the couple of miles back to my place. While we're doing this I ask Jonno where he'll be tomorrow and he says he'll be at Carno's all day, but maybe the Crucible after. Might see him there, I say. Then he roars off down the road like he's been released from a slow wagon train, and Paul and I cruise out to the small-holding.

In the yard everything looks normal, just like we left it. Didn't expect otherwise but still relieving. While we're unloading the bikes Paul says to let him know when I discover what's been going on and I say sure. I offer him tea, but he says he's knackered and he'd prefer to autopilot home and slump. Just as well, since Mam's out – left a note saying she's at Randolph's – and all Bethan and Dale want to do is slump too. Wouldn't mind a sit-down myself, except I got a visit to make. I pick up the phone and ring Carly's number and when Russell answers I put it down again. Poke my head into the sitting room but then decide I won't bother the two flaked bodies in there with explanations. Just pick up my helmet and go.

# 11

I bang on the door of the flat using the heel of my fist, so it makes a good thumping din. When no one answers I do it again and shout, "Oi! Carly!" Carly and Russell've got a housing association flat in a converted town house that used to be a health centre, till the doctors moved into purpose-built premises. Smart flats, too. Far too good for their shitty, troublemaking tenants.

I know someone's inside because I can hear a noise like rats scuffling. I shout, "Oi!" again, and the door opens a crack. I wait till Russell's taken off the chain, then bang it wide with my shoulder.

"OK, OK," complains Russell.

"Just being careful," says Carly. "Who rung us from home?"

"Me. Bit nervous, are you? Who wants battering first?" I grab Russell by the throat and sling him against the wall.

"Jay!" Carly screeches.

I give Russell's head a shake. "Now you tell me exactly what you done."

"Carly!" he gasps.

"And don't you lie to me," I say. "I know you been talking to Eileen. I know you torched Carno's place. And I know you been up to something last night."

"Jay!" cries Carly, wrenching at my arm. "Leave him!" She's digging her nails in but I'm not relenting. She gives up with an exasperated hiss and talks over to Russell. "We'll have to tell him. It's OK."

"It's not fucking OK," I snap, but I release Russell. He coughs, checking his tubes are still working. Eyelids flicker like strobes.

Carly sneers. "We were just doing what you didn't have the bottle for."

"What d'you do last night?" I'm not rising. "What you done?"

She shrugs. "Just his cars. Down his place."

"His cars?" What imagination. "Right. You're going to tell me everything. Now. As in now now."

She stares at me and says, "Nothing else has happened, has it?"

"Hope not, for your sake."

"OK." Gives a bad grace shrug. "Suppose you'd better come through."

We sit round her poxy oval veneer table in her shiny poxy kitchen/diner, me opposite the pair of them, like they're in dock and I'm an ill-tempered judge and jury. Just an ash tray between us. Not a heavy smoker when I'm calm but I'm stubbing out the second twenty minutes on, just at the moment when it comes to me why Russell had burn marks on his face a fortnight ago. Ha fucking ha, I think, grinding the stub out.

They share the story-telling. It started like Sparky says, in the Crucible. Russell takes this bit. He says Eileen comes over to him, introduces herself, and asks him straight out his opinion of Carno. Russell's had a few beers. He tells her he's nothing against the man himself, but Carno's the waste-disposal big shot who killed his wife's dad. Eileen says he's just killed her brother too and she wouldn't mind if they went somewhere private to discuss mutual grievances. Prat thinks she's coming on to him. Natural mistake, him being such a sex god. He's a bit blustery here, with Carly sitting large beside him, but my guess is that while he's seeing himself in wet dream territory, handsome chick marching up and playing promising word-games with him, Eileen's started to read it different, as him suggesting they might be able to do business if she puts out for him. No way of knowing the exact truth without thumbscrews. But at some point she calls him a wanker and storms off back to Sparky. It takes Russell a while to twig that Eileen might actually have been serious, and even then his first thought is that if he and Carly went along with something against Carno, they might make themselves some spending money. Wouldn't occur to Russell to do anything for free. But it does occur to Carly, when he tells her later that evening. He don't understand why she's so angry with him but then he's probably never talked Carno with her. He's telling it like it's a weird encounter with a weird lady, an opportunity passed up but maybe no bad thing, and she's hearing it like the angel of retribution finally made earthly contact and he fucking ballsed it up. She sees things calmer the next day though, and they make up – well, they were round at our place, saw them do it. Interesting thing is that Carly can't have even hinted to Mam what started the fight, or Mam'd have made connections later. Suggests Carly had hopes they might be contacted again.

And after Eileen fails with me – and it gives me a shit feeling remembering how she tried to persuade me, as if she'd taken tips from Russell and seen me as dick-led too – that's just what happens. Eileen knows Russell's surname from Sparky, and there's only two Parkins with local numbers in the book, and both are Russell's relatives. He and Carly haven't been in the flat long enough to be listed. It's Russell's uncle who gives her their number. This time she gets Carly who explains that Russell's short in the sensitivity department but she isn't – oh yeah? – and she'd welcome a chat. Eileen must be relieved she don't have to bonk Russell to get things moving. When they meet up Russell refuses point blank to mug Carno and he's such a shrimp I can't see Eileen or Carly pushing it. So they settle on hurting his business. But Russell still wants paying, since it'll be him taking the risk – Carly's the wrong build for shimmying up wire fences with a back-pack of petrol – and nobody does nothing for nothing in his books. Carly's sour about this but Eileen isn't. Gives him five hundred quid up front and promises him the same again when it's been in the local paper. 'Course they never get the second payment.

So that's the first arson. What I can't understand is why they weren't shitting themselves after, when they heard Eileen'd been arrested. Was me told Carly, wasn't it? Late Sunday, only two nights after the torching? She never missed a beat. Happy that night, for fuck's sake. Elated, even. Swinging her legs in the kitchen, teasing me, trying to persuade me to own up to it.

"When d'you hear Eileen'd been arrested?" I demand. Had to be before she came round – no other explanation.

"Saturday." Confiding all this has turned Carly smug. She's proud of herself. "Got a phone call. Bloke saying Eileen was banged up but not to worry."

"What bloke?"

"How'd I know? English. Her solicitor, I expect."

"So you didn't worry?"

"'Course I worried. But then, it happened so quick, her getting arrested, I got thinking. It's obvious. She turned herself in. Wanted Carno to know. Be no point otherwise. She'd got no connections with Carno, not direct, so how'd they get on to her so fast? She had it planned, must have. And no one turns up for us by Sunday. Cops have had her twenty four hours and got nothing out of her. She'd be counting on getting off light, what with grieving for her brother and that. Planned all along."

"You're so stupid," I say. And she thinks she's so clever. Thinks she knows everything. "Carly," I say, "why d'you think the cops went for me? Why d'you think Carno went for Dale?"

She pulls her chin back into her neck, pitying mouth, like I'm so thick she can't believe it. "You got a grudge," she says. "Obvious. And Dale's your mate."

"I got a grudge that's thirteen years old. Why'd people remember that?"

She sets out to reply, mouth opening and working, till it comes to her she's got no answer. A grudge thirteen years old's enough for her. It's still fresh in her mind – raw, more like – so she sees it the same for everyone.

"They went for me because I took Eileen down Carno's place to see him. Didn't tell you that, did she?"

Russell says, "Eh?" looking alarmed at Carly, who just blinks. Mam can't have told her. Not about the visit. I remember moaning at Mam for mentioning Eileen, but she must have just said that the woman had been round. Well, she wouldn't go into detail, would she; she'd know Carly'd only use it to get at me.

"And that's why they went so quick for her, too. She got her hands on him, tried to get me to hit him. Used my name in front of him. Stupid cow."

She thinks I mean Eileen. Her brain's working, feverish. Don't like having scary information sprung on her. She's casting around to prove she's not been stupid. "Doesn't mean it weren't planned. Could be part of it."

Hmm. Well. Can't disprove it. Except Carly's viewing Eileen like she was together and organized, planning revenge on Carno with a cool head. Not seeing her as a woman who'd just lost her twin, mad to blame someone, actions wild and all over the place.

"She tell you what Carno'd done, for her to go for him?"

She's got this off pat. "Told you. Killed her brother. Well, good as. Taken his wife and kid, bad-mouthed him, kept the kid away, all sorts."

"He didn't abduct them," I say. "Wives leaving happens all the time. And it was two years ago."

Carly's starting to get angry. She's losing certainty. "Since when did you start sticking up for Carno?"

"I'm not. Just wondering why you fall for crazy stuff when it could get you locked up."

"Eileen won't talk. Know she won't."

"It'd kill Mam."

"It won't happen."

"So if you never got the cash, how come Russell's still getting at Carno for free?"

"Didn't do the cars for Eileen. Did them for Dale. And I did them."

I've got to prop my chin on my hands. She's going to go down. Crazy as Eileen.

"How d'you think that's gonna help?"

"Someone had to pay him back. It's evil, what he did." She gets fierce. "Should have been you, but you're too chicken."

I wasn't chicken. Just not reacting right. And if I get to revenge Dale now I'll make fucking sure no one else pays for it.

"So what d'you think Carno's going to do?" I say. "Who's he going to blame?"

"You and Dale were away. I made sure of that. You got alibis."

"Had an alibi last time."

"Only Mam and Bethan."

"Carly," I sigh. "He thinks I got someone else to torch his place. Why else he go for Dale?"

"You were all away. All the boys."

"He don't know that. He don't know who my mates are. Probably thinks we went away just to get alibis. Ah Carly. He's got no one else to get back at. You don't know what you've done."

She's defiant. "He deserved it."

"You're going to get someone hurt."

She sneers. "You, you mean."

She's not thinking straight. Just getting one in automatic. She can't hate me that much. Even Russell's frowning.

"You want to see me nailed to a floor?"

She don't answer.

"Or who else is out there? Mam, Bethan, Dale...."

She still don't answer. Russell and I both got our eyes on her. Watch her swallow. Her lips pinch tight. Shit, it's hard for her.

"OK," she mumbles.

Even longer silence. Everyone contemplating the wonder of her taking fault on board. Then Russell gets up and says, "Need a drink." He opens the fridge and takes three cans out. Puts two down in front of Carly and me.

"It's done now," Carly mutters.

"Aye." I push back in my chair. "It is."

Neither of them got anything to add, so I say, "The cars. You do a lot of damage?"

She sighs. "Didn't hang around to see. Expect so. Tipped petrol over the Jag and trailed it half way to the gate. Two other cars, either side."

"The gates were open?"

"Nope. Chained. Easy climb though. No security light, or they hadn't turned it on. Only half ten, not that dark. Would have left it later, but I was worried it would rain. Threw a match and ran. Heard it go up as I climbed back over the gate. Saw the flare from the lane, too."

"Bet they had a camera," I say. Can't believe Carno would pay for cameras at the depot and not kit out the house.

"I was well wrapped up," says Carly. "I thought of that."

I look up at Russell, standing swigging by the sink. "And where were you?"

"Down the lane. Keeping a look out."

"In the Escort?"

"Aye. But muddied the plates. Didn't see no one anyway. She was fucking quick."

He says it admiringly, as if when he fired the depot it had taken him hours.

"You see fire engines?"

"Nope. Never heard them, either. Nearest fire station has to be Crickhowell, so took the Talybont road to be out of their way, cleaned the plates in a layby, and came back over the mountain."

"Shit." I shake my head. "He's gonna be tamping."

Carly was getting proud of herself again, recounting her arson prowess. This pulls her back. Chews her lip.

"We got to sort it," I say. "Before he does something."

"Sort it?" She barks at me. "How?"

"Go see him." Haven't thought it out but, as I say it, I know it's the only way. Just sitting there top of my mind, waving at me. Comes at a price, though. Heavy price. Means forgetting about revenge. Means letting things go. At least where Carno's concerned. Maybe still a chance for the nailgunners... but without Carno, where would I start? Oh shit. Shit. Gotta do it though. Carly being involved changes everything. And it's the only way.

"Tell him it's got to stop. Tell him we'll stop our side if he stops his."

Carly's disbelieving. "I'm not admitting nothing to Carno!"

"You don't have to. Just make it plain we got the power. That we'll sort it for him. That we don't want anything happening to our family or friends, so we'll deal with it. The price is that he backs off. Otherwise, well. He's got other things to burn."

"Suppose he calls the police?"

"Why'd he call the police? It's not a deal he'd want broadcast."

"Well, beats us up, then. He could do anything."

"No he couldn't. We just turn up at his depot. No appointment. No chance for him to set things up. He attacks us in his own premises he's going to have explaining to do. There's drivers in and out. Security men. Witnesses."

"All bent."

"Doubt that. One of them's Jonno. I'll check with him. Do it while he's there."

Carly stares at me. "So why've I got to go with you?"

"Because we're putting it to him as a family thing. Like we all feel threatened. And because he'll get leery if it's just me and Russell. Two blokes demanding to see him."

"I'm not going!" Russell cries. "No way!"

"You are," I snap. "You started this."

"No." Carly shakes her head. Looks suddenly convinced. "Don't think Russell should go. Three of us is mobhanded. And looks suspicious, like Russell and me've got more interest in settling things than you and Bethan. Keep it as a family thing. Just you and me."

I want to argue, because it seems like Russell is getting off far too light, considering his involvement and the fact that he's a shitty criminal wanker, but I can see her point.

"And if it works," Carly says. "We'll be one up, won't we?"

Shit, there's a glint in her eye. I reckon you'd have to torch half a town to match one nailing-down, but I'm all for giving Carly incentives.

"Aye," I say. "If it works."

"So when do we do it?"

"Mmm. Fast. Before he tries anything. I got to take Dale to the hospital tomorrow morning and check Jonno's on the gate. But if he's there we could try in the afternoon."

"I'll get a migraine at lunch time," Carly says. "Wait here, is it?"

"Aye. And, listen. In front of Carno, we're nice to each other. No snide digs. Nothing to get him wondering. Just protecting our family. Got it?"

She smiles sweet at me. See, she can do it. Well, it's obvious she can act. And lie.

I go into the sitting room to ring home then, because all this talk's making me jittery. Last time Carno took three days to retaliate, but he might be more geared up now. Or, of course, because he'd guess we'd be more geared up too, he might decide to leave it longer, wait for guards to drop. No way of knowing. Mam answers the phone and shouts at me for going off without telling anyone where. Oops. Bethan's told her about the cops visiting in North Wales and she got a call from Scott herself early this morning, asking where we were headed. So she knows something's up, but not what. I ask if Randolph's there and she says he is but he was just going and I say hang on to him till I get back. Then I ask her to fetch Dale for Evans' mobile number. Evans gave us both a card but fuck knows where mine is. Dale can't hold the phone so she reads it out to me and I write it down. Tell her I'm ringing him to find out what happened last night.

Then I cut off and ring his number. But I've got to put the phone down half way through dialling because I'm doing things too quick. Like my brain and actions are out of sync. Take a few breaths and steady myself. Tell myself I can do this. Well, I got to do it.

I remind myself that I don't know nothing, nothing, right, except that we had cops visiting in North Wales. Then take another breath and redial.

Evans' voice sounds like it's got an electrical fault. Hills round here, useless for mobiles. But at least he's answering. I tell him I'm ringing because we had our festivities interrupted in Cricieth by uncouth colleagues of his and I want to know what the fuck's going on.

"Ah, Jay, is it?" he says, after a moment. "You haven't heard, then?"

"'Course I haven't heard. Only just got back."

He sighs. Must be wearing, not knowing who's lying to you.

"Well, suppose you'll hear soon enough. Three cars scorched at Carno's house."

I wait a moment, like I'm absorbing it.

"Bad?"

"I didn't deal with it. Powys force. But yeah, seems so. All write-offs."

"Anyone hurt?"

"Physically, you mean? No. Luckily. But there's a kid there, you know."

"Aye. I know." I'm not sounding apologetic. "Tough. You'll be dealing with it now, will you?"

"Mmm. Could be the arsons are connected." Says this straight, the humorist. "In fact just been visiting now. On my way back."

He's in a car coming up the hill. That explains the shit reception. "Did you speak to Carno? Who's he blaming?"

He hums long enough for me to get the message. I say, "I want protection. I got Mam and Bethan and Dale to think of."

"Yeah." He sounds bleak. "Thought you might ask that."

"And?"

"It's not so easy. Not when there's nothing to go on."

"For fuck's sake."

"You know how much protection costs? Could go on for days."

"We'll stay away tomorrow. Mam can visit Randolph. Just need it for tonight."

He sighs again. I hear him thinking. Then he says, "You got a mobile phone up there?"

"Nope." He thinks I'm at home. Remember Jay, I tell myself, I'm at home. Phone line at the small-holding is just a looping cable.

"OK. You happy to leave long enough to pop into the station? Might be able to help."

"Right. Yeah. Randolph's here. Like now?"

"Fine. I'll be there in ten minutes. Ask for me."

Carly's place is only two minutes from the police station so I pace around the flat to use up time. Chomp a pork pie from her fridge but it gums up my mouth like glue and I have to swill the muck away with lager. Remember the pick-up Russell was going to buy and ask him if that was what he was going to spend his arson cash on. Only if the other five hundred came through, he says – still had hopes, the wanker, even after they heard Eileen was arrested, that's how sure they were she planned it – but since it didn't, he's let it go. Ah, shame, I say.

When I get round to the police station Evans is only just coming in himself, with another copper who isn't Baldy Scott.

"Be with you in a minute," he says, letting himself in the back room through the hatchway. He looks weary. Fat and weary. When he returns, couple of minutes later, he takes me into the front interview room. He's fiddling with a mobile phone, clicking numbers in, sighing and frowning at it. He looks up and stares at me.

"What've you done to your eyes?"

"Eh?"

"Amazingly red."

"Ah, it's the ride. It's nothing." The ride, alcohol last night, lack of sleep. Child of Satan look, know it well.

He puts the mobile phone on the table. Sighs again. "OK. Got you this."

"Right." I peer at it. "Er…." Gonna have to admit something here, fuck. "Not brilliant at remembering numbers, mind." The only PIN code I've ever remembered is for my cash card.

"Won't need to be. I've quick-dialled two numbers for you. Press four and hold, you get 999, five and hold, my number. Got –" he checks the phone "– at least 48 hours before it needs recharging."

"OK." He's made it easy for me. Well, he might have for anyone.

"So keep it with you. And no ringing Australia, or I'll arrest you."

"Right."

He runs a hand down his face. Looks knackered himself.

"I'm off now, but I'll tell you what else I'll do. I'll get a patrol car to pass your place a few times tonight. You leave your gate open and tell me what vehicles you got in the yard, and I'll ask them to shine their lights down. If they see anything different they'll call in. Can't do more than that."

"Right." I tell him to ignore a grey Subaru and Randolph's blue Ford van, which may or may not stay overnight. Not expecting any other cars. He says he'll pass the information on.

"Ta," I say. Kind of mean it, too.

He leans back, gives another sigh. Not a happy copper, Evans, tonight.

"Dale OK?" he asks.

"Fine. Bandages off tomorrow. Oh, and shit, he's remembered something."

I tell him about Dale recollecting the smell of burning.

"Mmm." He don't look excited. "Smell's a difficult one, evidence-wise. Nothing else?"

"Nope. Except he told me they put it in his mouth."

"He's withdrawn that."

"Still happened."

"Aye." He nods glumly. "Nasty."

"You haven't found the nailgun?"

"'Fraid not."

I get up to go. Taken too long already. He's still sitting there, like he hasn't got enough energy to stir.

"Jay," he says, swivelling before I reach the door. "You haven't got a problem with someone, have you? Apart from Carno?"

"Er. Don't think so. Why?"

He sucks his teeth. "It's just... well. It's his Jag again, isn't it? I know that's what Carno's thinking. You say it's not you, but –"

"It's not me. Was in Cricieth. And it's Carno that keeps having Jags, not me that keeps torching them."

"Mmm. Still.... It's almost like someone's pointing a finger –"

"I didn't torch his old Jag," I say.

"No. No, you didn't."

"I got to go," I say.

He gives a final sigh. "OK then. Sleep well."

"An' you."

Anyone would think it was bedtime. No such luck. By the time I'm back at the small-holding, letting myself in and bolting the door behind me, it's still not eight. The others have eaten and left me chilli beans on the Rayburn. I tell them what's happened down at Carno's and Randolph decides to stay over. He wants another prowl round the premises before it gets dark but I'm wasted so Mam says she'll do it with him. Occurs to me that Randolph always wants company on his circuits and that's what makes them so lengthy, because every few steps he's got to stop and muse. Must have been lonely when his wife died, having no one to muse to. First time I thought that.

I'm not telling Dale that Carly and Russell have put their hands up to the arsons, nor that me and Carly are visiting Carno tomorrow – not telling Mam either, makes me go cold imagining it – but I'm planning to tell Bethan both when we go to bed. Sense she'll never forgive me if I don't. I had to say something about where I'd been earlier so I've said I went to check Carno's depot, and that it looked same as usual, and then nipped into Carly's to ask if she'd heard anything, and when she said she hadn't, used her phone to ring Evans. I've shown everyone the mobile and told them we're promised a few cruise-bys over night. I'm keeping Dale in the dark about Carly and Russell because I can't face explaining that it's my sister and her husband got him injured, not tonight, anyway, and back of my mind I think the less he knows the better, just for now. I don't want to tell him about the visit to Carno's in case he tries to persuade me out of it. Not sure he would, but I sense he's wanting to move away from action, not towards, and I know I'd find arguing with him hard. All I've said is that I think he should stay somewhere else after his appointment, just for a while. Told him I'd worry less, though really what I'm afraid of is the chance of Carno retaliating fast. Where he stays is up to him, but I don't want him back alone in his flat even if his bandages are made smaller, because it's a place someone might just look for me. Maybe he could try Andy's, or one of his workmates'. Maybe even Paul. In fact Paul's seems such a good idea I ring him to tell him about Carno's cars and our overnight protection, and mention the subject of tucking Dale away somewhere safe. Don't have to say more; he tells me where the cottage key is hid during the day and says one the girls is usually home by four. I say I'm leaving the decision to Dale, but thanks. Bethan's back to late shifts this week, so she'll go in to the hospital early – maybe with Dale and me – and stay over in one of the spare on-call rooms when she finishes. I've fluffed over what I'm going to do. Run out of ideas.

We all go to bed early. We tell Floss to keep her ears peeled and treat the last remaining pup to a night by the Rayburn. Be puddles on the tiles by the morning but at least Mam won't worry. I've a feeling Bethan's got things to say to me, as well as me to her. It's the way we use the bathroom without speaking to each other, like we're both rehearsing lines in our heads. In the bedroom I put the mobile on the floor by the bed and sit down on the duvet to unlace my boots. Bethan draws the curtains and switches the lamp her side on. She's frowning.

Then she stands in front of the window table and says, voice quiet but hard, "I want to know what's going on. And don't tell me nothing is."

"Aye." I kick off the boots. "Sit down."

She sits down on the chair in front of the window and I tell her. She don't help me out like usual, just sits dead quiet staring at me and letting me muddle through. Find myself thinking how pretty she is. She's had a bad day and I'm unfolding a worse one. It shows on her face but it don't stop her being beautiful.

At the end she shakes her head. Like words aren't enough for what she wants to say.

Finally she says, "Bitch. Crazy, stupid, bitch."

Can't disagree with this, though I wonder why she sounds so bitter.

"Why now? After all this time...?" But she don't need me to answer. She knows Carly. How she's stuck in time, and how she needs other people. How she's never done anything against Carno herself. And then suddenly there's other people egging her on, her big chance.

"You can't go with her to see Carno. You can't."

"My idea. You got a better plan?"

"Yes. You ring Evans right now and tell him it's her and Russell."

"I can't do that."

"Why the hell not? What's she ever done for you?"

"She's my sister. She'd go down. Arson's heavy."

She shakes her head. "She'll probably go down anyway. All Eileen has to do is open her mouth."

"That'd be Eileen. Not me. This way she stands a chance."

"You're not going to tell Mam either, are you?"

"Not if I can help it."

"You're mad. Mad. Stupid." She makes a little choking sound in her throat, and starts to weep.

"Ah, Bethan."

I move down the bed towards her, but she bats at me to stop. Hisses, "You think you're going to talk to Carno, with Carly beside you, and she's going to do what you say?"

"She's got to."

"Since when did Carly ever behave herself with you? Never, ever. He's only got to say something shitty, and she'll flip. She's got no control. She's going to get you hurt. Oh God."

"She won't. She understands. I've told her. And I can look after myself."

"No." She wipes her eyes with the back of her hand. "I don't think you can. Carno and Carly... neither of them looking out for you. She'll spoil things, and if he doesn't hurt you, you'll end up hurting him."

"It's not what I'm planning."

"Christ, Jay. You've got a temper too.... Anything could happen."

"I don't see no other way."

"I'll ring Evans for you."

"No. You won't. Mean it. Carly going down would kill Mam."

"What about you going down? You thumping Carno because Carly gets him dangerous, and you go down?"

"That'd kill Mam too. I'm not going to do nothing that leaves her alone. It's in my mind. It'll keep me careful."

"If you get yourself in trouble over this –"

"I'm stopping trouble. Not starting it."

"– if you get into trouble –"

"I won't."

"Shut up. I'm telling you. If you do, it's over."

Just didn't want to hear it.

"It was different before. When we thought it was a mistake....

182

But Carly... always winding you up, getting you stupid. I can't take it. I don't like being scared."

No, I know she don't like being scared.

"And I don't want a man who's in trouble. With the law or anyone."

I know this too. "I promise, Bethan. I'm going to stop it. I won't do nothing stupid."

She starts crying again. This time she lets me pull her on to the bed. I cuddle her. She's so unhappy. Tired and angry and unhappy. I want to tell her something that makes her see it better. Gives her more faith in me. I know I'm right.

"Hey," I whisper. "Going with Carly's stopped me being stupid another way. I was talking to Dale last night. About the men who hurt him. They put the gun in his mouth, Bethan. Threatened to pull the trigger. While he was nailed down."

Bethan draws back from me, eyes huge with horror. I hold on to her.

"Don't tell no one, he don't want it spread around. But I couldn't take it. I was planning going after them, till I found out it was Carly. Now I'm not. I'm leaving it. I'm going to settle things. You got to trust me. I'll do it."

Bethan stares at me. And I never considered her, while I was thinking of revenge for Dale. Not once. Or Mam. Only thinking of Dale. No, not even Dale.

Bethan sounds breathless. "So... I'm meant to thank Carly, am I?"

"'Course not. Just telling you. Her being involved has made me see straighter. Made me see consequences. I'll be thinking of you and Mam, it'll keep me cool." I pull her close. "Promise."

She don't say nothing but grips me tight. Feel a bit teary myself. That'll do wonders for my red-eye.

"Can't you at least tell Evans you're going?" she moans.

"Don't think so. He's not stupid. Already casting around for someone connected with me. Can't hand him Carly. And he's not going to mount an escort, is he? Wouldn't want it if he did. Jonno'll be on the gate."

"Jonno," she says. Vicious.

"Better than no one."

She starts crying again. Seeing her like this makes me want to do more than cuddle her. But I don't want her complaining I'm crass. To save my feelings coming out inadvertent I loosen my hold. She gets up. Blots her eyes.

"I need my sleep. You do too. Your eyes look gruesome."

"Aye."

We get undressed. The room goes quiet again, because we're both back on tomorrow. Even when we're in bed we don't say nothing. It's just in our heads, and up there in the dark, pointing down at us like a row of swords. Or nails. But we're both dead beat and that's a blessing. Too tired to worry about night visitors. Bethan's asleep in minutes and I'm going fast. Floss'll look out for us.

# 12

Crowd of millions at hospital outpatients but we're lucky – Dale's sent up to the ward to have his bandages seen to. Doctors have got no bandaging skills apparently, so Sister's going to do it.

I wait in the dayroom. Watch Dale taken away by a nurse who says, "Ooh, look better, you do, Dale," winking over to another nurse behind him. Made an impact when he was here last, obviously.

We've all come in together in the Subaru. It's past eleven so Bethan won't have long before she's on duty. Both she and Dale got overnight bags and lists of phone numbers. Could be only hours before we all meet up again, or much longer. Before we left I moved the bikes round to Randolph's and locked them in one of his outhouses, leaving the empty shed at our place open, so no one does damage battering their way in for nothing. Mam's refusing to move out of the small-holding. Says she's got Floss and Randolph – makes them sound equal value – and she's too old for all this excitement, so she's just going to ignore it. Truth is she don't like upsets to her routine, specially dietary, or being in places where things aren't exactly where she left them. She'll be out at Randolph's business most of the day anyway, so I just got to accept it.

Had a nasty moment downstairs, saying tara to Bethan in front of Dale. Said, "See you later," and she said, "Mmm," not meeting my eye, and tripped off. Watched her disappear down the corridor but she never looked back. I was pulled out of it by Dale saying, "Oi, Jay, you coming?" Gonna weep if Carno takes her off me.

Suppose I really said goodbye to her early this morning, when I woke to find we hadn't been nailgunned to the bed overnight, and instead of drifting off again I decided it was a good time to fix her in my mind by exploring her. First her smooth curvy shoulder, then the knobbles of her backbone, then her hard round little bum, and then her soft sleeping tits round the other side. Think her body woke before her mind. She murmured, "Oh, Jay," tossing her head like we ought to think what we're doing before we do it, but by then I'd got her nipples between my fingers and her hips had already swung round, restless and searching. Stopped her head by kissing her and then her mouth won't let me go. Got to do the whole thing tongues delving each other, which means me hunching right up to make us fit, and it'll be a crime if that's the last time we do it because it made me feel we're connected more than ever.

There's three old guys in here, well, one's maybe only Paul's age, but he looks older because he's grey-gilled and hobbling around with a leg in plaster. I'd like a ciggie and I've parked myself by the window but I feel inhibited in company. None of them are doing much, just flicking over newspapers and hobbling, and I suddenly wonder if we're all of the same mind, hoping the others'll piss off so we can point our lungs outside. Once I've thought this I look at them closer and, bugger me, two of them got fag-packet bulges in their pyjama breast pockets. I get my own pack out and tap it on the sill, and instantly there's three pairs of eyes on me, and then darting at each other, all with the same thought. I slide both windows wide as they'll go and we huddle round pretending we've got dignity, striking up and puffing away furious before anyone else comes in. Mind, the two ancient guys got such disgusting coughs I wonder why they bother.

Dale returns soon after, smile on him like the sun came out. Waves his hands at me. Still got bandages on them but much smaller, fingers waggling free. Lot cleaner too, the old ones were getting insanitary. Sister's suggested he wear fingerless gloves, now he'll be able to get gloves on, stop getting these so grubby. Walking down to the car park he says she's told him not to worry about a bit of stiffness, it's natural and there's nothing to stop him using his fingers now as much as feels comfortable, give the hands some exercise. Just no strangling chickens or punching anything. I can tell that seeing the wounds for the first time has relieved his mind. Think he'd been imagining holes much bigger. He says once she'd wiped the gunge away it's just three little scabs like pox marks either side. She's said he can go back to work next week if he wants and that's really pleasing him.

I'm taking him down to Paul's now. Where he stays is meant to be his decision but he hasn't rung anyone. He's easy anyway – so chuffed about his hands he don't care. Keep catching him smiling at them. Makes me think he's been worrying about them a lot more than he's let on.

When we get down to the cottage it's all shut up but the key's under the flower pot like Paul says. Such an original hideyhole I dunno why he don't leave it in the door. Inside the cottage feels dark and cool and we find ourselves talking quiet, like we're intruders. I think Paul's a real friend for offering us an empty house, and he's even been thoughtful enough to leave a note on the kitchen table which says, 'Hi Dale – get Franny to help you with anything, she'll be back at four,' and giving his work number. Reading it makes us feel more at ease, gets us back to normal volume. 'Course, Dale shouldn't need too much help from anyone now.

I make us both a sandwich out of Paul's bread bin and fridge and while we're eating Dale starts to wonder how long he's got to be here. I don't think he's given it proper thought before, no room in his mind for anything except his hospital appointment. Hard for me to imagine, having a job so satisfying I'd be devastated if I lost it. Now I got him down here I think I'll tell him some of the truth. I say I'm going to try and see Carno this afternoon, sort things out with him.

"You're what?" He's shocked.

"Could go on for weeks otherwise. Can't live like this." I try to say it offhand. "It's OK. Not looking for trouble. Just want to find out who he's blaming. Give him assurances."

"On your own?"

I don't want to say about Carly. He'll want to know why.

"Gonna make sure Jonno's on the gate."

"Jonno?" He's like Bethan, scathing. He hesitates, and I see him inhaling for something difficult.

"Don't want anyone else," I get in quick. "And definitely not you. Thanks for offering."

The air slides out relieved. "One of the other boys? Just as backup?"

"Who? It's not their problem. All at work anyway."

"Does Bethan know?"

"Uhuh."

"And she thinks it's a good idea?"

"Mmm. Hasn't suggested anything better."

"You ought to tell Evans. Just in case."

"I've told you and Bethan. If you find me in a ditch later you can pass it on."

"Not funny."

"I'll be OK. Might even pick you up tonight."

"Ring me after."

"'Course."

I leave around two. I tell Dale I'll be going straight to the depot, do a cruise-past to check Jonno's there, then try and see Carno. Hope to get back to him maybe four, five. I can see Dale's not so happy now, facing being stuck out here with nothing to do except wait for me to ring in, but he don't have no choice. I tell him there's a piano in the sitting room. Heard him play chopsticks. He can give them fingers some exercise.

The car feels weird driving back to town. Like someone's adjusted the seat wrong; I got to keep straightening my arms and pushing myself back. And got a breath problem – too much air in my lungs. I'm blowing out like the dash is a birthday cake.

First time I coast past Carno's depot I can't see no one on the main gate. Shit, I think, Jonno's not here. I yank the wheel and take the turning that runs down the side of the yard where I know there's another smaller gate, but that's closed and no one's there either. A few cars inside parked back of the buildings. Wonder what Carno's driving now. I park down the end of the sideroad out of sight and aerate the windscreen for ten minutes, then creep back again. Can't do this too many times. Rear entrance still closed and quiet but this time at the main gate I see two uniformed blokes standing in the yard, a few yards back. Just a quick glimpse, but it's enough. Yep. Recognise that bull-torso anywhere. The other one could be the guard Carno called Seeger. Not sure. But we're on.

So now it's round to pick up Carly. Two minutes, zip zip. She's waiting in the hall of her flat and she don't look nervous at all. Ridiculous, but not nervous. She's wearing a button-through short-sleeved flowery dress, knee-length, bare legs, girly peeptoe heels, scarf holding her hair back. Reminds me of pictures of Mam as a girl. Miss Goody-Goody 1960. She grins at me and says she's been giving the meeting thought, reckons this would make a good impression. Bought the dress at Oxfam just now. I tell her to lose the scarf, don't want Carno crippled with mirth before we start. Does me good, criticising her. Feel instantly steadier. She says neither of us should wear jackets, because the less body covering we got the more relaxed he'll be. Don't want him worrying that we're harbouring sawn-offs. She has been giving the matter thought. I got no jacket anyway. Just a T-shirt over my combats.

I show her the mobile Evans gave me and make sure she understands how the quick-dial works. Just in case of calamity. Then I tuck it in one of my trouser pockets. It makes a small bulge but it don't look like a weapon. Looks like a phone. Nothing unusual about carrying a phone.

Carly then says I'm not to shout at her, but while she's been doing her thinking it's come to her that really she ought to do the talking. She reminds me I sometimes get in a muddle. Specially if

I'm worked up. I don't tell her to fuck off, because she says it tactful, like she's my devoted little sister already, and I can't deny it's the truth. And she does look confident. Not sure how I come across.

"You understand what we're saying?" I ask. "And what mood we're in?"

"Serious. Little stressed maybe. But diplomatic. And business-like."

"It's Carno we'll be talking to. He's gonna be rude. You think you can keep your temper?"

She nods, intent. "Be the same whether I'm listening or talking."

I dunno. Can't decide if she wants to do this because it's her responsibility and she could have more to lose – legally speaking, that is – if we mess up, or whether she just fancies centre stage.

"Mr Carno...." She puts on a voice level and mature, a hint of urgent. Hands clasped together at her waist. "We got worries. We know you got worries too. We don't want to point no fingers or make no accusations, but we both got family to think about. Matters are getting out of hand. We're not happy about that. And there's things we can both do to help...."

She's thought it out. And she can act. I couldn't do as good.

"Doesn't mean you can't say nothing," Carly urges. "Just let me start it off."

"Right. OK." Comes to me that a long time ago, before Dad died, she used to talk us out of all sort of scrapes. We'll be travelling back in time. As long as she keeps her cool. But maybe that's more likely if she's doing the talking, acting her part and feeling clever, rather than sitting beside me mute and frustrated. Have to say I'm not disappointed. It feels like a load off.

We drive to a street out of sight of the depot, then take to our feet. All this gearing up, Carno's got to be here. Feel the adrenaline rising, tap tap tapping inside. I remember Bethan saying that I got a temper too, and remind myself of what I stand to lose if I let fly.

And there's Mam. We do this right, there's a chance she need never know about Carly. Do it wrong – very wrong – and she'll be visiting both of us down Cardiff.

It looks like just Jonno on the gate. Good. He sees us coming and stares at Carly as if she's a vision. He knows her from the Crucible, and from down the benefit office.

"Hi Jonno," I say. "We come to see Carno. He around?"

He's still goggling at Carly.

"Hi Jonno," she simpers. Taking the piss, but Jonno can't see it.

"That's a beautiful dress, Carly," he says. "I never seen you in a dress."

"For fuck's sake," I sigh. Could tell him now, this romance is doomed.

"Aye, well." Jonno pulls his eyes away reluctantly. "He's round the office. What d'you want him for?"

"Little chat," I say. "Nothing offensive. You take us round there?"

"Not meant to leave the gate. Could buzz him."

"No." I say this firm. We need things to move fast, because Carno might have already seen us on video. Unlikely, unless he keeps his eyes glued to the screen, but possible. "Just take us round. A favour, mate."

Jonno shrugs and leads the way. Disobeying orders don't worry him. Well, getting fired don't either. He's same as me, not keen on working all year. And it's the only way to leave jobs, if you don't want to be benefit-less for weeks.

"You won't forget we're inside, will you?" I say as we cross the yard. A couple of men over by the skips, but no uniforms. "Not expecting trouble, but be nice to think there's eyes out here."

"I got you covered." He puffs out manly. Carly smiles sweet at him. Revolting sight.

The office is a large tin-and-asbestos shed up a couple of steps with a Portakabin bolted on behind. Saw the back of the Portakabin a few minutes ago, when I was peering through the side gate. The combination isn't impressive-looking. Still scorch marks above the grilled window.

Jonno raps on the door and half opens it. "Two visitors for you, Mr Carno." He stands back.

Carno must be close by when Jonno spoke, because he appears at the doorway straight away. Wearing a suit, tie. Far too smart for the building. He looks down at us. Me first, then Carly. Me again. Astonished, then alarm rising. I see his chest swell like he's going to shout, and I'm about to cut in when Carly does it for me.

"Sorry to bother you, Mr Carno," she says quick, "but we got to have a word." Wonder when she last clapped eyes on the man. Could be years. You'd never know. She dimples her cheeks. "We're not here to make trouble."

Carno checks my face and I drop my shoulders and try looking untroublesome. He turns his glare on Jonno.

"You break the rules once more," he snaps, "and your fat arse is out of here. Get Seeger. Now."

"Yes, Mr Carno." Jonno gives him a death-ray stare and stomps off round the corner. Carno's still blocking the entrance to the office, and it's obvious he's going to stay there till he's got back-up.

"It's kind of private," Carly ventures. Gives him a nervous smile. Can't tell if she's acting.

"You can speak in front of Seeger," Carno says, "or not at all."

I try to get the message to Carly that it's OK. If anyone's in on it here – and Dale's nose says someone is – I bet it's Seeger. Bet it is. Not as if accusations going to be made explicit, anyway. Not on our side.

When the man comes round I'm even more sure. Big bloke, forties, ape arms, hard eyes. Hair like steel wool. He's only seen me face to face once but he knows me instantly, like he's been doing his homework studying last visit's video. Can see him with a glove across Dale's mouth. Or pulling the trigger of a nail gun. I got hairs rising. Whoa, got to stop before I steam up. That's over, Jay. Let it go. Relax.

Carno says, "Jay and his lady friend would like a chat."

Carly tinkles, "Oh, no, Mr Carno. I'm his sister."

"Sister? Sister?" Carno almost smiles. Can't think why. Must be forgetting she'd have a grudge as big as mine.

The man Seeger says, "You want to speak inside, Mr Carno?" and Carno nods and moves back from the door. Seeger waves us up in front of him. When we're inside he closes the door behind us. There's a big desk one end of the room, filing cabinets along the side wall. Open doorway where they end into the Portakabin behind. Video screen up above the open doorway, cut into four pictures. All exterior views. Can't see a camera in here. Nobody else in the room, no secretary, office help. Pale chipboard underfoot, like someone's lifted the floor-covering. The place still smells of fire.

"Sit down." Carno makes his way round to his desk chair and stacks papers away. Seeger pulls up a couple of chairs. Brushes the seat of the one he offers Carly. Leaves mine dusty. We sit. Seeger stands behind us.

"You got five minutes," says Carno. "Less, if I'm not interested."

Carly clasps her hands on her lap, tips her upper body forward. She starts on the spiel she gave me in the flat. Sounds more nervy now, but not unconvincing. Just unconvincing for Carly. He don't know her, though.

"Stop!" orders Carno, when she's only got to the bit about thinking about families. "You two. You wearing wires?"

"What?" says Carly, like she's an innocent and never watches cop programmes.

"No," I say. "'Course not. Check if you like."

Carno considers, decides my offer could be a bluff, and says over to Seeger, "Check them."

I stand up and lift my T-shirt to my armpits. Show him a naked torso. Seeger pats my trousers, finds coins, Subaru keys, and the mobile.

"A phone here."

He takes it out and places it on the desk. It's just an ordinary phone. No *police issue* stamped on it. I sit down again.

Carly's turn now. She gets up, giving a good impression of a virgin about to be raped, but a rape she got to endure for her country. Pulls up the skirt of her dress to the top of her bare thighs and lets it fall again. Have to say, her legs don't look too massive in peeptoes. Starts to unbutton her dress from the neck. Carno waves a hand at Seeger.

"Just pat her." He's wincing. Nice young lady, subjected to this. Hasn't noticed she's not blushing. This is the nice young lady who once got so mad at a guy mauling her in the Crucible she whipped her top off, rammed his head into her Wonderbra, and then nutted him. Both pissed, of course. Well, he'd have to have been. Carly sits down again, smoothing dignity round her like a mink stole.

"OK, young lady," Carno says. "Apologies. Now. I want you to think very carefully what you're saying."

Carly nods. "I am, Mr Carno." She gives him a lash-flickering smile, forgiving him his unkind suspicions. "Not making any accusations. Not to anyone. But we both know what we're talking about. And maybe we both got the power to stop things."

Carno listens close to this, doesn't reply. Looks over to Seeger. Seeger's standing behind us so I can't see if he's sending information back. Carno lifts an eyebrow. Smiles at us triumphant.

"Your family finally had enough of you too, Jay?" he asks.

Fuck. Fuck. Should have guessed this would happen. I'm so stupid. Fucking Carly. What's Carno seeing? Mr Guilty having the mess he's got everyone in sorted by Miss Pure. Can feel my temperature rising. Maybe Carly can too, because she steps in quick.

"You know Jay hasn't done nothing, Mr Carno. You know that."

"Oh aye?" Carno's grinning nasty. "And that's why you're here. Because he hasn't done anything."

"We're here," says Carly carefully, "because we got family and friends to think about. Like you have."

He stares at her a moment, eyes narrowing. "I beg your pardon?" Considering a rethink. Unwelcome rethink. "Hope you're not threatening me, young lady."

"Of course not." Carly shakes her head, dismissive. Body demure, definitely unthreatening. "You've suffered damage and a lot of inconvenience, Mr Carno. And one of Jay's friends has got hurt. We'd just like to put a stop to it all. Now. Draw a line. For mutual benefit."

She must have written herself a script last night. *Suffered inconvenience. Draw a line. For mutual benefit.* Using her office-speak. Galls me that if we get away with this – which we just might, I'm beginning to think – they're going to imagine this is her, for real.

Carno looks past us to Seeger again. Receives a message and gives a brief nod, like it might be *your decision*. Then stares at us, taking his time. But his head's still echoing that little nod. Shit, I think, we're going to do it. Maybe details to work out, lectures to listen to, but we're getting there. More than half way. Gonna get the revenge squad called off. Carly's done it.

There's a noise from the Portakabin. A door banging, rumpus of footfalls. Carno frowns across to the doorway quick, startled even, like it's an intrusion he's not expecting. A man comes to the doorway. Behind him another. I recognise both of them. The front man is Baldy Scott. The slighter one behind, fuck me, fuck me blind, is Damien.

A game of statues been declared. Think I hear a breathed, "Shit," from Seeger behind me. Dunno what's going on, but whatever it is, we all got to recover from it. Can see the shock on faces. Bet mine's a picture too. Carly don't know who Scott is and may be vague about Damien too, but she's sitting rigid because everyone else is. The air's solid with paralysed brain cells.

Locking on to Damien jump-starts me. Gets the cells racing. If it had just been Scott, fucking cavalry, I'd think, always turning up when you least want them. But he's with Damien. Little gap-tooth Damien. Andy-and-Maureen lodger Damien. Security van driver Damien. Ah shit. And Damien's so shattered his face is comical. Not that I'm laughing. Not at all.

The first movement is Scott lowering the holdall he's carrying. Soft canvas. That's the clincher. Half empty, something heavy and angular in the bottom. Something similar's lodging itself in my guts.

Carno breaks the silence. He says, "Might have fucking rung first," to Scott. Sounds bitter. It's a safe thing to say, except for the way he says it.

I got to let Carly know what's going on. It can't make the situation worse. The worst has just arrived. Any agreement with Carno's off. That's not my decision, it'll be Baldy Scott's.

I say, "This is Detective Constable Scott. That's Damien. Might have seen him around. Scott's a bent copper. Carrying a nail gun in his bag."

I feel Seeger's hands clamp on my shoulders. Makes the weight in my guts shudder, but I'm not moving. No point. Four of them, even if one is Damien, only two of us. Well, I got my nailgunners. Red handed, with Carno. Just never imagined it like this.

Carno's face has gone pasty white. Only pink showing is two lines down his cheek. Shit, remains of those nail tracks. He shakes his head at me, jerky movement, and hisses, "That was such a stupid thing to say."

Wasn't. Scott knows he's blown it, it's on his face. If he were here official he wouldn't be using the back gate, letting himself in casual. The room wouldn't have been struck dumb the way it was. And it's him we're up against now, not Carno. But I noticed the way his eyes widened when I said Damien's name. Hang on to that. No wonder the boy looks shattered.

Out the corner of my eye I see Carly's feet shifting. She's trying to slip her peeptoes off. She's got good control of her face. Looking more herself now, but not enough to frighten anyone. What we could really do with is Jonno bursting through the door. Could give it a go, three against four. But he's on the main gate, not the back gate, and although I can't see the door behind us, it sounds restful.

Carno gets up. He's frowning deep, collecting papers, stuffing them in a bag. Locking drawers. Pressing buttons on his phone. Doing what business men leaving the office do. His mouth is tight. Don't like seeing him so upset. Don't like it at all. Prefer him furious. He stops what he's doing and looks at me and Carly. The sight of us gives him anguish.

He blurts out, almost wailing, "I got to tell you something. Your family. So fucking stupid."

Carly snaps, "Piss off, wanker." Not a flowery-dress thing to say, but we're past that.

"Your Daddy," he says. "I told him what was down that hole. I fucking told him it was poisonous. But he has to be a hero."

Nobody but us three grasp what he's on about. Carly's head rears up like a snake. Mouth foul.

"Liar. Fucking liar."

He shakes his head. He don't care whether we believe him.

"And because of that, he saves my skin. Funny, eh? Goes down while his partner's in the vehicle ringing in. All over in seconds. Total cock-up. So then it's obvious it's lethal, and I can say I didn't know. Dickhead."

I don't care what he's saying. I'm not listening. It's the fact that he's saying it. Like he's making connections. Can feel prickles rising back of my neck. They wouldn't. Oh fuck. Don't think about it, Jay. Keep a grip.

Scott is unzipping his holdall, lifting out the contents. Now I know what a nailgun looks like. Usually green or orange, Evans said. This one's red. Seeger's hands are still pressing down on my shoulders. Hot and heavy through my T-shirt. His fingers shift around, poking into me. Hate letting him do this, but I can't throw him off yet.

Carno pushes Damien aside to get to through to the Portakabin.

Shit, I think, shit. He's going out the back way. Should have thought – that's where the cars are. Should have checked with Jonno. Stupid, stupid.

Just inside the doorway he turns and says, "Give me twenty minutes. Then ring his Mam and make sure she hears him. And get her to check the time."

Scott nods. Not an obedient nod. Loaded. "Be in touch," he says.

The message isn't lost on Carno. He mutters, "Seeger'll deal with it, he knows the business," then whips round and disappears. Hear a door bang. I know his business too. Waste disposal. Don't think about it, Jay. Don't think it.

Carly stands up. Her feet are bare. She still looks girly, because of the dress, but tamping girly.

"Sit down," says Seeger. "Be a good girl now, like your brother."

This could be an insult but I'm not responding. I'm keeping my mind working. My eyes are on the video screen. Tiny pictures, but clear. Two of them show gates. Main gate open, back gate closed. Can't see anyone at the main gate. Jonno could be prowling the yard, keeping those eyes peeled. Could be. Really could use him bursting through that door. Carly hasn't obeyed Seeger. Still standing.

Scott steps closer, pushes the nailgun barrel against the side of my jaw, and says over to Carly, "Sit, you stupid bitch."

And she's *still* thinking about it. Perhaps this is the moment. My hands are free. I'm being held down at the shoulders, nailgun pushed in my face, but my hands are free. Perhaps it'd be worth being shot in the face and pulped afterwards to lose Carno his alibi. No. Too soon. Got to be other options.

"Carly," I say. "Please."

I get a sneer down her nose. It don't go with the Miss Goody-Goody look but she's blown that already. She sits.

And then we wait. Weird minutes. Heart beating so violent I

can hear it. Expect Seeger feels it, too. I'm waiting for Jonno, or, failing that, these blokes to move around. Always more chance with movement. Whatever they're planning, they got to move sometime. I can't see either of their faces, but they must be having to work things out. Must be difficult, keeping a man sitting tight, no spare hands to secure the situation, and not being able to speak. Damien's free, could be running errands, locking doors, or doing anything for them, but he's not. Maybe they're unsure of him. I knew his name.

I can see Damien's face. He don't look like he's waiting for anything. Looks like he's shitting himself. I stare at him. Not sure how intimidating I come across, two men bearing down on me, but I do my best. It helps, too, keeps my mind clear. He sees I'm looking, tries to keep his eyes away. They creep back and dart away again. My eyes tell him that I know he hurt Dale. That I know he helped Seeger pull him down, and hold him while Scott nailed him.

"Why d'you do it?" I say.

"Shut up," Scott says.

"Didn't know it was going to be Dale," Damien complains. "Just someone needing a talking to, that's all they –"

"Shut the fuck up," Scott snaps.

Seeger says, "Lock the door. This one. Then get over here. Stand behind her."

They're going to use him. Or test him. And Damien obeys. Least I assume he does. He moves behind us and I hear a click, then the pad of feet. Always does as he's told, little fucker. Can't see any faces now. I suppose they think they've got the muscle spread right. The two big boys on me, Damien on the little lady. This could be a mistake. Got to pin hope on something.

Then more waiting. Minutes take a long time to tick when there's a hard barrel pushing at your jawbone, and no Jonno breaking down the door. Might be locked, but one big kick'd do it. Dale and Bethan were right. He's useless. This must be a crap business too – not a single phone call. Or maybe Carno put the office line on divert. That's it, Jay, keep thinking, keep thinking.

Feels like hours before Seeger murmurs, "OK. Time's up."

Scott prods the barrel into me. "Right. Pick up the mobile."

Hoped they'd say that. Almost sure they would. They got no hands to do it themselves. Caught on the hop, no equipment, and no privacy to plan it out. They know I won't sit still with a nailgun in my face if someone's not holding me. I stretch out a hand and pick up the mobile. Scott don't know it came from Evans. May not even realise it's mine. I've kept cool. Just got to do what I've decided, and do it now, because there might not be another chance. Too late as it is, of course, but I still got to do it. I rest my hand over the mobile, find 5, and squeeze it down.

"Wait!" orders Scott.

Long enough. I'm connecting. I shift my fingers to block the sound holes. Don't shout, Evans, please. My hand's got a tremor in it.

It's OK, he thinks I was just starting to dial. "Damien?" he snaps. "You know his number?"

"Er. 305… shit, something like that."

Scott rams the nailgun in so hard he must be making a dent in my jaw. "Young lady?"

Carly's seen my fingers moving. She recites the small-holding number slow as she can.

"That's it," says Damien. "Yeah." He sounds definite. Don't think he's grasped what's happening.

"Right," says Scott. He jabs me with the barrel. "You ring now. You say, hey Mam, it's Jay here, tell us the time, Mam. That's all. Then cut off. Don't wait for an answer." He jabs me again. He's making my eyes water. "Got that, thicko? Dial now."

Fuck, I hate this man. Can really see how he scared Dale. I've broken into a sweat. Dimly wonder if all this is just to terrify us, too. Except we've seen him.

I dunno what it does to an open line to have numbers pressed on the phone. Just makes clicks, I hope. There's eleven numbers, including the area code, and Scott's watching me press each one. My finger's sticky. My eyes swimming. Could do with some wetness in my mouth. Just pray, if doing this cuts me off, Evans was listening before and heard enough. But he could be miles away. Even down the station would be too far. And he don't know where I am. At the end of the sequence I omit the Call. Gotta risk it.

I lift the phone. Hear nothing the other end. Tell myself I'm gonna get hurt sometime, whatever. I say, "Hi, Mam. It's Jay. I'm at Carno's –"

Something slams into the side of my face. Carly screams. Phone shoots off across the desk. I'm falling off the chair. Shit, I think, quite clearly, as I go down, he's done it. He's shot a nail into my jaw.

Nothing's too clear after that, because I'm trying to get up and Seeger's lunged between the chairs and is crushing me down. Carly's flowery dress flew away out of sight. I get a few heel-kicks and elbow jabs in, but get a volley of thumps back. Ah, can hear the girl now, bellowing rage. Someone just trod on my ankle. I'm spitting blood and my face is getting near the chipboard. Now they're both on me. My cheek hits the floor and it's the first time I feel pain. Would say something to express it but my mouth's not working right. Someone climbs onto the small of my back, wrenching one of my arms round. It's Scott, can hear him swearing. If his hands are free he must have put down the nailgun. Small relief. Must be Seeger on my feet. The weight of a buffalo. Oh shit, Scott's hauling on my other arm, he's trying to cuff me. Fucking coppers, carrying shackles. No, not having it, not having it. But I can tell he's done this before. He's breaking my arms. Can't stop him. And now he's done it, the metal's got me. Ah fuck, fuck, fuck. That's it, just hurting myself now, I lost. Ah fuck.

He's lifting his weight off now, leaving me useless. Never want to be here again. Worse than horrible. Bethan, you were right, we've screwed up, and now we're really gonna get hurt. Oh shit. I can't hear Carly no more. Yell, Carly, I think, yell, girl. Please.

More noise. Only chance. I'd do it myself, but I can't. Just gobbing mouthfuls of blood.

Someone does yell then, but it's not Carly. Seeger? More a yelp, like something bit him. The weight jerks off my feet. I lift my head but all I can see is Damien. Damien, fuck me, on the floor in front of me. Something felled him. He's thinking about rising, but only got as far as his forearms. Looks ill. Head sagging. I think about rising too but I can't do it. Can't work out how. Putting my face down again hurt too much, it's clouding my brain.

Somewhere behind me a man's voice – Scott's, has to be – says, "Give it here now, love," ice-steady and wary, and Carly's comes back wild at him, "You just try!"

I hear Seeger rap out, "You take that side," and then there's a pop and one of them – can't tell which – gasps, "Fucking hell!" like they've been bit again.

Then the door crashes open. No sound like it. Bang, like gunshot. Knew it would, sometime. No I didn't. Just imagined it. Willed it. And a lot of tumultuous noise soaking like silk into me, shouting and thumping and swearing and yelling. Carly loud, screaming, 'Don't help him, Jonno, he's one of them!' and Jonno roaring, like he always does fighting. All voices I know: them two, Seeger, Scott, and then another familiar one, shouting, 'Leave it, Carly, just leave it, let them go!' and fuck knows how that voice got here. But I'd know it anywhere. It's Paul's. A miracle's happened. Maybe Dale did it, I think. Fucking beautiful Dale. Not got holes in his hands for nothing.

Then there's doors banging out the back, bam bam bam, like a machine gun, and the place is suddenly quiet. Can hear Jonno's roar somewhere outside. Engine firing up, screaming away. Knees slide in beside me. Paul's knees.

He whispers, "Jesus Christ," running his hands light over my head and shoulders, checking I'm still joined together. "Oh Jay," he murmurs, like it's all his fault and he's so sorry. Somewhere close by Carly's snarling, "You try, Damien, I'll knock you down again," and Damien's voice is whinging back, "OK. OK."

I need to tell Paul to get me up, because it's hurting my face lying here, but I can't get the words out. I try bringing my legs up and pushing against him, because I know that's the way to do it; I got a desk blocking me the other side. Then I see bare feet. Carly's come to lean over me too.

She says, "You OK, Jay?"

Yep, I think. Never better. Oh shit, I'm hurting.

"He's got a nail in his jaw," she tells Paul. "He's lying on it. He wants to get up."

I dunno if Paul would have helped me if I hadn't kept struggling. Got a thing about leaving casualties alone, these first-aid trained types, even when they're being urged not to and the casualty's face down in blood. But in the end he helps me roll over and sit up. Leans me back against the desk. I got the shakes, dunno why, must be relief. He apologises for not being able to do anything about my hands, but promises Evans'll be here soon. He's on his way, knows I'm in trouble. He pulls out a phone and says he'll just ring for an ambulance

I can see the whole of Carly now. Amazing sight. She's dancing about, dividing her time between finger-threats at Damien, who's tucked with his knees up in the corner, and little smiles back at me. Flowers got a few dust smudges, but she looks unhurt. And fizzing. Nothing like the high of a fight you won. At least she's put the nailgun down, so no danger of victory salvos. I see her like she's glassed off from me, a trembly moving picture, not real at all. Good picture though. Good. When Paul finishes on the phone she bobs up and down at him and cries, "We did it, Paul! We did it! We'll have the lot of them!"

Paul rams the phone into his breast pocket. He's not fizzing at all. He snaps, very harshly, "And you can just shut up now, Carly."

Dunno why he's so angry. Can't understand it. The girl's done OK. Better than OK. And she's right. I'd give her a little smile, if I could.

# 13

I'm getting so many callers that the nurses have put a note on the door saying *Visitors – check with Sister first.* So now they barge in saying, "Hey? What's the note about?" Like whoever it's aimed at, it's obviously not them.

Got a second line of defence though. Bethan. My spitting angel sharing the pillow.

Two local press men been sent packing. Likewise Jonno. Not unkindly. Just isn't room for Jonno in here. Then a dribble of Bethan's mates, no favours, same treatment. Then Andy – gets half a minute. Looks sad, Andy does, like one of his kid's turned out a severe disappointment. Expect Maureen's cut up too. They give the boy houseroom, teach him how to brush his teeth, and how does he repay them? Andy insist there's no way Damien would have hurt Dale if he'd known he were the target. No way. The boy was just a driver, stupid enough to fancy action with the big boys. Wouldn't have known the weapon, even. So how come he was still with Scott, Bethan sneers, if he were such an innocent? Andy's got no answer to this. Looks distressed. Can guess myself, though. Not easy to pull out of bad company. Scott would wonder why, and I can't see him being tolerant of divided loyalties. Damien'd got himself deep in shit, however you look at it. Still, he's going to be useful now, doing what he's told and giving Evans all he needs to know. I'm wondering if I should have thought of him earlier. Knew he worked in security. Saw him near faint at Dale's bandages. Already suspecting security types involved, and how many outfits are there round here? But wimpy Damien? Na. I'd never have guessed.

Evans and another copper get short shrift too. I might have been more tolerant with Evans, but Bethan's as fierce as I've known her. "He can't speak," she snaps, "so what's the point? Go ask Carly." She says 'Carly' with her lips twisting like she's a foul taste. Carly knows what's good for her and hasn't been in. Yet. She'll wait till dead of night, expect, hoping even spitting angels go home to sleep.

Dale's here sometimes, sometimes not. Can't tell unless I got my eyes open and see him. Takes up no space at all. I got a memory of him here last night, soon after I came in. Maybe Simone drove him up. I see him standing next to Bethan and she's swung away from me, eyes blind with feeling, and her head suddenly butts into his shoulder. Grinding too and fro. He's holding her so their hair's mingling and murmuring in her ear. See his strapped hand pressed on her shoulder blade. Funny thing is, the sight don't worry me at all. Just glad he's there, taking care of her.

No tears from Bethan since, mind. Not a glitter since I was brought up here. This is Dale's old ward and Dale's old room, too, next to the nurses' station. Could be a coincidence, or maybe it's where they always put problem patients. Saves calf ache. Haven't seen the old Sister yet, but I expect she'll be on later.

I've made up a little pile of my own notes, for when Bethan can't answer for me and I need to do more than nod or headshake. Fucking unfair – Dale gets nailed in the hands, the one place he cares about, and I get nailed in the jaw, making me temporarily speechless, which means I got to communicate by writing. Justice would be the other way. Dale could afford a small blemish in his face, might make it more manly even, and I'd have the excuse not to put pen to paper for months.

I can't speak not because of my jaw – they fixed that last night and not a new cut outside to show for it either, amazing – it's my tongue. Must have ripped it on the nail end when I hit Carno's floor and what with the stitches and swelling it's like I've got a snaggy rubber ball in my mouth. Everyone says tongues heal quick though, plentiful blood supply – certainly saw evidence of that yesterday – and they say in a couple of days I'll be mumbling good as new. Worse thing is I can't drink more than a lip-wet so I got to have a drip in my arm. It's either that or a tube down my nose, and since I need that for breathing and it's a bit bunged up with bruising anyway, they've decided against more obstructions. Haven't asked for a mirror.

Bethan's sat up on the pillow beside me and I got my head resting on her breast bone. Not my choice of snoozing positions but I've got to be propped up for my airways and it's surprisingly comfortable. If I turn my head so the good side's against her I can hear her heart beating. She's got one arm across my shoulder and chest, the other down my arm. Like now she's got me back I'm her prisoner and I'm not escaping again. Definitely some of that fierceness aimed at me. The hospital staff don't tell her to get off the bed when they come in and see us. If they're female they go, "Ah, love 'em," pulling soppy faces to whoever else is in the room and if they're male they grin at me and say nothing. They nearly all know Bethan, 'course.

It's early afternoon and I've just heard Paul outside. Must have seen the note on the door – he's asking permission to come in. That's a first. I only realise Dale's in the room when he gets up from the armchair. I must have been dozing. Bethan says, "You can stay, Dale," but he shakes his head and murmurs, "It's OK, be back soon." As Paul comes in he slips out with a smile.

"Where's he off to?" Paul says. Fuck, he's got a loud voice. Peaceful it was, just now.

Bethan says, "Only meant to be two to a room," though it's not a rule anyone else has stuck to. I can't stop Paul visiting and I don't want to because I love the man, but I'm finding him exhausting. It's not the first time he's been in – he was here late last night after chatting with the cops, and early this morning – and he's so hyped up he makes the room judder. Think Dale finds him tiring too.

Paul flings himself into the armchair. I rest my hand on my lap notes in case I need them. Top one says, 'Painkillers please' – no prizes for guessing who wrote that, but the rest are my own work. Range from 'Piss', for when I want a bottle, through 'dOnt kNOw' – Bethan added the 'k', once she'd twigged what I meant – to 'exPlane' which I gather has something wrong with it but people seem to understand anyway. I also got one that says 'PiGfAce', which I'm confident is spelt right. Not written with venom, mind. More in hope I get the chance to use it.

"Well, I've done it," Paul announces. "Went to see the Director just now. Told him he could stuff his department. Gave him my resignation. He tore it up and told me to take six months sabbatical. We'll see."

Not sure how to respond to this. 'Piss'? 'Painkillers please'?

"What's a sabbatical?" Bethan asks.

"Unpaid leave. Doesn't believe I'm serious. Ha!"

I don't believe him either. Maybe he should see a social worker. I would ask him what Simone thinks, assuming he's told her, but it's too complicated to write down. Ponder how to spell Simone. 'S', obviously....

"It was yesterday, when Dale rang me. That was the moment –"

He's off again. Sure he said all this this morning.

"– there we were in this meeting, talking about Mission Statements. Fucking Mission Statements. I'm thinking of suggesting 'We Talk up Our Arses'. Then being dragged out to speak to Dale, well... and he's asking my advice about something that really matters. Looking for action. Organization and action. Something I'm actually rather good at –"

I close my eyes. He's hooked on the story. Got to keep saying and saying it. Suffering from too much excitement, Paul is. I know what happened already from both him and Dale. It was Dale who performed the miracle, though he didn't need saintly powers to do it. Just the phone. Soon after I'd left him he rang Paul, got him pulled out of that meeting, and Paul said he was dead right, Evans definitely ought to know what I'm doing – neither of them knew

Carly was with me, of course – and I ought to have back-up besides Jonno. Paul says he'll go himself, and it's him who contacts Evans. Tells him he's going up to Carno's to check Jonno's there and watch my back with him. Evans says ta for the information – not that there's much he can do with it – but he does take Paul's mobile number. So when Evans gets my weird call he rings Paul straight off, and he and Jonno rush in. End of story. Might have helped if Paul had rung me and told me where he was – saved me having to say "Carno's" and maybe stopped me getting nailed – but he thought I'd be going straight to the depot and was worried that a phone trilling would spoil things. When he got there and Jonno said that me and Carly had only just arrived he realised he could have rung earlier. But too late then. My fault for not being straight with Dale. Still, if I had been, and warned him off ringing Evans like I did Bethan, he might not have contacted Paul at all. And then fuck knows where I'd be.

Both of them know Carly did the arsons. Paul guessed the moment Jonno said she was with me – well, he had her in the frame way back, but was put off by me. And Dale knew because of me not saying I was taking her. He said, "Arsons down to Carly, were they?" this morning when Bethan went out for a piss, and I nodded. I put my finger to my lips after, because writing a note that says 'Keep it quiet' seemed unwise. Didn't know then how savage Bethan was going to be with coppers, and imagined having to write dozens of notes giving variations on 'No comment'. Bet Evans guesses too, mind, but unless he can get Eileen to talk he's still got nothing to go on.

"Sorry, Jay," Paul says. "You asleep?"

"He's a bit tired," Bethan says. She's hinting, but she won't tell Paul to piss off outright because she's so grateful to him. Him and Dale.

"Your Evans is a funny copper, isn't he?" Paul muses. "When I first rang him he sounded like a man plodding round in a fog. But then efficient as anything last night, and today he's zipping."

"You seen him today?" Bethan asks.

"When I was leaving here. Had a few words. No love lost between him and that Scott. Must be grim, when it's someone you work with. The other's got a collapsed lung, by the way."

"What? The security man?"

"Yup."

I knew Seeger was in hospital. He's being detained in The Heath, Cardiff, where Scott threw him out of the car. Carly'd only got one nail in him, but in the back. Must have been when he was pinning my feet. I heard the yelp. She put two nails in Scott, arm and shoulder, but they didn't stop him driving. He tried to get back on the M4 after dumping Seeger but got stuck in traffic and a lorry driver looking down noticed blood everywhere and got him pulled over. Don't know where he was making for. I'm looking forward to finding out more about Scott. Discovering if he was settling other people's scores for love or money. Both, maybe. Bastard.

"He says I can tell Jay that Carno's being cooperative."

"Oh yes?" Bethan presses my arm. "Hear that, Jay?"

I nod. Carno was picked up at his home. Before that he'd been with his bank manager in Crick having an alibi-securing chat. Or so he thought.

"My guess is that the thugs were running the show, and Carno'd had enough. Carly's said he was about to call things off when Scott came in, hasn't she?"

Bethan says stiffly, "Wouldn't know. We haven't spoken."

Can't see her face, but I hear her tone. Feel it, too, hardening her chest. I want Paul to go now. Don't want to think about Carno. Reminds me what he said about my dad. Maybe I'll tell him about that later, when he's had time off and calmed down. Carly won't have said anything because she'd never believe anything Carno said, but I believed him. Didn't want to, but I did. I wonder if Mam ought to know, or whether she definitely ought not to know. Need advice on that. I got so used to thinking of Carno as a killer. 'Course, Dad and that bloke still died, but there's killing and killing. And I see his face before he left us with Scott and Seeger. Looked ill. Shit, would Scott really have done it? Don't like thinking that direction, either.

On the other hand, Carno's the one who promised he'd nail me. And nails are what they used. So even if he didn't pull triggers, that's still down to him. Still a nasty-minded, criminal bastard.

"You and Carly," Paul sighs. Sounds almost contented. "You're Carno's nemesis."

I snap my eyes open. That's it, he's out. Not having philosophy in here. I reach for the pen and scrawl 'OF' on a blank sheet. Put it next to the 'Piss'. Bethan peers over my shoulder and indicates I need another 'F'.

Paul leans across to see. "OK," he says. Still smiling. Nothing's denting him. "Just going."

Around tea time – not that I get any tea, mind, but Bethan and Dale tuck in – flowers arrive from Sparky. Ah, Bethan coos, sweet of him. Encouraging, I think. Can't be too out of touch. I hope he's not blaming himself for me as well as Dale. No. He's a clever boy. Once his mind's clear he'll see things straight.

Soon afterwards Randolph brings Mam in. Randolph hates hospitals. His wife died here, down in Intensive Care. He's had to escort Mam up because she got lost last night. She can't read the signs and all the corridors look the same. Randolph leans round the door, face rigid, and grunts, "Right, Jay? Ah, don't look so bad now. I'm not stopping. Half an hour, I'll be back to fetch her."

"It's OK." Bethan climbs off the bed. The only visitor she's moved for. "One of us'll take you down, Mam."

Randolph nods and says, "As you like." He disappears.

Dale's already murmuring, "Be in the day room," and slipping away. Bethan adjusts the pillow support behind me and says she'll get Mam a cup of tea. I wish she'd stay. Mam was so upset last night she wouldn't speak to me. Just sat there kneading my hand, hurting my wrist because she couldn't see the marks from the cuff, and twisting my fingers. Could feel a lot of anger.

It takes her a while to settle in the chair because she's got to get over the indignity of being guided up here. She organises her coat and bag, stares around, getting her bearings. I don't like seeing her in places she don't know. She's not the Mam she is at home. She scrapes the chair closer to the bed, so she's very near to me.

"We're alone now, are we?"

I nod. Shit. She's never seemed so blind. Make it a big movement.

She takes my hand and says softly, "I been having a chat with Carly, Jay."

I feel her hand shift on mine. Wait.

"I don't want you feeling you got to keep secrets from me. I don't like it. I'm not so feeble I got to be protected."

I wait again. Don't know the movement for *what you saying, Mam?*

"She's a grown woman," Mam goes on. "And I've told her that. I'm not having her hiding behind you. You say what you like to the police. I won't do nothing to hurt her, but I'm not having you in trouble because of her."

I shake my head. Definite. Reach for the pen and paper. Write 'NO trUBUL' across the sheet in big letters.

Mam reads it. Nods her head in little movements. A body-load of relief falling from her. She mutters, "Not improving, are you?" looking choked up. Feel a bit choked myself. Giving me permission to ditch Carly to protect myself.

Bethan pokes her head round the door, eyebrows enquiring. I start to shake my head when Mam sees her. She sits back.

"It's me, Mam," Bethan says. "Sorry to interrupt. You want that tea now?"

"Come in," Mam says. "I've said my piece. Just telling Jay he's not Carly's Daddy. Not up to him to sort her out."

Bethan glances at me. She comes over and gives Mam the tea. Mam stirs it, frowning. "I've told Carly she'll not be welcome for a while, and she's brought it on herself. She's got to show she can behave. If she's given the chance, that is. And poor Dale too. I know she didn't mean him to be hurt and she didn't do it herself, but she don't think, and she's been wild too long." She shakes her head. "You're too like your Daddy, Jay. Always trying to stop people hurting. He wasn't always right either."

I get really choked up then. Not at all comfortable, having a stuffed nose and a stuffed mouth. Bethan gives me a tissue and mopping my nose isn't painless either.

"It's the anaesthetic," Bethan says. "Can make you a bit weepy."

Mam sips her tea and then says, blunt, "She wants to come up here, Jay."

"No." Bethan's violent. "You can see he's not well enough."

"Just a couple of minutes, son." Mam's fixed on me, trying to read me, not listening to Bethan. "She's down in the van now. Just wants to say she's sorry."

Bethan's still shaking her head, but looking anguished because she's seen my nod. Mam knows I want to see Carly. 'Course she'd know.

Mam puts her tea aside and stands up. Like Carly visiting is something she understands has got to happen, but she wants it done quick, over and out the way.

"You take me down now, Bethan," she says, "and I'll send Carly up. Just two minutes, I'll tell her."

Bethan gives a sighing groan and leads her out. They must pass the day room but Dale don't reappear, so I expect they warn him Carly's coming. While I'm waiting I remember something else Dale said earlier, same time Bethan was in the bathroom. He said he'd told Evans to change his statement back. He wants Seeger and Scott to go down hard. He don't care either way about Damien, and Damien may not go down at all, being small fry and keen to spill all he knows. But Seeger and Scott were the ones who held his head and pushed the gun in his mouth, and it was Scott who bullied him

212

to confess it to Evans. He's seen the nastiness of that and it's really offended him. So now he wants to say it where it counts. There's going to be two of us in court now, describing what they did to us, and maybe that's a comfort to him too.

There's a knock on the door. Fucking hell, Carly, I sigh to myself. Get a brain.

The door opens a crack and Carly's eyes are darting round. When she sees I'm alone she grins and comes in quick. Closes the door and hurries across.

"Hey." She stands over me scrutinizing my face. "Don't look too bad. How're you feeling?"

The only note I got relating to how I feel is the 'Painkillers please'. I give a shrug.

"You really can't talk? Not at all?"

I shake my head.

"So you haven't said anything to Evans yet?"

She's wide-eyed. Like she can't believe her luck.

"Well, listen." She becomes confidential, pushing her bum in the chair. "You thought what you'll be saying when he asks why you took me to see Carno?"

Ah shit. So this is why she wanted to visit me.

"Only I've thought of something. If you said it was my idea, kind of an assurance to Carno that the cars were nothing to do with you, and I was just going along to make sure you said it right –"

And I thought she was coming up here for a little celebration. A little just-between-us celebration. Ah well. Business as usual. If that's the way she wants it. I find the 'piss' and the 'OFF', and show them to her.

She looks uncomfortable. "So what you going to say then? Thing is –" she dips her mouth, making it awkward "– he's already asked me, and I had to say something... I'm really sorry...."

And that's the apology, is it? Not quite what I'd been promised. Cow. I feel my jaw tensing, which isn't a pleasant sensation right now, but then suddenly I think, oh fuck, I don't care. What was I planning to say anyway? I don't know. Haven't thought about it. The luxury of being speechless. But I'm not agreeing to anything now. She's a disappointment. Leave her to stew.

I dig around in my bundle of notes and find the one right down the bottom. Show it to her. Wrote it as a joke, but sincere will do.

"Very funny," she says. "But you will do it, won't you? It's not as if it's evidence against them. Just explaining why we were there."

I stare up at the ceiling. I'm sulking. I'm not giving her the satisfaction.

She seems to take it anyway. Sighs and sits back.

"If I do go down," she says. "I mean, if Eileen says anything now, I'm going to say I did both arsons. I think I'd get off lighter than Russell. Don't you think?"

I continue staring at the ceiling. Lifting out of my sulk, reluctantly, experiencing a twinge of admiration. Novel feeling, in relation to Carly. She waits. I nod.

"Have you told Dale?" she asks. "Saw him in the day room. You told him I did the cars for him?"

No, fuck, this is going too far. Thinks he's going to be grateful, does she? Rip his togs off and thank her?

"Maybe I'll tell him myself," she says. "Really sweet, Dale, isn't he? Bound to see him around."

There's a few seconds silence. Carly's Dale-dreaming, while I'm fuming. I'm rehearsing telling Dale that if he ever, ever, gives her the pleasure our friendship is over. Got to draw lines somewhere. Show some discrimination. And I'd make sure Russell found out. And I'd –.

"You know Mam says I'm not to visit for three months?" Carly's voice has dropped low. She's switched mood. "I had to tell her. She was really angry with me. Thought she was going to cry. Horrible. Says I can ring her but I'm not to come bothering any of you till my birthday."

I pick up the pen and write 'GOOd' underneath the Pigface. Was going to add 'idea' after it – slightly softer reply – but can't think how to spell it. Tough.

She nods, sighs. Takes it square. "Think it is, actually. Let everyone cool off." She hesitates. "And I am sorry, Jay. Didn't mean for you or Dale to get hurt. I just wanted to do like you'd done, when you did his car. Wish I'd done something then. It worked for you. You were OK. Wasn't fair. 'Tisn't."

And suddenly she can't get on from this. Like what she's said is stuck in her mouth and she's having to taste it. Can't chomp it away. Her eyes are blinking, glistening, and then she starts to cry. Not raging crying, just crying crying. She's sitting there with tears trickling down her cheeks and a tugged-back gargoyle mouth. Fuck me. Never seen her cry like this. Never. Ah, poor cow. But I can't take it. I'm ill.

I reach out and pat her forearm. She snatches the arm away, but then gives me an agonised headshake, like she's stupid and didn't mean it. Just automatic.

I reach for the pen again and write four little words below the 'good'. Push the paper at her. I can't smile too well, but I catch her gaze and try to convey it. The words I've written are 'wE GOt thEm AwL'.

She holds the paper up in front of her. Sniffs, reading it. Then gives a little sobbing bark of laughter. She turns her head and nods at me. Carries on nodding. Her mouth isn't quite smiling because she's still crying, but it's close. I mime tearing the piece of paper up, trying to show her it's just between us. Our satisfaction, just ours. We did get them. All of them. Both got what we wanted. Carno and the nailgunners. And maybe we haven't quite walked away, but we've come close. I've made it, and if she's lucky, if Eileen keeps her mouth shut, she just might too.

The door opens and Bethan's caught us. Dunno what she thinks. Carly in tears but smiling too. Nodding and smiling. Maybe it looks like she's been remorseful, I've forgiven her, and she's grateful. That's near enough.

Can't say Bethan looks impressed though. She rolls her eyes. Then props the door wide and says, "You'd better go now. Jay needs his rest."

Carly comes over brisk. She snatches up a tissue from the box and blows her nose like an air-horn. Dries her lashes on the back of her hand. Then turns to me and says, "Seeya. Three months."

I nod. She won't have changed, I know it, but she was fucking good at the depot, and I'll give her the benefit. Poor cow. Waited a long time, and then everything fouls up for her. She didn't mean no one except Carno harm. But Bethan's right too. And Mam. She's got to learn consequences.

Bethan closes the door after she's gone, sighs long and deep, and climbs back on the bed. I adjust my position to lean my head on her chest. It's restful, not being expected to speak. Don't think I need those painkillers. I'm beat. Drop my lids. Dale'll be in in a moment, but he's quiet as a ghost. Anyone else calls, I'm out.

**Scott Clark** is a photographer, artist and designer. His work has been widely exhibited across the UK. He has been known to customise cars and airbrush images without getting arrested. Recent exhibitions include *Misunderstood* at Snickerdoodles, Caerphilly. His large-scale photographic images can be seen at many coffeehouses in Cardiff.